Imploded Lives

Imploded Lives

The Invisible Robbery and the Human Fallout

David P. Warren

Acknowledgment of fine work and many thanks to my incredible editing and insight team:
Nancy J. Warren
Melanie Sue Prisuta
Jan Hernandez

Contents

Part 1
The Hostages

Chapter One
Paul Mason and Brian Gallagher

March 14, 2018
Twenty-Eight Days Before

Brian Gallagher stood at the open door to Paul Mason's office looking around to assure that the lights in the surrounding offices had been turned off, and the occupants were no longer lingering. The building was dark and empty as far as the eye could see. He looked back at Paul and said, "So, are we going through with this?"

"I'm not talking here. Let's go outside and take a walk."

The two men took the elevator down to the ground floor, staying silent throughout the ride. There was no one else in the elevator and very few people seemed to inhabit the building. They signed out at the guard desk and slid their personal access cards through the reader at 9:20 p.m. They walked outside to the street to find that the almost perpetual Los Angeles rush hour was slowing and the traffic was about as light as it was going to get. There was a slight drizzle, noteworthy because any rain was rare in Los Angeles. As they walked down the street toward Mulligan's Brewery, Paul Mason ran a hand through his short black hair and said, "I don't know, man. It is a big risk." Paul was six foot, two inches and slender, with the body of a rider in the Tour de France. He wore wire-rimmed glasses over penetrating blue eyes. Brian was two inches shorter and muscular, his regular workouts keeping his body almost as fit as it had been when he played linebacker at Stanford. His brown hair was longer than Paul's, and matched a well-trimmed beard that showed little gray.

Brian shook his head. "We've been planning this for three months. I thought you got past the hesitation."

Paul replied, "Yeah, but this is a big fucking deal. This is not just career ending, it is prison time." He shook his head. "And we agreed that unless we were all on board, we kill this plan, right?"

"We did and I agree that we need to be fully committed. So if you're not, we need to walk away from this project now," Brian said. "We've already put countless hours into this project and if we're still not committed, we never will be," Brian added, sounding frustrated.

Paul sat down on a bench outside the watering hole. "Look, we know that they will figure out what happened. That's a given. There will be some lag time before they catch on, but after that, they will start tracking everyone who could have pulled it off and I keep thinking that could somehow lead back to us. That's when I start thinking that maybe we should walk away."

Brian nodded. "I get it, man, I do. And at some point we might be among the suspects, but how do they get back to us? They won't be able to prove anything."

Paul shook his head. "I don't know. This is like betting your future at the crap table."

"Déjà vu. We have had this conversation. And if you want to, we walk away. But if not, let's commit. Role the bones, man."

"Don't you have any second thoughts? I mean, we both have kids under ten. Don't you get nervous that you just might leave Alison and the kids to do a long prison sentence? That's the part that unnerves me. I believe in what we are doing, but I don't want to leave Ann to spend time in a cage with nothing to do but replay my regrets."

"I get it," Brian said. He smiled. "Like I said, we can walk if you want, Paul. I'm not in if you're not, so it all ends here if you choose. What keeps me in is the thought of what a couple of guys might be able to accomplish in terms of the immediate results, and the message we get to send. And if we do it right, maybe no one learns who sent the message. I just think..."

At that moment, Brian's phone rang. He hit a button and said, "Brian Gallagher." After a moment, Brian said, "Pretty timely call. I was just talking to Paul about the project." He paused and then asked, "What's the news?" There were a few more moments of silence and then Brian said, "Okay. See you tomorrow night."

Paul said, "I take it he's in?"

"Yep, he's in."

"I guess I'm not surprised," Paul replied. "He's almost as outraged by all this as you are and he's single."

"And you're not as outraged as we are?" Brian asked.

"Yeah, I am." He thought for a moment and then added, "I'm just not convinced that three guys can fix this."

"We can't fix it, but that's not the plan. What we can do is send the message that they are vulnerable, too."

Paul furrowed his brow. "Do you ever have visions of the FBI surrounding your house and dragging you away in cuffs? Have you considered that part of the downside? I mean, if we get caught, we are totally fucked. We will likely know some of the people in on the arrest."

"Yeah, but it'll be a heck of a book when you get paroled." He grinned and then added, "Of course, you won't be able to make any money on it because of the conviction, but we know a number of good causes ready for donations."

"Funny stuff," Paul said, shaking his head. "And I guess I'll always have you to keep me amused."

"Exactly, but more importantly, we are not going to get caught. We have this honed to perfection, man. It's beautiful."

They stood up and walked into Mulligan's. They selected a twelve-dollar beer from one hundred and fifty on tap and then found a table in the back of the bar. They looked around at the tired figures in suits that populated the bar. Lawyers, politicians, lobbyists and investors, all capping the day at the watering hole. Some planned to persuade Congress to change laws for the benefit of corporate clients, while others worked on transactions to make them richer, while still others tried to find a way to escape a deal gone bad. There were big players here, but none of them dealing on the scale of what Paul and Brian were contemplating. There was an extended silence while they looked around at this world of behind the scenes business. After a time, Paul looked at Brian and said, "Okay, I'm in. Let's roll the bones, my friend."

Brian grinned and gave a satisfied nod. "I think we can make a difference."

Chapter Two
Linda Caldwell

Twenty-Four Days Before

Linda Caldwell yelled up the stairs, "Come down for dinner you guys."

"Just a minute, mom," said a twelve-year-old voice from one of the bedrooms. "I just have one more life."

"We only get one life and we don't delay it or our dinner based on video games. Let's go."

"Okay, be right there."

The front door opened and Brad stepped inside. "Hi, sweetheart," he offered. "How was your day?"

She wiped at her brow and then shook her head. "Chasing kids all day. I feel like I've been trying to move frogs across a football field in an open wheelbarrow. I'm hoping we can do dinner, but apparently Jason can't emerge until he uses up one more life."

"Sorry, honey, sounds like a tough day. I'll chase these guys."

"Give me some lips before you disappear up those stairs, never to be seen or heard from again—I think that's what happens to people who go up there."

"I've heard that. Maybe we should tie a rope around my waist and you can hang on to one end."

"Hey, guys, time to come down for dinner," Brad said. Jason came racing out of the first door and started down the stairs two at a time. He wore a T-shirt and blue jeans with countless pockets. His hair was uncombed. Brad met him half way and hugged him. "Hi, buddy. What's new?"

"Not much. What's for dinner?"

"Liver salad and cod liver oil dressing." Brad said, walking to the top of the stairs and pulling off his tie. "That hair of yours seen a comb lately? You look like you were dragged backwards through a hedge. And where's Matt?" he asked the disappearing boy below.

The answer was screamed back. "He's putting the lip lock on Claire at the back door."

Brad thought that Matt was too young to be lip-locking anyone. He had just turned fifteen and he had another year before he was allowed to date.

Brad changed into jeans and went downstairs to the kitchen as Matt came in from the back porch. Brad grabbed silverware as Linda put chicken stir-fry onto plates.

"Hi, buddy," he said to Matt.

"Hey, Dad."

"You and Claire spending a lot of time together these days?"

"Mom was just all over me about that. No big deal."

"Looks serious to us when you're kissing on the porch."

Jason walked into the room and Matt glared at him. "Jason, you little jerk. Quit spying on me."

Jason shrugged and sat down. "You do your thing on the porch, people are going to see it, he said, and then added, "We got any hot sauce?"

Linda put the plates on the table and sat down. She grinned widely at Brad. "The news is in," she said.

"You got it?" he asked with wide eyes.

"Yep. I fly to Vegas in three weeks to be installed as the new Vice President of Human Resources." She grinned widely.

"That is so good, honey. Congratulations!" He took her hand. "I'm going to open a bottle of wine and we are going to celebrate."

She nodded. "You know, it feels good just to get the nod above all of the other applicants. There were some impressive characters applying."

"Not as impressive as you. And that's my objective opinion," Brad replied with a smile.

"Can you get more time away from the office to keep an eye on these guys during the four days I'm there in meetings?" she asked.

"You can count on it."

Matt shook his head. "We don't need watching," he said emphatically.

"Yeah," Jason added, taking a big bite of the stir-fry. Hot sauce rolled down his chin and onto his shirt.

"Nice going, nerd," Matt offered, shaking his head.

Brad looked at Linda and smiled widely. "That is so awesome."

She grinned, basking in the moment.

"Should we come watch?" he asked.

"It's an announcement, not a coronation." She laughed and added, "Thank you for the thought, but it will be fifteen minutes of announcement and then off to four days of meetings."

"Okay, but you've worked up to this for eight years and it is a big deal."

"Thank you, sweetie." She came around the table and kissed him.

"Please," Matt responded, "I'm eating."

Linda gave him a sideways look. "Seems like you should be the last one to complain about kissing these days. You've been trying out, what does your brother call it?–your lip lock on Claire."

"Mom, stop," Matt said, fighting embarrassment.

Linda kissed Brad again. "Thanks for being so supportive," she said.

"I only wish we could all be there to see the promotion." He looked at Matt and Jason. "Mom kicked butt, right guys?"

"Yep," Jason said. "She is awesome!"

"How about you Matt?" Brad asked. "You have something to add?"

"If an HR executive is in everybody else's business, she's probably pretty good at it."

Brad frowned. "That wasn't nice."

"Relax, Dad, just kidding."

"It didn't sound like a joke."

Matt was a little fidgety, having painted himself into a corner. "Yeah, yeah. I know she's really good at what she does." He put down his fork. "Can I be excused?"

"What's your plan for tonight?" Linda asked.

"Going to study at Claire's." Linda and Brad both looked at him and waited. "Relax, both her parents are home."

"Okay," Linda said, "be home at 9:00."

"Going to study Claire you mean. More lip lock," Jason said grinning.

"Shut up, you little twerp."

"None of that kind of talk or you'll both be grounded."

Matt shook his head. "Why does he have to be such an asshole?"

Linda snarled, "We don't talk like that around here. Next time you spit out something like that you can tell Claire you're unavailable for the next week."

"Okay, I'm sorry," Matt said. "He's just such a..."

"Quit while you're ahead, Matt," Brad directed.

He nodded and walked toward the door.

"You're forgetting your homework," Brad yelled in his direction. Matt grabbed his backpack from the living room and headed out the front door.

"Can I be excused, too?" Jason asked.

"Yeah. And you don't need to stir it up all the time, young man," Linda replied.

"Me?" Jason said indignantly. "I'm just stating facts."

"Well, stop stating facts that are your brother's business and you'll get along much better."

"All right. Can I go?"

"I said yeah," Linda responded. "Go, before I change my mind."

As he ran up the stairs Linda and Brad looked at one another and laughed. "This is how parenting is supposed to work, right?" she asked.

"Beats me. I'm faking it, just like you are."

"Want to do dishes?" he asked.

"No. You?"

"No." He paused. "Want to have sex?"

She smiled and said, "Yeah, in the kitchen or in the car?"

"In any room we can keep kids out of. The downstairs bathroom's free."

"I'm in," she said, smiling, "anywhere they can't find us or call us."

Chapter Three
Kevin Roper

At 10:30 a.m., the phone rang and Kevin Roper hit a button and said, "Roper."

"Hi, Mr. Roper. Ashley Gibbons here."

"Hi, Ashley."

"Mr. Eaton and the executive board would like to meet with you now if you can be available."

"What's the status of the negotiation?" Roper asked.

"The Veritable team has been left in the conference room pending our discussion with you. Mr. Eaton instructed me to keep them there until he meets with you. How soon can you be here?"

Roper considered and said, "I can be there in about twenty minutes."

"Great," Gibbons said. "We will leave word downstairs that you are to be taken to the Chairman's suite as soon as you check in."

"Fine. On my way," Roper said and hung up. He sat back in his seat and grinned. This was going to be interesting. He ran a hand through his short, black hair, and pushed his glasses back on his nose. He looked part accountant and part professor—handsome in a nerdy kind of way. His appearance was Clark Kent meets Chris Isaak. At thirty-seven, he had already discovered success in an independent and entrepreneurial way.

Roper grabbed the file he needed for the meeting. He turned off the playlist as Asia's "Holy War" was beginning and looked around the office. It occurred to him that the corporate battles he inhabited were "Holy Wars" in their own way, with big stakes and corporate careers on the line. He grabbed his jacket from the hanger behind the door and raced through the unoccupied reception suite to the bank of elevators. He loved his office because he made it just what he wanted it to be. Inside the double glass doors was a large, well-furnished and uninhabited reception suite, two conference rooms each having three computers on long conference tables, and Roper's private office, complete with fireplace. The reception suite was simply a large room he passed through coming and going, with two desks and no occupants. It was simply a buffer between him and the outside world. He had plenty of space in what had once been an executive condo, and he had no need for employees. Besides, if employees knew what he did, they would put him, and potentially themselves, at risk. So what Roper did, he did alone. After one try at marriage that lasted only a year, he was unattached at age thirty-nine. His life was as he had designed it. He was free to date, to have fun and to work eighty hours a week without guilt.

Roper made his way downtown and parked in a reserved space under the building. He walked into the massive three-story lobby of the latest glass and steel monolith on Fifth Street in downtown Los Angeles, the upper fourteen floors of which were occupied by Bryant International. As he walked toward the desk, a uniformed security officer and a man in a suit stood next to the security desk ready to greet him.

"Good afternoon, Mr. Roper," the young man greeted, extending a hand. "I'm Mike Sanchez, Mr. Eaton's assistant."

"Mr. Sanchez," Roper responded, shaking the hand.

"If you'll follow me, sir. I'll take you to the private elevator that is waiting."

Roper followed the man down a corridor and around a corner to where a woman waited by a large gold and glass elevator.

"Good afternoon, Ms. Cole," Roper said, greeting the woman.

"Hi, Mr. Roper," the thirtyish brunette said softly. "They are waiting for you." They climbed into the elevator and the woman turned a key and pushed the button at the top, which simply said 'Penthouse.' They rode silently for the twenty-five seconds it took to climb fifty- three floors. As they stepped out of the elevator, Ms. Cole said, "Let's take the short cut." He gestured that she should lead the way and then followed her through double doors of smoky glass. They turned down a narrow corridor and walked to an unmarked door at its end. A code box and card reader were mounted beside the door. She ran a card through the card reader and then punched a series of numbers into a code box. She lifted the handle and they were in a back corner of Jack Eaton's private reception area. Roper followed her past three desks and into a conference room with a massive oak table that would have seated forty people. The room was currently occupied by seven people, a couple of whom Roper had met. The rest were strangers to him.

From the end of the table a man in his late fifties, with white hair swept back, stood to greet him. As he smiled, Jack Eaton greeted him, "Kevin, thanks for coming."

"My pleasure," Roper said.

"Please, come down and sit here," Eaton said, gesturing to a chair that awaited him adjacent to Eaton's.

Roper shook Eaton's hand and sat down. The faces around the room regarded him with anticipation, waiting silently for Eaton to lead the conversation.

Eaton swung his chair to face Kevin directly. He smiled and said, "So, it looks like you've done it again. Tell me what you've got."

Roper opened his file, pulled out a couple of documents, and laid them in front of him. He said, "Your team let me know that during your negotiations Veritable stated that its subsidiary, Monarch Industries, no longer had issues with potential liability for the way it has been disposing of its two controversial solvents, right?"

"Affirmative," Eaton said. "That's what they represented and we haven't found anything to the contrary."

"Well," Roper said grinning, "you will. They are not exactly being forthright with you." He handed Eaton the first of the documents in front of him. "This is the notice to Monarch Industries that a full government investigation is now underway. It is dated two weeks ago." He handed the document to Eaton and waited.

Eaton shook his head as he read. "Those bastards," he muttered.

"And there is one more important document," Roper said, passing the second document. "Here is an email from legal counsel at Monarch advising executives that this investigation will be extensive and is likely to consume several months to a year. Note that the addressees include top execs at Veritable as well as Monarch, so it will be hard for them to suggest that they were unaware of these developments."

Eaton silently reviewed the document and then said, "Holy shit. Two of the addressees on this email are in the conference room down the hall right now." He looked to the elegant looking woman on his left. "Theresa, can your team put together an analysis of costs, including PR, staffing costs, fines and corrective actions costs."

"You got it, Jack," the woman said, taking the documents and walking toward the door.

As Theresa walked out, Ms. Cole appeared at the door. "The visitors are inquiring about how much longer they need to wait," she said.

Eaton smiled. "I'd like to say until hell freezes over, but just send in sandwiches and tell them we will be with them as soon as possible. Thank them for their patience."

Ms. Cole nodded, spun and moved out of the room.

"Any questions?" Eaton asked the other executives in the room.

There was a moment of silence, and then a bald man sitting five seats from Roper responded. "Kevin, I'm Bob Timmons. My question is, how sure are we about the information you've provided?"

"Mr. Timmons, I would say as close to one hundred percent as you can be about anything. I mean, these are documents that Veritable and Monarch created."

"Any other questions?" Eaton posed.

"Yes," said a thin man with hair only above his ears and large dark-rimmed glasses, "I have a question. How did you get this information?"

Roper glanced at Eaton, who looked angry. Roper just grinned. "Well, sir, I'm a researcher. Finding out things is what researchers do. Like reporters, I can't give up sources or my sources dry up."

Eaton, perturbed by the last question said, "Okay, enough questions." He looked at Roper and said, "I know I've offered this before, but if you ever change your mind, I'd love to have you come work for me. I will make you a hell of a deal."

Roper smiled. "Thank you, Mr. Eaton, and if I ever decided to join an organization, it would likely be yours, but I am content right now."

"Well keep us in mind and keep doing good work for us."

"My pleasure, sir," Roper said as he stood up. He waved to the room and then turned back to Eaton. "Let me know how this comes out, will you. I'd love to know if the Veritable deal is remade, and if so, what I've helped you save. And don't worry, your savings won't affect my price structure."

Eaton said, "We will. And don't forget, I want you here full time. Think about a package that might persuade you to join us."

"Thanks," Roper said and headed out of the room thinking that this had been a pretty good day so far. Not only was he being courted by one more Fortune 500 company, he had made a hundred and fifty thousand dollars for about three weeks of work.

Roper had several other projects underway, and when he checked his phone found that a new corporate client had called during the meeting to tell him that they had some work they needed on a priority basis. The first time a client called, they always had the notion that they could call him today and he could do the work tomorrow. They were shocked to learn that he considered every assignment for one to two weeks before he would tell them if he would take it. It made no sense to them and he gave them no explanation. Without payment, he spent days evaluating how the assignment could be done, as well as the risk posed by the project. That analysis was critical. Kevin's work would be regarded by many as corporate espionage. It was a fascinating niche and there was no shortage of work, but he had to stay cautious. Not just cautious, but also invisible. If he was exposed, he never knew how far his corporate targets might go to get even. They might come after him through law enforcement or even more directly, as they also had the ability to work in the shadows. Every action creates an equal and opposite reaction. Newton's laws of physics were in play in the corporate world, and when your actions cost a company millions, that reaction could be quiet warfare.

Roper returned the call and began his initial inquiry. "Is this Joseph Barry?"

"Yes."

"Kevin Roper returning your call. First, how did you get to me?" If there was no good answer to this question, the conversation went no further.

"We were referred by Michael Jefferies."

"Okay. What assistance do you need?"

"We need to know if our technology has been stolen. Can you assist?"

"Maybe. I need more information. Can we meet tomorrow?"

"Earlier the better," Barry said.

"How about 8:00 a.m.?

"That works. Tudor Tower, 53rd Floor. Someone will meet you in the lobby."

"Please have materials available to show me the technology and the reasons you suspect it was stolen, Mr. Barry."

"Done. See you then."

As Roper hung up, he had the familiar feeling of excitement that came from operating on the edge. The excitement of the work and the fear of detection created an addictive high like no other.

Chapter Four
Chris Morgan

Thirteen Days Before

Chris Morgan was five feet six and had always been thin. His thick rimmed glasses completed the weak and nerdy image that had chased him for as long as he could remember. He had struggled with being bullied at school and he was socially nervous and clumsy. The world never seemed to go his way. But, maybe all that was about to change. He wanted the Operations Director job so badly he could taste it. With a new baby on the way, his third, he couldn't hope to survive on a teller's wage; not even on a senior teller's wage. The Operations Director position would change all that, almost doubling his earnings, and after eight years, he felt sure he had the inside track.

Branch Manager, Hank Mercer, had a way of keeping distant, but Chris knew that was just his management style. Chris would be a part of management in the near future and he couldn't wait. The most exciting part of it would be rushing home to tell Connie that he got the promotion and everything would be all right. Their money worries would be a thing of the past. They could buy a new cradle for the baby and new clothes for all of the kids.

Maybe they could even find money for a deposit on a house. It would all be within reach.

At 6:00 p.m., when the last of the tellers had gone for the day, Chris spent some time reviewing the revisions to the cash ordering policies that had just been distributed. He wanted to learn it all, so that he knew all banking operations inside the branch. At 6:30 p.m. he got ready to leave. He stopped at Hank Mercer's office door and said goodbye on his way out. Mercer barely looked up as he mumbled good night. He was distant and cold, even for Mercer. If it had been anyone else, Chris would have been concerned that there was something wrong, but, this was Mercer being Mercer.

As Chris turned and walked toward the door, Mercer called out, "Just a minute, Chris."

Chris returned to Mercer's office door.

"Sit down for a minute," Mercer said in harsh tones. When Chris took a seat in one of two visitor chairs, Mercer said, "We have a problem, Chris."

"Really? What is it?"

"We received a complaint about you violating bank policy."

Chris sat back in shock. He had no idea what this might be. "What do you mean?" he managed to say after a brief pause.

"There has been a harassment complaint against you. We are going to have to put you on leave while we investigate the matter," Mercer said.

Chris was in shock and feeling panic rise up. "What am I accused of? And who is accusing me?"

Mercer said, "That will come out in the investigation."

Chris took a moment and then said, "Hank, I didn't do anything wrong. I have another baby coming and I can't afford to be off work right now."

"I'm sorry Chris, but that's the way we have to do it. I don't get a choice in the matter."

Chris felt like he had been kicked in the gut. He mumbled, "Okay," and then he stood up to leave.

"The investigator will be contacting you next week and set up a time to interview you. You will be told what the accusations are and have the opportunity to respond to them."

Chris sat there in stunned silence. Mercer repeated, "I'm sorry, Chris, I have no choice."

It was like an out-of-body experience. This just couldn't be happening to him. "Okay," Chris managed to say again as he walked from the room. He felt weak in the knees, like he might just collapse under his own weight. Driving home, Chris tried desperately to figure out what he might have done to offend anyone at work. He liked his coworkers and tried to help them learn. As long as he could remember he had been the "go to guy" for tellers with questions. His stomach was churning and he felt a sense of helplessness. He began to cry as he thought about having to tell Connie that he had been suspended. To make it worse, he would earn no money for the next several days while this investigation happened, at a time when they needed every dollar. It was all so sudden and so unfair.

Chapter Five
Josie Everett and Don Silver

Ten Days Before

The calendar said it was almost the beginning of spring, but Des Moines was still winter cold. The latest storm left the roads difficult to travel and a number of communities without power. Josie Everett looked at her husband, Tom, who was still in bed, and then turned and walked to the kitchen without speaking. When she had been a prom queen and he had been a football star, they were a match made in high school heaven. But after twelve years of marriage, forever had become harder to see. Tom was in and out of construction jobs with the demand and the weather. Over the years they had both grown in different ways and they slowly had grown apart. She had studied accounting, and to her way of thinking, he had studied nothing but football and craft beer. There was a distance between them that was hard to navigate. When he wanted sex, her first reaction was to resist. She would tell him that she had a headache or there were other things she had to get done, but he knew the truth. Her desire for him had waned with the growing distance between them.

Josie grabbed a travel cup and some coffee and carefully drove the fifteen miles she commuted to work, but it was hard going in the harsh weather, with cars randomly strewn across and beside the road like pieces arbitrarily left on a game board. She parked in her usual spot and walked into the building. She proceeded to the restroom and checked herself. She was satisfied with what she saw. Her large breasts were always noticed first, and guys had been staring at them since junior high. She had a good figure that she maintained by intermittent jogging and random periods of starvation. She had considered one of the newer, short haircuts that had become popular, but she wasn't there yet. Her long black hair was attractive, and the contrast to her penetrating, dark green eyes still drew stares and smiles. Her high cheek bones and small nose completed an image of elegance and intelligence. Josie would celebrate her thirty-fifth birthday next week and had decided she wanted big changes in her life. She walked back to her office and checked email, responding to several before turning her attention to the documents awaiting her attention and analysis.

At 10:30 a.m., Josie walked down the corridor from her small office to her boss's larger one. She entered and closed the door behind her. He was surrounded by documents as the office was slow to make the turn to paperless. Don Silver was forty and graying at the temples. He was a white-collar guy who was handsome in a Marlboro Man kind of way. He looked up from his laptop and asked, "Any word on my meeting with Encore?"

"Yep. It's all set for Thursday during the L.A. trip."

"Good news, thanks. What about the pitch to Winston Marble?"

"Waiting to hear back from them," she said. "If I don't hear today, I'll call them again."

"Great," he said and smiled warmly at her.

Josie walked to the door and twisted the lock on the handle. She turned and faced him and then reached under her skirt to slide her panties down to the ground. She stepped out of the panties and walked over to him. She smiled and then reached down and rubbed him over his pants. She got an immediate response. She undid his belt, and pulled his pants down, and then straddled his lap and slid him into her. She began to move, at first slowly and then more rapidly. When the chair began to squeak loudly, they stood and she leaned over the desk. He entered her from behind and tried hard to remain silent so they couldn't be heard by the community of workers not far from the office door. She smiled as he came with deep thrusts and held her tightly. She felt warm all over. It was just the way lovemaking was supposed to feel.

They stood and got dressed.

"Wow," he said, "that was incredible."

"Yeah," she said, "it was."

He smiled and took her hand. "I can hardly wait to have you all to myself for four days in Los Angeles," he said.

"It will be wonderful," she said.

"Where does Tom think you are going?" he asked.

"He thinks I'm visiting my sister in Minneapolis," she said.

"Your sister will cover for you?"

"Yeah, although she doesn't like it. What about your wife? Is she suspicious about us?"

He shook his head and then said, "No, I don't think that she has any clue at all. She doesn't behave like she is concerned when your name is mentioned."

She ran a hand through his hair and kissed him softly. "Obviously she should be, though."

"Yeah, I guess so," he replied.

She combed her hair and straightened her blouse and skirt, and then she emerged from Don's office back into the world of work. She was suppressing a smile and had concerns that an after-sex glow might be seen on her face. No one should look like they just got laid on a busy day in an office, so she made herself ponder her lengthy to-do list. She felt a flash of guilt about Tom, realizing that at some point there were decisions to be made there; decisions she had been deferring for some time. She still cared about him and a breakup would be hard, but maybe not as hard as staying together when the love was slowly leaking out like air from a punctured tire. Those hard realities brought her back down in a hurry and she was instantly back in work-mode.

Chapter Six
Kelly Parson

Eight Days Before

Kelly Parson finished her lunch-time workout and showered. She dressed quickly and returned to the hospital, donned her blue scrubs and headed down to radiology. Kelly looked younger than her thirty-eight years and kept herself in good shape. Her gorgeous hazel eyes were usually the first thing people noticed when they met her, and those eyes were set afire by her soft blonde hair. She had delicate features and the kind of a smile that made people like her right away. She was smart and witty, and drawn to people with a good sense of humor—people who didn't take themselves too seriously.

She had a full schedule this afternoon, including consults with two physicians to review MRI's. She had been a physician in the nuclear medicine department at Cedars-Sanai in Los Angeles for five years and had never been happier in her professional life. She was well regarded for her expertise and her manner. She also made enough money to do whatever she wanted to do—which would have been nice but for the fact that she didn't have time to do much of anything.

Work was rewarding, but her private life was, as she characterized it, non-existent and her opportunities for correction bleak. Kelly had tried web-dating, just lunch dating, blind dates set up by her friends, and none of it worked. To the contrary, the thought of going out with another of these unattractive strangers was more than she could take. The supply of self-absorbed, uninspired, inarticulate or just plain boring men out there was inexhaustible. Some of them wanted to talk about past relationships, while others wanted to tell her about their skills in sports, at work or in bed. These dates were so hard to endure, and typically, she could hardly wait to say goodbye to the guy at the end of the date. They never seemed to notice her lack of enthusiasm and clock watching.

There had been a guy she loved in college—really loved. But everyone told them they were too young and somehow, they both let it get away as they chased other dreams. They went away to different universities for post-graduate work after receiving their Bachelor's degrees and lost the future they might have built together; a possible future she let herself contemplate only occasionally. When she got to medical school, where there was hardly time to sleep, let alone build a relationship.

After working as a practicing physician for nine years, the relationship she wanted to find seemed further away than ever. Any free time was hard to come by, and Kelly would rather spend that time listening to a podcast or reading a book than interviewing another random guy who wanted to get laid and get back to football.

During the afternoon, Kelly met with other physicians to consult on interpretations of scans for a liver cirrhosis patient and a hepatitis patient. She spent the remainder of the afternoon training newer practitioners in analysis of CT scans and MRI's. She interviewed an applicant for a radiologist position at the end of the day and made her way home at about 8:00 p.m. She fed her tuxedo cat, Poco, who everyone thought was named after the band. It was actually a short form of Hippocrates—a little nerdy, but she liked it. Kelly made dinner and cleaned up around the condo. Then, she climbed into bed with a book, and Poco took his position, purring beside her. As she settled in for the night, she found herself wishing that there was someone other than a cat next to her to share the day's events and to kiss goodnight. All in good time she told herself. Love would find her if that was supposed to happen, even if she had no time to look for it.

Chapter Seven
Chris Morgan

Five Days Before

Chris Morgan had been at home and constantly worried for five days before they called him to schedule a time for him to meet with the investigator. When he first told her what had happened, Connie had just looked at him, silently appraising, conveying that he had let the family down without saying a word. He had assured her that he had done nothing wrong and everything would be all right. She nodded, but he was not sure that she believed him.

Since the day he had been suspended, Chris had been obsessing about what was going on. Was someone out to get him? And how would they pay the rent and buy food this month? They had nothing in the bank and nowhere to go for money. They had borrowed from her parents and owed plenty already. He was feeling trapped and had far too much time on his hands, most of which was spent replaying the suspension and trying to determine what policy he had allegedly broken.

Now that the day of the interview was here, Chris could hardly wait. He wanted to hear what he had been accused of and to make it right. He wanted to put this all behind him and get back to work. He drove downtown and pulled into the parking lot of California Bank's corporate headquarters. He parked, taking the ticket the machine spat out at him so that he could have it validated. He signed in with security in the lobby and rode the elevator to the fourteenth floor as directed. The receptionist took him to a small conference room where no one waited, flicked on the light, and told him to take a seat and the investigator would be with him shortly.

He straightened his tie and took deep breaths to fend off the nervousness. After about ten minutes, the door opened and a short-haired woman in a business suit stepped inside. She looked about forty years old, was slightly overweight and had a serious expression.

"Mr. Morgan?" she asked.

"Yes, ma'am."

She took a seat across the small table and said, "I am Roberta Fisher, an attorney and investigator for the bank."

"Yes ma'am."

"Mr. Morgan, I am here to ask you questions about accusations that have been made against you at the bank. I have to let you know that depending on what we find, you could face discipline or termination. Your job is just to answer my questions truthfully and completely. We want to get to the truth. We will attempt to keep all of this quiet and only those within the company who have a need to know will be kept informed. Any questions?"

Chris's head was spinning. He couldn't think of any specific questions, so he said, "I don't think so."

"All right, so let's begin. Do you work with a teller named Amy Cooper?"

"Yes, sure."

"How would you describe your relationship with Amy?"

"Good. We are just coworkers, but we get along fine."

"Did you tell Amy that she looked really good in what she was wearing?"

"I might have, I don't know. If I did, I was just complimenting her."

"Did you tell her that a certain outfit made her ass look great?"

Chris froze. It had happened once about a year ago. "Well, it was a year ago and I was only telling her how hot she looked."

"So you did say it?"

"Yes, one time. Like I say, it was a year or more ago."

"Chelsea Wilkins is another teller who works with you regularly, right?"

"Yes."

"Did you tell Chelsea Wilkins that she had great tits?"

"No, no, I never said anything like that."

"Did you stare at her breasts?"

"No."

"Did you ever put your hand on her buttocks while she was bent over a file cabinet?"

"No way."

"Did you talk to Chelsea about her boyfriend?"

"Depends what you mean. She talked about him, so I would like ask how he was and how they were doing."

"How they were doing as a couple?"

"Yeah."

"Why did you need to know that?"

"I didn't need to know it, I was just being social, asking how it was going with her and her boyfriend. She talked about him a lot, so I would just ask how they were doing."

"How often?

"I don't know. Occasionally."

"Did you ever tell her that you wanted to fuck her brains out?"

"No, never. I wouldn't say that to a woman."

"Ever ask her to show you her tits?"

"No, never. I do not talk like that to any woman."

"You ever touch her breasts?"

"Never."

"Mr. Morgan, can you think of any reason that either Chelsea or Amy would want to lie about such things?"

"I have no idea. I can only say that I did not do the kind of things you're asking about. I never would."

"Did you ever ask Amy if it was hard to take her jeans off?"

"What? No, I..." He stopped when it occurred to him that they had a conversation about jeans a couple of years ago. "I can't believe we are having this conversation," he said. "This is really not right."

"What do you mean," Fisher asked him.

"A couple of years ago we talked about our favorite jeans. She said she liked Trend Brand, and I told her I tried them but I didn't like them because they were too hard to get on and off. That was the end of that conversation."

"Did you ever go over to a co-employee's house?"

"One time, yes."

"Whose house did you go to?"

"Amy's."

"Why?"

"She left her coat at work on a Friday night. She called and asked if it was there because she wasn't sure where she left it. I told her I could drop it off on my way home."

"And did you?"

"Yes."

"What did you say to her?"

"Here's your coat."

"And what did she say?"

"Thanks."

"Any more to it?"

"Not that I recall."

"Did you make any comment about her appearance that night?"

"What?"

"Did you say anything about the way she looked?"

Chris sat back in his chair and thought.

"What was she wearing?"

"A dress."

"Did you comment on it?"

"I might have said she looked pretty."

"Anything else?"

"No."

Fisher regarded her notes for a few minutes and then said, "Okay, that's all I have. Is there anything you would like to say?"

Chris drew in a breath and said, "Only that I love my job and I respect women. I would not say sexual things to the women I work with, so none of this makes any sense."

She nodded and made a brief note. "Okay, we are all done here, Mr. Morgan. We will get back to you when the investigation is concluded. It will likely be within the next few days."

Chris stood and shook her hand. "Okay, thank you."

"Will you guys validate parking?" he asked.

"Yes, sure. See the receptionist out front and tell her I said we would do it."

"Thank you," Chris said. He walked to the receptionist and she put a stamp on his parking ticket. As he walked to the car, he replayed the interview in his mind. He wanted to think that this was all behind him soon, but he was worried. He couldn't believe that he had been accused of behaviors like that. He asked himself why they would do that, but could come up with no answer.

As Chris drove home, the questions were spinning around in his mind and he tried to replay them as accurately as possible. The people that he worked with every day and liked—they thought he was a harasser? It just couldn't be right. He would tell Connie everything that happened and she would help him make sense of all this. Nausea rose up in him like a wave and he had to pull over to the side of the road to vomit. It was a nightmare.

Chapter Eight

Three Days Before

Paul Mason stood on the beach watching the sun turn the distant clouds a deep orange-red as it prepared to disappear over the horizon. He dialed Brian Gallagher's number and waited.

"Yes," Brian said when he answered.

"Are you on schedule?"

"Yes. You?"

"Affirmative. I just checked into the Coronado Hotel for the next week. Just going to be sitting on the beach and seeking out untried umbrella drinks."

"Nice. Well, have a wonderful vacation."

"You all set, too?"

"I'll be working from home all week if you need to get hold of me."

"Great. Have fun."

"Yeah, you too. Bye."

* * *

When Chris Morgan told Connie about the interview with the investigator, she stared at him silently. At first she listened attentively and supportively. As he described the sexual comments, comments about clothing, about breasts and alleged touching he had been asked about, he had expected that she would understand that none of these things were true. But somewhere in the process, it felt like a line was crossed and she began to look at him differently. Like a guy who might actually be making sexual comments to the women at work. It struck him suddenly, as her transfixed stare became one of shock rather than support.

"You don't think I did these things?"

She was quiet and then said, "I hope not."

"Do you have faith in me?"

"I do, I do. It's just that these are the kind of comments women always hear. We are subjected to men talking about our body parts all the time. They talk about the way we look, what we wear and what they want to do to us all the time. I've heard it a lot, especially when I worked in the warehouse." She paused and then added, "It just sounds like the kind of thing that is real—the kind of thing that women get to hear wherever they work."

"I know, but that doesn't mean I did it. Honey, you know I'm not out there chasing women."

"I do know that, but I also know that harassment isn't always about chasing."

"So you think I did this?"

"No, I'm not saying that I think you did it. I am saying that it sounds real and I am concerned that these two women think it happened. Do they have any reason to make this up?"

His heart sank. Even the woman who knew him best had the same questions—the same hesitations. "I don't know. They know I want the Operations Director job. Maybe…"

"You think both of these women are making this up to stop you from getting a promotion?" She was quiet a moment and then said, "This is bad, Chris, this is really bad. They are thinking that you harassed these women."

"Do you think I did?"

"Why were you telling a coworker how hot she was or making a comment about her ass? Even if that's all you did, that's not okay." She was getting more upset as she spoke. "We can't afford to have you out of work, Chris, we're barely making it now. And I don't want my husband talking sex or body parts with other women." He saw anger and resentment in her eyes, and then she turned and walked away from him.

Chapter Nine

Two Days Before

Linda Caldwell sat on the sidelines in a folding chair near other parents, watching Jason run back and forth on the soccer field. She knew that they actually planned plays, passes and scoring runs, but it always appeared to her to be random movement. One team got near the goal, the other took it away and moved back to the other side of the field to do the same. They were now nearing the end of the fourth quarter and neither team had managed to score.

Linda glanced about twenty feet down the sidelines to where Matt and Claire sat holding hands. They couldn't stop staring at each other. This can't be good, she thought, seeing the raging hormones that filled the air between them. They were just too horny for kids not yet sixteen. She and Brad had better talk about this and make a plan, as she had no desire to be a grandmother when her oldest son graduated from high school.

She walked down the sidelines and said, "Let's pick everything up and get ready to go." They couldn't stop staring at each other long enough to respond. "You guys hearing me okay?"

"Yes, sorry, Mrs. Caldwell," Claire said.

Linda had an urge to tell Claire to stay away from Matt's pants, but didn't think it would do much good. These two weren't far from some experimentation, if it hadn't started already. "Matt, let's go."

"Okay, Mom, I'm getting ready."

"Getting ready? You're still sitting there staring at Claire."

"Mom, you're embarrassing me."

"Well, I don't mean to, but we need to get ready to go. I want to do some work and then start packing for my trip."

"Why? It's still three days away."

"You know me. I'm not one to wait until the last minute."

"That's for sure."

A whistle blew in the distance and the teams lined up to congratulate one another on a game well played. Jason found them and helped carry chairs to the car.

"Did you see me out there?" he asked. "I had three shots on goal."

"You did, Buddy. Nice work," Linda replied.

"Aren't we overlooking the obvious?" Matt said. "As I recall, none of them went in the goal and the game ended in a scoreless tie."

"You're an asshole," Jason said.

"Don't talk like that Jason. I don't want to hear words like that from you. And Matt, you could be a little supportive. Your brother worked hard out there."

"I think you did a good job," Claire said, smiling at Jason.

"Thanks, Claire."

"Matt? How about an apology to your brother?"

"All right, I'm sorry. I get that you worked hard, even if your team suc..."

Linda interrupted him. "Quit while you're ahead Matt. You almost said something really nice there." She paused a moment and then said, "Can you have dinner with us tonight, Claire?"

"I think so. Just have to check in with my mom."

"Jason, you want to have Trevor over?"

"Yeah, sure. I'll call him now."

Linda smiled. It was one of the unwritten rules of parenting that if one kid gets company, so does the other. Though it was easier where Jason and Trevor were concerned, because she didn't harbor silent fears that she would come home early and find them naked in her bed.

* * *

At noon, the phone rang. Chris was almost sitting on top of it and picked it up on the first ring. "Hello?"

"Chris, this is Hank Mercer. We need you to come into the branch at 1:30 today. Is that okay?"

Hank wasn't his usual, abrupt self. Instead, his boss sounded concerned. "Yes, sure. I'll be there. What is happening?"

"We'll talk about it when you get here, Chris."

"Okay," Chris said. As he hung up the phone, he felt nausea rising.

"Who was that?" Connie asked.

"Hank Mercer. He wants me to go into the bank at 1:30."

"Okay," she said, and then added. "Just be the good guy you are."

He nodded, "I will."

They had a sandwich together, with conversation at a minimum and nervousness filling the air around them. Connie walked out to the car with Chris and gave him a kiss. "It's going to be all right. Think positive."

He nodded and then climbed into the car. He waved as he backed out of the driveway. As he drove toward work, it occurred to him that he still might get the Operations Director promotion once all this was over. His mood brightened and he turned on the radio. This nightmare would all be over soon.

He pulled into his parking spot and walked into the bank. Hank met him at the door and said, "Come with me."

It sounded a little ominous. He followed Hank to the conference room in silence. The attorney he spoke to, Roberta Fisher, and the HR Manager, Gladys Newell were both already in the conference room when he and Hank Mercer arrived.

"Good afternoon, Chris," Newell said. "Please, sit."

Chris sat down and waited. Newell started the conversation. "As you know, the bank has a zero tolerance policy concerning sexual harassment. We have to make sure that all of our workers have an environment free of any sexual harassment. You understand?"

"Yes, ma'am. I understand that."

"In this case, we have two credible women who have stated that you made them very uncomfortable with talk about body parts, sex and inappropriate touching."

"I didn't do that," Chris blurted out, surprised at how angry it came out.

There was a moment of silence and then Fisher said, "Chris, it is our assessment that you engaged in conduct that is a violation of law and a violation of the bank's policy and it is very significant. We have thought long and hard about it, but we think we have to let you go."

"No, no, please. I love this bank. I've worked hard here for eight years and I never intended to offend anyone I work with, I like them all. Please, let me stay with the bank."

"We just can't, Chris. We will give you the chance to resign if you want to so that you don't have a termination on your record. If you do that, if we get calls from any prospective employer, we will tell them only that you quit."

"Please," Chris begged, "don't do this. I am a really good employee."

There were a few moments of quiet and then Newell said, "The decision has been made, Chris. Now it's just a question of how you want this to go."

Chris was angry at this betrayal. He glared at them finding no words to express his panic, then, without saying another word, he stood and walked from the room.

Chapter Ten

The Day Before

At 8:00 a.m., Josie Everett walked into Don's office carrying a bag and wearing a smile. He grinned at her while talking about the estimated time to complete a project to someone on the phone. She opened the bag and showed him a short dress, holding it up to her so he could enjoy the prospects. Then she reached into the bag and came out with a see-through negligee that would cover nothing much at all. Now Don was smiling and having a hard time keeping his attention on the call.

"Okay, so I'll call you when I get back from the LA trip and we'll update the forecast." A moment of quiet and then he said, "Shall do. You too."

Don put down the phone and said, "Wow. Very nice. If we had time I'd want you to try it on for me."

"All in good time. Right now we have to get out of here because our flight leaves in two hours."

"I'm ready. Call an Uber and let's get out of here," Don said, walking to the corner of the office to grab his suitcase. "Let's go have some fun." He thought for a moment and then added, "Maybe we can join the mile high club on the flight."

"Are you kidding? There's hardly enough room for one person to pee in airplane restrooms. I don't know how couples can have sex in a three foot-closet."

"Creative," I guess.

She smiled. "I'd rather have beds, couches or even a rug by a fireplace."

"Don't get me worked up, we have to go."

"Well, I can always give you a personal massage under a blanket while others are sleeping on the plane."

His eyes grew wide. "Now you're talking. In the meantime, put on your business face and let's get out of here and head for the airport."

* * *

When Chris told Connie what happened at the meeting, she became very quiet. As he told her all of the details, her expression became sad and he could see that she was doing her best to be accepting. When he finished, she asked, "Did you tell them that you had made mistakes and that none of this would happen again?"

Chris froze. He wasn't sure he had said anything like that because he didn't believe that he had done anything wrong. "Does that mean you think I did all these things?"

"No. I'm saying that women you work with were obviously offended by some of the things you said and did. You can say that you will be careful without admitting everything that was alleged, right?"

"Yeah, I guess so."

"So how did the meeting end?"

"They told me I could quit or be fired and I walked out of the room."

"You just left?"

"Yeah. They were clearly not listening to me."

"If you quit, then they don't tell people that you were fired for harassment, right?"

"Right."

"Doesn't that make it a whole lot easier to find a new job?"

"It probably does, yeah."

"So do it."

"Okay, I'll call the HR Director and confirm that I quit." She shook her head woefully. "What?" he asked.

"I'm worried, Chris. We can barely afford the mortgage as it is. I just don't know how we're going to make it."

"I know. As soon as I talk to the company, I'll go down to the unemployment office, and then I'll start looking for a new job."

She nodded and quietly moved toward the living room where the kids awaited her attention.

Chris felt a rising panic in his gut. "Oh my God," he said to an empty room. He dialed HR at headquarters and asked for Ms. Newell.

"Hi, Chris," she said softly.

"I've decided it's probably best if I resign. Then you don't give out any reason for me being gone, right?"

"That's right, Chris. Anyone who asks will simply be told that you elected to leave or resign. We will give no further explanation."

"Okay, write me down as a resignation."

"You're sure? Because I can't change it once it goes into the system."

"Yeah, I'm sure."

"All right, Chris. That's what your file says as of right now. I am entering it as we speak."

"Okay, thanks," he said, and hung up.

Chris checked the clock. He still had time to get to the Employment Development Department and file his unemployment claim today. He said goodbye to Connie and raced out the door. He arrived at the unemployment office at 4:05 p.m. and there was a long line ahead of him, but there should be plenty of time to get to the front of it before they closed at 5:00. He saw an open window and walked up to it.

"Yes, sir," a blonde woman in her mid-twenties said.

"I need to apply for unemployment benefits."

"Certainly, sir," the polite blonde said with a big smile. She handed him a small stack of forms and said, "Complete these in one of the cubicles over there," she said pointing, "and then get in that line when you are done." He looked at the stack of forms and then back at her. "Don't worry," she said, "it moves pretty fast."

He nodded and moved away from the window, finding a seat in one of the cubicles and filled out the requested personal information as fast as he could. At 4:45 he stood and got into the line. There were ten ahead of him. At 4:58 there were still three ahead of him. 'This was not going to work,' he thought, feeling frustrated.

Some of the windows were now showing closed signs and he knew there was no way he would make it in one more minute. At that moment, a balding man in a suit appeared behind the woman seated at the window in front of him and said, "Don't worry. If you are in this line now, we will not close before we see you."

Chris drew a deep breath, fending off some of the anxiety that had overtaken him. 'All right,' he told himself, 'this will all work out and then I will find another job.'

Chris made it to the front of the line at 5:15. The woman looked at his documents and then looked back at him. "Did you resign your position?"

"Yes."

"Why?"

"Just ready to do something different," he mumbled.

"I'm so sorry, sir. You are not eligible for unemployment benefits."

"What?" he asked too loudly, the anxiety returning immediately.

"When you quit your job you don't get benefits, sir. Here, it's in the rules." She handed him a booklet and all of the documents he had completed. "Thanks for coming in and so sorry we can't be of assistance to you."

Chris walked over to a nearby chair and sat down, afraid that he might fall down if he didn't. "That bitch," he said audibly, and others turned to give him disapproving glances. Newell never told him that if he agreed to resign, his unemployment benefits would go away. He was breathing deeply through his mouth as anger rose up inside him.

"Are you okay, sir?" a man walking by asked him.

Chris stood and ran from the building, having no idea what to do next.

* * *

The phone rang just before 7:00 p.m. Linda grabbed it on the second ring. "Hello?"

"Ms. Caldwell?"

"Yes, who's this?"

"This is Adrianna Newby at the California Bank. We are processing your refinance documents and found a problem."

"What's that?"

"There is a place on page 52 that does not have your signature. Can you come by the bank tomorrow and provide the missing signature?"

"Page 52, huh? I guess I stopped reading the small print when I got to page 51."

The woman laughed. "I know. I stopped on page 10 and I see these documents all the time."

"Okay, I'll come by tomorrow."

"If not, we can arrange to do it all electronically, but it's easier at this point to provide the single missing signature."

"Yeah, I'm leaving town the day after tomorrow, but I can find time to stop by tomorrow. What time?"

"How about between 12:30 and 1:00 p.m.?"

"You got it. I'll be there."

"Thanks so much and sorry for the inconvenience."

"Not a problem. This is an easy fix."

"Thanks. I will look forward to seeing you tomorrow."

"You bet," Linda said. As she hung up the phone she added this latest task to her to-do list for tomorrow. There was a bunch to do before she left for Vegas.

Part 2
The Invisible Robbery

Chapter Eleven

The Day Of

Chris didn't sleep all night. He paced around the kitchen and drank too much coffee while Connie and the kids slept. He had been silent when he returned from the unemployment office, unable to tell Connie that he could not get unemployment and they were in big trouble. He wanted to tell her, but each time he tried, he couldn't find the words. The sun would rise in the next hour and he had not come up with a plan. There was nothing he could do. There would be no money when the bills came in this month.

Chris paced faster, calling Gladys Newell a 'fucking cunt.' That bitch had ruined him. Hank Mercer was worse. He hadn't even tried to stand by Chris, just threw him under the bus with the first bullshit complaints. For eight years he had given everything to the bank and he had been betrayed. They had taken everything from him; his earnings, his self-respect and maybe even his family. This could not stand.

Chris walked to the hall closet, pulled out the step-stool and reached up to a box at the tallest point on the shelf. He pulled down the box and took out the Saturday night special he had purchased for seventy dollars a couple of years ago. It wound up in this closet and out of view because Connie wanted nothing to do with guns and wanted to make sure it was never within reach of the kids. But, now he needed it. He tucked the gun inside the water heater cupboard for easy access and walked upstairs. Maybe now he could sleep for a little while, then, he would make things right. They would be held accountable for what they had done to him.

* * *

Josie and Don got off the plane at 2:30 a.m. and went to the airport Sheraton, where they got more exercise than sleep. They fell asleep at about 4:30 a.m., then awoke and made love again at 9:00 a.m.

"You feeling spent yet, cowboy?" she asked him with a wide grin.

"Yeah, but every time I look at that ass of yours, I get excited all over again."

"Take me to breakfast and then we'll come back here for more," she said.

"Yeah, okay. I don't have to be at the meeting until 2:00 p.m."

"I'll shop a little while you're at your meeting and then we can have a romantic dinner somewhere."

He was quiet a moment and then said, "You sure Tom isn't suspicious about us?"

She gave him a curious look. Why did he bring that up? Was he worried Tom was going to come after him? "I don't know," she said and then paused. "He knows that I am not sleeping with him much anymore, so he might think that there is someone else. We just don't talk about it."

"Yeah, I get it. It just isn't like it once was. The passion slowly leaks out of relationships, right?"

She paused and then said, "I don't know. Tom and I are both sad about what we lost along the way. I'm not sure I should tell you that, but I'm doing it anyway. I guess I'm trying to figure out what's real in the relationships we built our lives around. What about you and your wife? Is it a relationship you plan to save?"

"I don't know. I haven't thought about it because I'm not sure she even suspects. She never raises any question anyway. I just don't want it to be more complicated than it has to be."

Josie paused a moment. She furrowed her brow and asked, "And what do you want out of our relationship?"

"I want to fuck your brains out, gorgeous. I just can't get enough."

"And that's it?"

"I don't know," he replied. She gave him a stern look. "Truly, I don't know what I want," he said.

"I know we're having fun, but I was wondering whether I was more to you than a fuck buddy."

"You are. You really are," he said. "It's just complicated."

She nodded. "Yeah, it's complicated, but I'd like to know what you feel about us."

He smiled and said, "Let's go to breakfast now and talk life later. I'm starved."

* * *

Chris slept for about an hour. He awoke and it all came crashing back down on him. The loss of his career, no money and no unemployment. He dressed and drank coffee, avoiding conversation with Connie, then made his way to the water heater and grabbed up the gun. When he made his way back to the kitchen, Connie asked him if everything went okay at the unemployment office and he told her that he thought so. He couldn't bring himself to tell her that there would be no money. Later in the morning, he told Connie he was going to do something about their situation and left the house in a hurry. He drove to the downtown branch at 11:45 a.m., but Hank Mercer's car wasn't in the parking lot. He called the bank's customer number.

"Good morning, California Bank, this is Denise, how can I help you?"

He was quiet a moment and then said, "Hi, Denise, this is Chris." There was a silence on the line and it was clear that Denise did not know what to say, "Everything is okay. I was just calling with a question for Hank about my benefits. Is he in?"

"No, he had a meeting outside the branch but I expect him back in the next fifteen or twenty minutes. Shall I have him call you?"

"No, I'm going to be out for a little while. I'll give him a call later on. Thanks Denise."

"Sure. Take care, Chris."

Chris bought a cup of coffee from a mini-mart on the corner and walked around the block. By the time he returned, Hank Mercer's Lexus was in the parking lot. He touched his belt line to assure himself that the gun was still in place. All was good. At 12:24 p.m., he walked into the bank.

* * *

The morning was incredibly hectic for Linda Caldwell. Jason had a field trip and, naturally, hadn't obtained the necessary consent or even remembered he needed one. Linda took him to the drop-off point at school, found the teacher in charge and signed the missing form. With Jason on his way, she and Matt picked up Claire and she gave them a ride to school in the other direction. None of this was that unusual, it was just that today she had a lot of work to do before she took a late afternoon flight to Las Vegas. She was also stressed because of the raging hormones that filled the car. Claire needed to be fitted for a chastity belt or something. These two were going to experiment anytime they could find thirty seconds and a quiet corner.

After she dropped off Romeo and Juliet, Linda returned to the home office, responded to emails and worked on the two critical projects at the top of her list. At 11:30 she put her bag in the car and left the house for Los Angeles International Airport. She was feeling better because she had plenty of time. She would make one stop at the bank to sign the page that had been overlooked in their refinance documents and she would be on her way. By tonight, she would be checked into her room at Mandalay Bay and watching the craziness that was Las Vegas. Linda parked and walked into the bank at 12:26 p.m.

* * *

Don parked the car on the sixth floor of a massive parking structure and he and Josie made their way down to street level. It had been a quiet ride. Since their exploration of what the relationship might be, Josie had been uncharacteristically quiet and Don was feeling a little awkward, unable to find words to push them past that conversation. He wanted to get back to fun and laughter, but the road back was hard to find.

When they got to street level, Don realized that he had parked in the wrong building, which would make getting reimbursed for a big parking fee impossible. They walked toward the building where his meeting was to occur, which was right next door to the bank. Maybe he could get past the emerging rift between them by giving her money to shop with while he was in his meeting.

"I need to stop here for a minute," he said, gesturing toward the bank. "Is that okay?"

"Yeah, sure," Josie said.

He walked up to the ATM, but then changed his mind because this is money he could not account for when he got back home. But there was another account he could use.

"Let's go inside," he told her.

"Okay," she said, agreeably. They walked into the bank at precisely 12:28 p.m.

* * *

Kelly's twelve hour shift at Cedars-Sinai was scheduled to begin at 2:00 p.m. She stopped for a chicken wrap and iced tea at Cabana, a small sandwich shop without outdoor seating. She indulged herself with the time needed to read those portions of the Los Angeles Times that caught her attention. She reflected that her life had become so busy that taking the time to get the news was now a guilty pleasure. How would she ever find time for a personal relationship?

She finished her iced tea and paid the check, giving the young server a big tip. He had done nothing extraordinary, but Kelly believed in tips. People who worked hard for near minimum wage needed all the help they could get.

She walked out of the restaurant and it was then that the bank caught her eye. She checked her watch and saw that she still had some time before her shift. This would be a great opportunity to set up her IRA, something she had been planning forever and never found time to do. She walked into the bank at 12:30 p.m.

* * *

At 12:31 p.m., Kevin Roper checked his watch and then walked into the bank. He walked over to the tables where deposit and withdrawal slips were completed prior to getting in the line for teller service. He pulled three checks from his wallet and began to prepare a deposit ticket. He glanced at the others around him and instantly saw a face that was familiar. It was a face he had known years ago, but it hadn't changed much from the one he remembered. She was pretty back then and now she was more mature and pretty had become gorgeous.

She was looking directly at him, apparently going through a similar recognition process. They stared at each other for a few moments and then she said, "Kevin?"

"Kelly?"

"Yes. Oh my God, I haven't seen you since high school graduation." She threw her arms around him and gave him a hug that he willingly returned. "I can't believe it," she said.

"You look amazing," he told her.

"You're looking pretty good yourself," she said, and then looked momentarily embarrassed.

"What are you doing now?" he asked. "I remember that you were planning to go to medical school, right?"

"That's it," she said. "I did it and I'm now practicing at Cedars-Sinai."

"Wow." He smiled and then added, "You always were impressive."

She looked embarrassed again. "What about you?" she asked. "What are you doing?"

"I'm in technology. I find new ways of using it creatively," he said. He knew this intentionally cryptic response told her nothing.

"I have to work at 2:00 p.m.," she said. "How about we make a time to get together and catch up?"

He caught her looking at his fingers. "Divorced," he said. "Three years now."

"You?"

"I never found the right guy," she replied. She wrote on a deposit slip and then handed it to him. "Here's my number," she said. "Call me."

"I will," he said.

* * *

When Chris walked into the bank, he looked around him and saw nothing out of the ordinary, but he was sweating, overcome by the weight of what he had come to do. Chris scanned the bank lobby. It was another busy banking lunch hour, with three tellers open and ten people in line behind those now occupying the windows. He wiped his brow with his sleeve and he could almost hear his heart beating as he walked slowly down the hall in the corner of the bank toward the manager's office. On impulse, he touched the gun beneath his jacket. It was still there and ready. The walk down the hall to the manager's office had never been this long before. Each step took minutes and the sound of his shoes on the tile echoed across the bank. He felt suddenly heavy and it was hard to keep his feet moving. Then he felt the nausea rise inside him. He reached his destination and knocked on Hank Mercer's door.

"Come in," Mercer said. The moment Chris heard Mercer's voice, he realized he just couldn't do it. He couldn't shoot Mercer. He couldn't shoot anyone, no matter how they betrayed him. And, he couldn't leave his family to fend for themselves while he went to prison.

"Come in," Mercer said again. Chris retreated quickly back down the hall to the center of the bank and then accelerated, moving quickly toward the front door. As he moved faster, people looked up at him. He looked straight ahead and went faster yet. The front door was only fifteen feet away now.

* * *

Paul and Brian parked fifty feet away from the bank in a handicapped spot, putting the blue and white disabled placard that identified the car as legitimately parked on the rear view mirror. They wore long beards that covered them from their nose to their chest. They each grabbed a back pack and a gym bag from the back seat and they made their way toward the bank. As they approached the building, they quickly put on ski caps and eye masks. They pulled handguns from their pockets and pushed through the door to see a man walking toward them at top speed.

"Stop," Brian told him in an altered, electronic voice. "Stop right there."

Chris Morgan stopped in his tracks.

Paul located the guard and ordered him to drop his weapon, which he did. "Everyone on the ground, face down," Paul screamed across the bank lobby.

As Paul watched the group, Brian walked down the hall and came back with Hank Mercer and two other employees who were in the break room.

Paul yelled toward the tellers. "Put the money from your drawers into these bags. No marked bills, no dye packs and no GPS. Got it?"

There was nodding all around. "Everyone else in here," Brian said, gesturing to the conference room.

Once they were gathered inside, Brian said, "Everyone face down on the floor."

Kevin Roper stayed standing and Brian yelled, "You too, man."

Kevin seemed to be frozen in place. Brian hit him in the gut and doubled him over. Kevin found himself on his knees and trying hard to catch his breath.

"Stay face down. No one moves," Brian said, looking around the room and assuring that all were frozen in place. He closed the door and the room was silent.

Brian walked over to the storage room next to the vault. On the wall inside the door, he found a grey box that looked like circuit breakers with a lock built into the front. He reached into his pocket and pulled out a small tool kit. He opened the kit and selected what looked like an ice pick. He inserted the device into the lock on the box and began to twist. Brian had it open within thirty seconds. He connected a device to three distinct wires inside the box. He walked out into the lobby and confirmed that all cameras had been disabled and then gave a nod to his partner.

* * *

In the conference room everyone stayed face down on the floor. After a long two minutes, a voice said, "What do we do?"

Kevin said, "We survive this." He looked over at Kelly, who was just a few feet away. She looked his way and her expression was pained.

"Are you okay?" he whispered.

She nodded and said, "Yes. You?"

"Yes," he replied.

A male voice somewhere across the room from Kevin said, "These guys aren't professionals."

"What do you mean?" a woman asked.

"I mean they never even collected our cell phones to keep us from communicating outside the bank."

"Okay. Someone call 911," another voice said.

"You do it," someone else said.

Finally, someone said, "I just sent a text message to my daughter to call 911. We should get some help soon."

Josie was positioned near the conference room door and was crying. Don told her that everything would be okay, even though he was scared shitless and didn't know if he believed it. His assurances had little impact on Josie, who continued to sob. In that moment, Don realized that this was going to be national news and this is how his wife Naomi would learn that he was fucking Josie. Maybe they would have a chance to discuss it and he could apologize. Or the cruelest possibility of all, he would die today and her last memory of him would be that he had been cheating with a younger woman and had taken her away on his last trip anywhere. His parting gift to her would be to ruin every memory they had shared together.

The door opened and Brian stepped inside. "All right," his electronically distorted voice said, "You," as he pointed at an elderly woman, "you," he said and pointed at Linda Caldwell, "and you," he said, pointing at Kevin Roper. "The three of you come with me. Keep your hands in the air where I can see them clearly."

The three stood with hands vertical beside their ears, and began to follow Brian. As they started moving toward the door, Chris Morgan decided it was up to him to stop this. Maybe he could protect these people and make up for the mistake in judgment that brought him here today. He pulled the Saturday night special from his waist band and lifted it toward Brian. Brian saw the initial movement and pivoted. Brian had his gun trained on Chris before Chris could complete his move. In that instant, Kevin Roper kicked the gun from Chris' hands away as he walked past Chris. Chris and everyone else in the room was in complete shock. "Are you trying to get yourself and all the rest of us killed? I want to get out of here alive, you crazy son of a bitch," Kevin yelled at Chris as the gun went skidding toward Brian, who grabbed it.

Brian looked at Chris and the electronic voice growled, "You stupid shit. You want to be responsible for getting people killed?" He looked around and said, "You can all get out of this without injury or you can do something stupid and die today." Chris shook his head, unhappy that his attempt to save them had been undermined. He could have taken that guy out.

Brian walked out the door with his three chosen followers. He led them down the hall to where the offices were located. He made a stop at the first door down the hall, the Operations Director's office. Paul came walking towards them and said, "Mr. Costello." He handed the three bags of money that he had been given by the tellers to Brian.

"Thank you, Mr. Abbott," Brian responded. He then pointed to Kevin. "You, in here. Go through this bag and pull out consecutive bills, dye packs and GPS devices. You have ten minutes."

"You," Brian said to Linda Caldwell. "You do the same with this bag." He pointed to the adjacent manager's office and handed her the bag. She disappeared inside and he closed the door. Linda walked to the desk and put the bag down. She sat down in Hank Mercer's chair and cried, realizing that the life she had built was over, whether she lived through the day or not. This day would cost her everything she loved. She put her head in her hands and tried desperately to think of some answer, any answer; some plan that would allow her to believe that she could make it through this and keep her family, but she could come up with nothing. It was so ironic that the life she had worked so hard to rebuild would be destroyed in a single day, simply because she was in the wrong place at the wrong time. She thought of Brad, Matt and Jason and how she was about to lose them and they had no idea. She loved them beyond all words. She needed a chance to explain. Would she ever get that chance or would she die here today, leaving them with a secret that would tear her family apart? One way or another, it was all going to come out today. She wanted to live long enough to explain it herself and to ask for their forgiveness. As she took everything out of the bag and began to search as instructed, she said her prayers aloud. "Please Lord, help me figure out what to do. There has to be something I can do. Please help me figure out what that is and I will find a way to make it right. Please, please."

After Linda Caldwell entered Mercer's office, Brian walked further down the hall. "Now you," he said to the elderly woman, who was now shaking almost violently. "You do the same in here." He pointed to the break room. "You do what we tell you and you will not be hurt. Understand?" The woman forced a nod and moved into the break room. The door was closed behind her.

Brian walked back to the desks of the loan officers and personal bankers, where Paul was seated. Paul said, "Okay, we are eleven minutes in. First contact should be between seven to ten minutes from now. Let's get to work."

They walked back to the conference room and Paul said, "All right, Mr. Mercer and Ms. Jacobs, get your keys and let's go."

"We can't open..." Hank Mercer started to say.

"Save your breath," Brian said. "We know exactly who can do what. Don't waste time and don't endanger the others. Let's go." The electronic voice was commanding and confident.

There was no Operations Director, so senior teller, Sophie Jacobs, had been designated as the other key carrier. Somehow, these guys knew that.

"Follow Mr. Costello," Paul said. He in turn followed them to the vault. "You have two minutes to get it open," Brian told them.

Mercer and Jacobs scrambled to the locks and got it done in less than a minute. They stared straight ahead, nervously. "Back to the conference room," Brian said. He followed them and closed the door once they were inside and back on the floor with the others. Paul and Brian then began moving the money from the vault—nothing smaller than twenties.

Linda Caldwell was feeling desperate. She had to try to get out of this. There had to be some way out before it was too late. She moved to the door of the manager's office and opened it just enough to give her a view down the hallway. She could see that there was nowhere to go. But as she started to close the door, she saw something else. There was someone walking out toward the two bank robbers; someone who shouldn't have been out there. She watched in fascination as the man approached the robbers. This guy was either crazy or was one of them. Mr. Abbott and Mr. Costello did not seem surprised by his arrival. They began to engage in conversation with the new arrival, who turned slowly in her direction as he spoke. His face came into view and it was a face Linda recognized. She stared in disbelief, and then slowly closed the door before anyone noticed her.

After ten minutes of moving money, Paul asked, "Got as much as we need, Mr. Costello?"

"Yeah, we're there."

As they completed the task, another voice said, "Are we ready for the next step?"

Paul said, "Yeah, let's get to it. We're going to get the first call in just a few minutes."

The newly arrived man simply said, "Good."

Brian said, "I'll be with you as soon as I handle cash, phase two."

The two men seated themselves at the financial service reps desks and began working the keyboards. Within three minutes there were recognizable sounds outside the bank. Paul knew that police would be clearing this block and everyone within a two block radius. There would be patrol and unmarked cars lining the streets and providing a protective barrier between the officers and the building.

It took eight additional minutes before the expected phone call. Paul let the phone ring three times before picking up. "Hello, who is this?" Paul asked in his electronic voice.

"This is Lieutenant Marshall Briggs, LAPD."

"Well, Lieutenant, I'm going to need to speak to a trained negotiator. Is that you?"

"I can help you," was the reply.

"Not if you can't answer my questions," Paul replied.

"No, I am not a negotiator. I have one on the way, but I can help now."

"Have that person call me, please," Paul said and hung up, anticipating that he had just bought another ten minutes or so.

Brian emerged and sat down at an adjacent desk, entering information into the computer. "Estimate?" he asked simply.

"I'll need at least another half-hour," the new arrival said.

"No problem," Paul said.

They worked for an additional seven minutes before the phone rang again. On the third ring, Paul picked it up. "Hello," Paul said.

"This is Emery Caplan. I am the negotiator you wanted. What is your name?"

"You can call me Bill."

"Okay, Bill. First, we have a direct line to you. You pick up the phone and I will be on the other end."

"Okay, good," Paul replied.

"We want to bring you out safely. Isn't that what you want, too?"

"First, I want to convey that everyone can make it out of here safely if you don't do anything to jeopardize them. Second, I need a plan from you to get about twenty of us out of here and to the airport in about three hours. Work on that and I'll get back to you in about a half-hour."

"Work with us," Caplan said. "Release some of the hostages in a show of good faith while we work on your request, okay?"

"We'll talk about releasing some hostages in a while. First, I need to know that you are sincere about getting us out of here safely," Paul said in electronic tones.

"Is everyone okay in there?"

"Everyone is fine. No injuries so far and I want to keep it that way," Paul said.

"I'd like to come in and verify that, Bill," Caplan said in his most friendly voice.

Paul paused briefly to make it seem like he was thinking this over. "We can talk about that later if you do what I ask."

"Okay. I want you assure me that all the hostages remain safe while we work on your request."

"You have that assurance as long as no one out there does anything stupid. I will call you in a half-hour for an update," Paul said and then hung up.

* * *

Caplan called Lieutenant Briggs and said, "Give me some kind of an exit plan that I can take to them."

Briggs said, "I know you are all about buying time in these situations, Caplan, but don't have any misconceptions. I am never letting these guys leave here without surrendering."

"I know, Lieutenant, but I have to give them something to keep them talking."

Briggs said, "Tell them we'll pick them up in golden chariots and fly them to the stars for all I care. But as soon as what you're doing stops working, my team will enter the building."

Caplan was quiet and then said, "Get me a bus that I can pull out front to show them their means of departure."

"This is such bullshit," Briggs said. "All right, I'll order you a bus. Tell them it will be here in an hour."

"Thanks, Lieutenant. If I can keep these guys in the game, maybe we get everyone out before the shit storm hits."

* * *

The phone rang after twenty minutes, but Paul ignored it and continued working. Fifteen minutes later, he picked up the phone and said, "So, what have you got for me?"

"We will have a bus here within the hour," Caplan said. "You release the hostages and that bus will take you to the airport or anywhere you want to go. We will not approach it."

Paul had to suppress a laugh. There must be some dumb fucking criminals out there if that kind of stuff works.

"Okay, that sounds alright. But first, we are going to be here for a long while, so I am going to need food, maybe pizza, for about thirty people."

"I can't guarantee your safety for a long while," Caplan said. "You need to work with me here. Send out some of the hostages to show good faith."

"All in good time," Paul said. "First the food. Pizza for thirty people. How long will that take?"

"You'll have pizza within forty-five minutes," Caplan said.

"I'll bring it in myself."

Paul grinned. "As long as I can see that you are unarmed before you get to the door, I'm okay with that."

"Anything else we should talk about to make sure everyone stays safe?" Caplan asked.

"Just make sure no one comes close. You know that one officer who goes renegade can turn this whole thing upside down, right?"

"Yes, I understand. We'll make sure everyone stays back."

Paul hung up and nodded to Brian. "As planned."

"That's a lot of pizza," Brian replied.

"Yep. The cops can eat it. It's about time the department bought them all lunch."

"For a guy who had so many reservations about all this, you seem awfully fucking calm," Brian said. "Aren't you even a little nervous about all this?"

"Yeah, of course. But I'd rather be concentrating on what I'm doing than focused on the fact that I'm scared shitless. Besides, the decision is made, so there's no point in further hesitation."

"Maybe I should have been more nervous earlier, so I didn't have to do it now," Brian replied and stared at the screen in front of him.

The three men work in silence for about twenty more minutes. "You got time to go let the money inspectors loose?" Paul asked.

"Five more minutes."

They could hear sirens, the occasional bullhorn warnings of the voices of command outside. Paul checked his watch and nodded. Right on time.

Ten minutes later, Brian and Paul nodded to one another and then to the third man. The third man walked away first. A minute later, Brian walked down the hall and began retrieving the bags from the three selected hostages who waited in separate rooms. He opened the door to the manager's office and asked Linda Caldwell, "Any sequential serials, dye packs or GPS in there?"

"Yes." Linda replied. She pointed to a dye pack and a GPS in a stack of currency on the desk.

"Good," Brian said, in his electronic voice. "Leave that on the desk and let's go."

He entered the break room and asked the elderly woman the same question. "I didn't find anything that you were worried about," she said.

"Okay, good. Follow me." Brian, closely followed by Linda Caldwell and the older woman, stopped at the Operations Director's office and opened the door. "What did you find?" Brian asked Kevin Roper.

"Nothing. It's all okay," he said, pointing to the bag of money.

Brian simply nodded and then took all three bags away. Paul led the elderly woman, Linda and Kevin back to the conference room while Brian took the three bags away. "You three get back down on the floor."

Paul left all of the hostages on the conference room floor. The room had grown silent, but worry filled the air. The hostages were shaken and shaking, wondering if they would be executed, freed or caught in the crossfire if the police came pouring into the bank. Many had texted information about their situation and "I love you" to family, just in case it was their last opportunity. Josie sent a text to Tom, telling him that she loved him. Kelly wrote to her parents to say the same. There were periodic sighs and sobs around the fear-filled room and the room was full of the group's collective anxiety while they waited for something bad to happen.

Finally someone said, "Should we do something?"

Another voice said, "Like what? If you know a way out of here, let me know. Otherwise, don't do anything to antagonize these guys. I want to get out of here alive."

Paul checked his watch and then picked up the phone. "Caplan?"

"Yes, I have the pizzas now. It took a little longer than I thought, but I'm ready. Can I bring them in now? We can talk while people are fed."

"Give me a few minutes and I'll call you back," Paul said.

Paul and Brian returned to the conference room carrying gym bags. There was an eerie quiet that filled the room as everyone waited, frozen with fear, to see what was next. Brian said, "Everyone stand up, slowly."

The hostages all slowly climbed to their feet, some with hands raised protectively.

Paul and Brian threw the gym bags on the table and began pulling beards, ski caps and eye masks from the two gym bags they brought with them. "Put these on," Paul instructed. "When you have them on, I don't want to be able to see any part of your face other than your nose and the bottom of your ears. Got it?"

There were nods around the room and everyone covered their faces as directed. When they were done, Paul said, "Everyone follow me. We are going to walk over to the area of the lobby near the front door, but stay out of view from everyone outside. I'll show you where and you will sit down and wait for the next instructions."

They followed Paul to the designated area and he gestured to everyone to sit down. He said, "Clasp your hands behind your head and don't move. We are going to be leaving in the next ten minutes. You will walk out of here and go back to your lives. You are very close to freedom. Don't do anything to mess it up at this point."

Paul walked over to the desk and picked up the phone. "Caplan?"

"Yes, I'm here."

Paul nodded at Brian. "Okay, you can walk the pizzas inside. Move toward the bank until you are about fifteen feet from the front of the building. Then stop and show me your inside pockets, waistband and legs below the knee. Got it?'

"Yeah, I've got it."

"Okay," Paul said, "start walking now."

Paul hung up and he and Brian walked to a point where they could see through the glass doors onto the street. A tall, clean shaven man with thick red hair was approaching carrying pizza boxes. Officers knelt behind cars fifteen feet behind him and guns were pointed at the bank. Paul and Brian watched as the red haired cop got to a point about fifteen feet away and set the pizza boxes down. He turned out his pockets and lifted his shirt to display the waistband of his pants. He lifted his pant legs as requested and then turned 360 degrees slowly and then gathered up the boxes.

At that moment, Brian walked over to the hostages. He instructed, "You are all going to walk out of here in a single file straight line and go directly over to the police cars. Slowly. No one runs and no one steps out of line. You follow one another until you get there. Got it?"

Brian started the first hostage out the door slowly. Scores of police raised guns and held them at the ready. Someone yelled, "Hold your fire," as the hostages began walking across the street to where the police cars awaited. They walked slowly, as instructed, remaining in single file. When half of the hostages had exited the bank, there was a sudden explosion somewhere close. Hostages ducked momentarily, and then continued moving toward the waiting police line. Some of the police officers were directed toward the explosion while others stayed behind to watch the hostages continue their journey from the bank to safety. Almost immediately, there was a second explosion in the same location and more police ran that way, with high-ranking officers screaming orders and the fire department preparing hoses and gear.

When the last of the hostages left the building, Brian and Paul darted further inside the bank. There would be confusion while the first responders tended to loud explosions and minor damage in the adjacent vacant building. They would take time to determine that the explosions did not provide an escape hatch for the perpetrators on the other side of the bank. Then they would try to determine whether the perpetrators had exited the bank along with the hostages. Brian and Paul had a few minutes while all of this was sorted out. Finding minor damage and nothing else at the explosion sites, the cops would all focus attention back on the bank. Then those in charge would decide to deploy the SWAT team and backup officers. Paul and Brian anticipated that they had about four minutes before the building was under siege.

* * *

Police officers lined the street in front of the bank, using strategically parked cars for protection in case the perpetrators commenced firing. Police tape and officers assigned to maintain the perimeter, kept both onlookers and reporters at bay. The perimeter had been established at two blocks in all directions. Traffic was redirected, and no entry was permitted beyond the perimeter, even to those who lived or worked within the boundaries. The press was the biggest pain in the ass because they somehow believed it was part of their jobs to overcome such orders. They would sneak past boundaries with cameras, they would look for places where officers weren't stationed, and they would roll cameras using helicopters hovering above the danger zones—crazy dipshits.

Lieutenant Marshall Briggs had rigged a trailer as his mobile headquarters. From there, he and the negotiator, Emery Caplan, had the only direct line contact with the interior of the bank. Briggs wanted these guys badly and he wanted them at first opportunity. He had to do this by the book, but as soon as he got the hostages out, he would order a massive assault on the bank. He had deployed snipers to nearby rooftops at every angle that might provide a clear shot into the bank. Briggs was intolerant of those like Caplan, who seemed to him to be psychologists disguised as cops. He didn't want to psychoanalyze these assholes, he wanted to bust them or shoot them—whichever came first.

He shook his head as he watched Caplan carrying pizzas toward the bank, then stopping to assure the assholes inside that he wasn't armed. Briggs knew that his superiors endorsed this bullshit, so he had to try it before he would be allowed to unleash the SWAT team on the doorstep. He had three police agencies strategically placed on all sides of the building and he was ready for anything.

Briggs watched carefully, with one screen inside the trailer blowing up the image of Caplan as he walked toward the front of the bank, and a second screen locked on the front door of the bank. Other cameras focused on the back door of the bank and views of the bank from three other angles gave him three hundred sixty degree coverage of the bank. Two other cameras focused on police lines at the front and back of the building. The whole building was surrounded by police. From his perch in the trailer, Briggs could see everything that was happening, quickly visualizing all scenes around the bank as events unfolded. If an officer fired a weapon, or any unauthorized action was taken, they would know it instantly and they would have it recorded.

After Caplan showed the perps that he was carrying nothing but pizza, he was then apparently given the signal to move forward. Briggs watched as he slowly advanced toward the bank. He got to within ten feet of the building and then the front door of the bank opened slowly. Briggs thought this was to let Caplan in, but instantly, the scene changed. People started to slowly emerge from the bank, one after another, wearing hats of some kind, masks and beards. They kept moving across the road toward the waiting police cars as Caplan stood there watching.

"Caplan, pull back. Pull back," Briggs yelled into his walkie-talkie. Caplan hesitated a moment and then backed away a few steps. He then walked with the emerging hostages back toward where the police waited.

There was a sudden explosion. Nothing on any of the monitors in front of Briggs showed the place of explosion. "Jesus, what was that?" he yelled. To his team in the trailer he said, "Find me the location."

A voice said, "The building next door, sir. Don't know what the building is."

"Dispatch officers to see what the fuck just happened over there."

He grabbed the phone in front of him and hit a button. "Sergeant Mills?"

"Yes, sir," a voice responded.

"You see what's happening here, right?"

"Yes, sir."

"I don't know what that explosion was, but maybe it was the exit used by the perps. Keep your eye on the ball. The hostages have all been disguised the same for a reason. It's likely that the perps either exited at the explosion site or they are among the hostages."

"Yes, sir."

"The hostages are under stress and may be too nervous to point anyone out."

"Agreed."

Briggs commanded, "I don't want anyone among the hostages walking away from us. We hold all of them while we..." His words were interrupted by a second explosion. After a moment, he added, "Same location, sir."

Briggs said, "Okay, dispatch additional officers and get me a report from them and the fire department."

Mills heard the second explosion as he watched the flow of bodies continue toward him. "Donavon," he yelled to an officer a few feet away.

"Yes, sir."

"Have your team greet the hostages, make sure that they are unhurt and then get the garb off their faces. Unless someone is seriously hurt and needs immediate hospitalization, get names and addresses as well as pictures of every one of them before anyone goes to the hospital to be checked out or leaves the area, got it?"

"Yes, sir."

Mills hit a button and spoke to the officers all around him. "I think the perps may be hiding among the hostages and will make a break for it at some point. We have to be ready for anyone making a move."

"Roger," was returned by each of five deployed senior officers at assigned points around the building.

Three EMT vehicles were placed together in a semi-circle to allow a preliminary review of the condition of the hostages as they emerged. The first to arrive was a woman in her early twenties. The mask, ski cap and beard were removed to reveal fearful eyes and hard breathing.

"You okay, ma'am?" one of the paramedics asked. The woman groped for words but found none. She could only nod. "Are you injured in any way?"

It took the woman time to find her voice. She shook her head and then managed a very soft, "No."

"May we take your vitals?"

"Yes," she said, barely audibly.

They took and recorded her vitals and then looked her over superficially. Finding no signs of injury, a paramedic said, "Okay, ma'am, please walk to the officers over there." He gestured to card tables that had been set up on the other side of the line of police cars. She nodded and walked slowly toward the waiting officers, who greeted her with bottled water and again asked if she was okay. By the time she reached the waiting officers, she could see that the press, although being kept out of reach, were getting pictures of her and the others streaming out of the bank.

A tall officer said, "Ma'am, we need to take your picture, okay?"

The woman, still in shock, just nodded. Photos were taken and then she was shown the way to a waiting chair at one of the tables. There an officer began inquiries. She was asked her name, address, circumstances surrounding her trip to the bank and the basics about what happened inside.

The second to reach the paramedic circle was Josie. She heard herself tell the questioning paramedic, "No, I am not injured. I am okay." As her vitals were taken, she saw the press filming in the distance and she focused on the fact that Tom would know that she was here with Don, fucking his brains out and not visiting family as she had told him. She had a feeling of impending doom. Josie was asked three times and each time assured the paramedics that she was not hurt. She was given smiles and coffee at the table where a police officer waited to talk to her and to take her picture so that all of Des Moines would be aware of her visit to Los Angeles with Don.

Next in line was Chris Morgan, who assured everyone he was fine. As his vitals were recorded, he felt only relief. He was relieved and grateful that he had not gone through with what he came here to do and that all of this was not about his actions. This whole scene could have been about him being carted off to jail for murder or attempted murder. This could have been the end of his life, but he made it out of all this and it was like he had been given another chance to make things work. He would find a new job and make everything right with Connie. He was also relieved that he no longer had the gun. It would be way too hard to explain why he was coming out of the bank with a gun. He told the officers he was unharmed and even smiled when his picture was taken.

Then came Kelly Parson. She was shaken, but the doctor in her was at the surface.

"Are you okay, ma'am?" one of the paramedics asked her as she took her ski cap and mask off.

"Yes, I'm unhurt. I'm also a doctor, so if anyone needs help, just point me in the right direction and I'll see what I can do."

The man smiled. "You are something else. We have a couple of other doctors who weren't hostages on hand to do that job. All you have to do is get through this ordeal yourself."

She nodded, but said nothing more.

"You sure you're okay?"

"Yes, I'm fine."

She was directed to where the officers waited. She provided her name and address and as her picture was taken, she found herself looking around for Kevin Roper and wanting to be assured that he was also okay.

The next to reach the paramedic circle was Don Silver. They took his vitals and seemed satisfied as they recorded the numbers. He assured them that he was okay and then asked if Josie had been there. A reassuring paramedic told him she had already checked in and that she was fine. He followed directions toward the police tables and the police photographer who waited. He could see that the press was getting video of all the hostages as they emerged from the paramedics to where police waited. One thing was clear, the secrecy that it took to keep two relationships going was a thing of the past. Maybe he could now figure out who should share his future. Maybe when he did, the woman he chose would no longer have any interest in him. In either case, his life was about to change in big ways. He sat down next to a waiting officer and started to provide his name and contact information.

Kevin Roper emerged next and went through the same initial process with the paramedics. He asked about Kelly. He began to describe her and then said, "She's a doctor."

At that point there was recognition in the paramedic's eyes. "Yeah, yeah," he replied, "she checked in. She wanted to know what she could do to help if you can imagine that—after all you guys have been through." The paramedic grinned and directed Kevin to where about twenty hostages sat around tables answering questions from the officers. He scanned them until he saw her. Then his heart lit up and he walked directly toward her.

A waiting officer said, "Over here."

Kevin said, "Okay, I'll be right back. I just have to check on someone."

The officer looked concerned. "I understand. I'll walk over there with you because I can't turn you loose until I have the information I need from you."

The officer followed Kevin over to Kelly, who was on the phone to the hospital informing them of why she had not appeared at the beginning of her shift. She saw Kevin approach and looked in his direction.

"Are you okay?" he asked.

"I'm fine. How about you?"

"Yeah, I'm good." He touched her hand and she smiled.

"I guess I have to go with this officer," he said.

She nodded. "Yeah." She paused and added, "Call me."

"You can count on it," he said, "I think we can have a better first date than this." He saw her smile and then followed the officer to his assigned table. As his picture was taken and he began to provide information like name, address and where he worked, he was still thinking about her. He hadn't reacted to a woman like this in a long time and he could hardly wait to call her. Between thoughts of Kelly, he considered all that had just happened. He felt good.

Linda Caldwell was one of the last hostages to emerge. She didn't want to meet with an officer, didn't want to give them any information and certainly didn't want her picture taken. She searched for any way around all this—any kind of a back door, but could find no way out. As she passed through the paramedic circle and was assigned to an intake officer, she could feel the weight of it all. Her picture was taken and as she gave the officer her name and address and she began to cry. The officer was understanding, telling her he understood how traumatic the experience had been and that everything would be all right now. He was kind and compassionate and had no way of knowing that her concerns were unrelated to the robbery, but were all about what would happen when her photograph was processed and when she appeared on televisions across the nation. She thanked him for being so understanding. She was trapped and terrified.

* * *

"Lieutenant, the adjacent building has small fires, no way out," an officer confirmed.

"Okay," Briggs said.

After the line of hostages made it across the street to the waiting paramedics, Briggs hoped that they were all out, but had no information about how many hostages had been taken. He considered his options for a few minutes and then ordered the waiting SWAT team to advance into the bank. They entered in rapid succession, clinging to walls with weapons pointing the way. Other officers followed, staying back to allow the SWAT team to clear each area within the bank. The team moved with trained precision as corners were turned and doors were flung open. The unknown was around every corner, as they had no idea whether they would find someone ready to open fire or another explosive device. Adrenaline ran high as each officer readied for what might confront them and stood ready to protect the other members of the squad. They moved through every room in the bank, clearing each until they had covered it all and take a breath.

The team leader radioed Briggs. "All clear. No perps, no hostages."

"You sure?" Briggs asked in frustration.

"Yeah, we've cleared every room."

Briggs radioed over to the hostage intake leader. "The perps must be among the evacuating hostages; the building is empty."

"Roger," the man said. "Although everybody out here looks like Joe citizen."

Briggs ordered, "Turn the forensics team loose on the bank now." His phone rang. "Briggs."

"Lieutenant, the fires are now out in the unoccupied store next to the bank. Two small explosive devices were used. We'll have the experts ID the device and source."

"Yeah, okay." Briggs hung up and called Mills.

"Has everyone who emerged from the bank been photographed and documented?"

"Yes, sir."

"And what have you got?"

"Nothing, sir. Everyone documents like Mr. and Mrs. America. The only possible exception is one guy who used to work at this bank and was fired this past week. No weapons, mellow guy, doesn't seem like one of the perps."

Briggs shook his head. What a fucking day. "All right, make sure to notate that on the report. The case has already been submitted to the detective bureau for assignment. There should be a team on it within the hour."

"Yes, sir. They all expect to be contacted for further interviews in the morning."

"All right, thanks Miller. Let's turn the scene over to forensics and see what we can get." He paused a moment and then added, "Any thoughts on how the perps exited?"

"No, sir. They sure didn't walk by us." He was quiet a moment and then added, "We know that there were two of them from what the hostages have told us. They seem to have just fucking vanished. David Copperfield would be impressed with these bastards."

At 6:00 Josie and Don had dinner at the hotel, largely in silence. It felt like a meal with a stranger.

"Let's talk about the elephant in the room," Josie said. "We know we've been discovered and we need to decide how we handle this. I'm not sure what there is between us."

Don looked down at his plate and said, "We've had a good time, but I think we should get you a separate room. You know, make everything look on the up and up."

"I see. You know that your wife is going to find out we are in Los Angeles together, so you want to pretend that nothing ever happened between us." She shook her head. "I guess that answers my earlier question about how you feel about me. Just fun to fuck when no one is looking." She was calm. "Don't worry, I'll get my own room." She stood up and looked at him, perhaps seeing who he was for the first time. After a few moments, she said, "I think I knew we were not real. I should have known better." She walked from the table without looking back and made her way directly to the hotel reception desk to check into a room of her own. By the time she walked away with her room key and headed for the elevator, feelings of guilt and shame had started to find her. It had all been a fling and nothing more, and she would get to tell her husband that she was that trite woman at the office who had been fucking her boss.

She put the key in the door and walked inside the room. It was undisturbed and looked almost sterile. She would have to get her suitcase back from Don's room, but that could wait. She would call Tom first. He would learn about all this from her, not putting the pieces together from hostage names provided by the press. She had to do it as soon as she could muster the courage, because this was already national news. She was shaking and her stomach hurt. She could feel the blood pulsating through her head as she considered that with this call to Tom, she could lose everything. She would likely be all alone at this point in her life. She deserved it, she knew that much. Perhaps she would remember this day while she grew old alone, with nine cats and no visitors.

It was 8:00 p.m. in Los Angeles and 10:00 p.m. in Des Moines as Josie dialed home. Tom answered on the first ring.

"Hello?"

"Hi, Tom, it's me."

"Hi, Josie." He paused and said, "I miss you already. How's your sister?"

She knew he had not had the television on yet. Her heart sank as she said, "Tom, I have to tell you something."

"Okay, go ahead."

She had to get right to it or she wouldn't make it. She paused and then blurted out, "I didn't go to Minneapolis to visit my sister. I'm in Los Angeles."

He was quiet and then said, "So you went with Don Silver to his meetings. Why wouldn't you tell me that?"

"I should have."

His turn to pause and then he asked, "You want to tell me anything else?" There was a protracted and uncomfortable silence, and then he asked, "Like how long you've been sleeping with him?"

"Tom, I'm really sorry. I didn't want to tell you this way."

"I've been suspicious for a while."

"Really?"

"Yes, really. It's pretty apparent. You stopped having sex with me and you light up whenever his name is mentioned. I thought I might hear that you are moving out to be with him."

"I don't want to do that," she said. "I want to stay with you." More silence. "Is that what you want too, Tom?" she asked, fearful that she would hear the answer she deserved.

"I don't know." He paused and said softly, "You've always been my dream girl, Josie. I always felt like I was so lucky to have you, but now that I know that our vows didn't count for much, I don't know what I want." She could hear him softly crying as he said, "It makes me really sad, Josie. I feel like everything is lost."

"I'm not going to leave you for him."

"I don't think it matters, Josie, I'm not okay with my wife sneaking around and sleeping with some other guy. I can't trust you anymore." He paused a moment and then said, "so I think we are done."

"Tom, I still love you. I wish I was there to hold you right now."

He was quiet and then said, "I'm glad you're not because when I hold you, I start to believe anything is possible again. Now I know better. Goodbye, Josie."

She cried out to the empty room. God, what had she done? For the first time in months, she thought back to her long walks with Tom on cool evenings, the feelings that she had shared, the decisions that they had made together. She thought about how he was always there to cheer her and support her. Then she thought about the vows that he wrote for her. He told her that she was the light in his eyes and that love was wherever she was. He told her that he would love her forever. And she told him that she was his, now and forever. That he was the man of her dreams and that they would grow old together. She could remember it all in such detail now. Why had she let all of that get away? Why had she cheated on the guy who was her forever love? It had all been a desperate attempt to find romance that had drifted away. Josie knew that Tom was the right guy. Hadn't she always known that? She cried with the realization that she might never have the chance to make things right with the man who was meant for her. She had known he was the one and he had always been there for her. She somehow let it all slip away.

* * *

Don Silver ordered his third Tanqueray and tonic, working up the courage to call Naomi. He emptied the glass and then walked from the restaurant. He tried to think of the right words that could explain all this—a man strays sometimes, but it doesn't mean he doesn't still love his wife. He would make her understand.

Don called Naomi at 8:30 p.m. California time, so it was 10:30 p.m. for her. The call woke her and she sounded groggy. "I didn't expect to hear from you when it got this late," she said. "I guessed you were out at a late dinner."

There was silence. Silver took a deep breath and said, "I have to tell you something."

"What is it?" She sounded worried now. "Are you okay?"

"Yes, I'm okay. I was a hostage in a bank that got robbed today. They let us all go after a couple of hours, so everyone's fine, but you're going to hear about it on the news in the morning."

"You're sure that you are okay?"

"Yeah, I'm fine."

"Thank God," she said.

Another moment of silence. "There's something else."

"What?" she asked, "What is it?"

"Josie is here with me." There was no response. "Did you hear what I said?"

"I heard you. Anything else you want to say?"

"It's not serious. I want to be with you," he said hurriedly. She was silent again. "Naomi, are you there?"

"Yeah, I'm here."

"It was a mistake," he said, apologetically.

"This is so sad," she said. "So cheap, so trite. I don't know why men think this is okay. Don, our vows were important. The fidelity vows we made are part of a loving relationship. Doesn't that matter to you?"

"It does. It really does. I screwed up," he said, beginning to weep.

"You screwed up everything that counts." After a quiet moment, she said, "The life we built means nothing to you. You tossed it all away just for a fuck on the side. I don't know why you would do that. Goodbye, Don." The phone went dead.

He called back and got no answer. He didn't leave a voice mail message but called again. He tried five times before she answered.

"Hi, Don. Was there something else?"

"I'm so sorry. I want to save us."

"You said that, I have it. Anything else?"

"We can make it through this."

"Don, you have been fucking another woman. I don't want to know how long, so don't make anything up. But the only reason I'm learning that you took a secret trip with your lover is because it's going to be on the news."

"Don't let all we have go, Sweetheart."

"It doesn't seem that we have too much," she replied. The phone went dead again and he sat alone in the dark.

Part 3
Chasing the Wind

Chapter Twelve
Stacey Gray and Jeff Butler

The Day After

The detective bureau was a vast open space with desks placed in seemingly random locations and files inhabited every inch of horizontal space. The conversion to paperless files was a slow process, particularly given that detectives took handwritten notes as part of their DNA and there was insufficient staff to input all of their observations and conclusions into electronic format.

"I need to see Gray and Butler before I meet with the Chief," Lieutenant Spencer said, standing at the door to his officer.

"I'll get them in here," his assistant said. She picked up the phone and pushed some buttons.

Stacey Gray was the first to appear. At thirty-eight, Gray was a twelve year veteran of the Department and had been a detective for the last six. She was an attractive woman with a face that featured dark penetrating eyes which were constantly assessing and black hair that she wore just above the shoulders. She was 5' 7" tall and had a nice figure, which she kept from drawing attention with her chosen clothing and jackets. She moved with an air of confidence.

"He's inside?" she asked.

"Yep. Go on in. I'll send Butler in when he gets here."

Stacey knocked briefly and then walked in. "You wanted to see me, Lieutenant?"

Spencer sat behind his desk with his hands behind his head. Before he said anything, Jeff Butler gave a brief knock and walked into the office. Butler was six feet tall and solidly built. At forty-two, he was a sixteen year cop who had entered the detective bureau three years ago. He was clean shaven and had black hair that was cut short, with only traces of grey emerging around the edges. He had a naturally serious expression and always looked as if he was deep in thought.

"Morning, Lieutenant."

"Gray, Butler, both of you sit" he said gesturing to his visitor chairs. "You've seen the headlines this morning?"

"Yes, sir." Stacey said. Butler nodded.

"And you've reviewed the reports from yesterday, including the one from Mendosa and Carter, who handled the initial appearance from our team at the scene?"

"Affirmative," Stacey said.

"So you know that this is already a clusterfuck and it won't be leaving the headlines anytime soon. This is going to get lots of attention within the department."

"Yes, sir," Jeff Butler said.

"So I decided that you are the team I want on this case. Get me some answers. Gray is senior on this and any formal statements to the press are approved by me and communications before you speak. We okay on all this?"

"We are," Stacey Gray said. Butler nodded.

"All right. Get out of here and go find out how two guys robbed a bank and turned invisible in the process."

"Yes, sir," they both said and left the office together.

As they walked out, Stacey said, "Let's go talk."

They grabbed coffee and walked into a small conference room.

"Congratulations, by the way," Butler said. "I heard you nailed the dirtbag who kidnapped the Wilson kid."

"Yeah, we had to put two rounds in him to stop him from shooting us, but we got him. He's going to pull through. Then the son of a bitch can stand trial."

"That's two big ones in a row for you, right?"

She shrugged. "Luck of the draw."

"I'm not sure about that. I hear you're doing good work." He paused and then added, "That history is probably why you're the lucky soul assigned to this investigation."

"Maybe. If that's true, then you're here because of that counterfeit bust you helped engineer."

"So, aren't we lucky," Butler said, grinning.

Stacey smiled. "Yep, we should definitely be careful what we wish for—I'm already yearning for the days of investigating something the press isn't all over in the first five minutes." She sipped her coffee and then said, "Ready to climb into this one?"

He nodded. "No time like the present."

She pulled out her notes and said, "So, here's what we know so far: We've got two perps who were heard calling each other Mr. Abbott and Mr. Costello in distorted, electronic voices. We have no camera shots of these guys because they wore disguises and then they promptly disabled the cameras. We have twenty six hostages who never saw what either of them looked like. By way of description, we have only that both were average build and one was a couple of inches taller than the other. Right so far?"

"Right on."

"So Abbott and Costello ask for a negotiator. When they get the negotiator and have a couple of conversations, they ask for a bus they never use and then pizza for all of the hostages. Then, just as the pizza is being delivered by the hostage negotiator, who is trying hard to get inside and get a look, they put everybody in the same disguise they wore into the bank and let them walk out. Now, we know that everyone who came out of the bank appears to be a hostage and none of them appear to be perps. Then SWAT clears the building and finds no sign of life anywhere. All correct so far?"

"Correct," Butler replied. "Correct and pretty mystifying. With SWAT and three police agencies surrounding the building, only hostages emerge."

"Right," Stacey said. "So I think we begin by talking to all the hostages again. Doesn't it seem that two of them, who come out dressed just like the perps went in, have to be our targets?"

"Yeah, I think so," Butler said, "but when you read the accounts, all of these people are regular folk who wandered into the bank for some mundane reasons."

"Yep, Stacey Gray said. "So let's look closer at all of them. Maybe the mundane reason offered by one of these guys is a perp's alibi. We'll get them in here and interrogate all of them and see where it leads." She paused. "I know where I want to start. One guy, let's see, Chris Morgan," she said looking at the report. "This guy is a former bank employee fired a couple of days before this went down and happens to be back in the bank at the wrong moment. This guy may have a motive for being at the bank."

"Do we cut the list of hostages in half?"

"Yeah, we'll each do half and compare notes. But before we do that, let's talk to forensics and see what they have. We also need to go out to the site. The bank manager is going to show us the set up and should have an update on missing money."

Butler shook his head. "I'm not sure how anything could be missing. The only ones who leave the bank are dressed just like the perps when they arrived or are cops. They all walk out in front of more than two hundred cops and the media, carrying nothing. So we think the perps were two of those in the disguise, but how did any money possibly get out? Neither cops nor hostages carried satchels out, so it seems to me that the bank is going to tell us nothing is missing."

"Makes sense. Let's find out," Stacey said, and they walked out of the conference room past the coffee pot for a refill and then headed out to the unmarked Ford.

On the way to the bank, Butler called in to the forensics lab. "Carlos Morton, please," he said to the answering operator.

There was a pause and then a voice said, "Morton."

"Carlos, this is Detective Jeff Butler. I have you on speaker so that my partner, Stacey Gray, can hear you. What have you guys got for us that wasn't in the initial report?"

"You aren't going to be happy," Morton said.

"Why?"

"Because we have a whole bunch of nothing. We found nothing collectible at the site, there's no DNA, no recoverable photos and no prints."

"Wow. Nice start. Got any good news? What about the explosive devices?"

"Made from common products found in the average kitchen. Nothing unique. Designed for maximum noise and minimum damage."

"Anything else?"

"Yeah. We also looked at the disguises that the hostages wore. Nothing on them except, in some cases, the DNA of the wearer."

"Where do they come from?"

"We're tracking the suppliers now."

"Let us know as soon as you get anything on that, okay?"

"You got it, Butler," Morton said. He then said, "One more thing though. We found dye packs from the cash drawers in two of the offices where the three hostages were taken and a GPS that came from one of the drawers was also in one of them. We are doing a forensic analysis on them now. The results of that analysis should be available in the next day or two.

"Thanks." As Butler hung up, he looked over at Gray. "Can you believe that? A whole bunch of nothing."

"Yep. No help at all."

Gray and Butler arrived at the bank and pulled into the parking lot where four other cars were parked. The lot was cordoned off to keep people, including some lingering members of the press, away from the bank's front door. They checked the parking lot to find nothing conspicuous and then checked camera locations. They made their way past the cordoning tape to the front door of the bank.

Bank Manager Hank Mercer unlocked the door and let them in. "Hi. I'm Hank Mercer, the bank manager. The other people here are from corporate. They are helping me assess what happened."

"Mr. Mercer, L.A.P.D.," Stacey said, showing her badge. "I'm Detective Gray. This is my partner, Detective Butler." They shook hands and then Stacey asked, "Have you figured out what's missing?"

"We have. Seven hundred sixty-three thousand four hundred dollars was taken from the vault and another eight thousand from the registers."

"Are you sure?" Butler said, his shock evident.

Mercer nodded. "Yes, we have it to the penny."

Gray and Butler traded glances with questioning eyes. How the fuck did these unidentified people manage to get seven hundred and sixty-three thousand four hundred dollars plus the teller money out the door? Everyone had to walk through a line of paramedics and a bunch of cops. How was any of this possible?

* * *

The press was waiting outside when Gray and Butler emerged from the bank. They set up cameras in the bank parking lot and took shots of the building as the backdrop to the anchor's pronouncements about the robbery. The world was getting a good look. The country's biggest daily newspapers' websites and the cable news shows all displayed pictures of the bank and each of the hostages, along with their names and cities of residence. There were catchy headlines like, 'Hostage Watch,' 'How did they do it?' and 'What happened to the Pizza?'

Cable news focused on the robbery, engaged in rampant speculation about what occurred and presented various experts on everything from the homemade explosives to the psychological effects of a hostage situation. Podcasts and documentary specials focused on bank robberies, solved and unsolved crimes and psychological effects of short term hostage situations were already under construction and already being advertised.

* * *

Kelly Parson saw her picture on the front page of the paper, three pictures away from Kevin's. The whole experience was surreal. She wasn't sure how one was supposed to feel about having been a hostage, but she knew that there was a persistent uneasiness that bothered her this morning. Maybe it was knowledge that it all could have come out much differently—much worse for all of the hostages. Maybe it was hours spent not knowing if you would live to the end of the day. Whatever it was, she felt more vulnerable to things beyond her control than she had ever felt before.

She arranged for the day off work and had an appointment to meet with the lead detective in a couple of hours. Not that she knew anything. She told them all she knew after they walked from the building, but if they wanted to go through the motions again, maybe she should could help in some way. She was shaken by yesterday's events, but she told herself she would get past it. What she wanted was to see Kevin again—to talk to him about what happened and what they had been through together, and to spend time with him. When they met at the bank, she had been excited. In all likelihood, she'd already have a date with Kevin if their reunion hadn't been interrupted by the robbery.

* * *

Stacey Gray walked into the conference room where Chris Morgan waited. "Mr. Morgan, I'm Detective Gray."

He stood and reached out a hand, which she shook. "Good morning," he said, forcing a nervous grin.

"Please, have a seat, Mr. Morgan. Do you want some coffee or water?"

"No, I'm okay."

"Well, let me just make sure that we have a few basic facts correct. You live at 1652 Westerbrook, Apartment 59?"

"Yes, that's right."

"Your wife is Connie and she resides with you?"

"Yes."

"And you have three kids?"

"Right. And one more on the way."

"Well, congratulations."

"Thanks."

"Where do you work?"

"I used to work at the bank."

"The bank where the robbery happened yesterday?"

"Yes ma'am."

"Until when?"

"Until this past Wednesday."

"And now you are unemployed?"

"Right. Yes, at the moment."

"Did you get fired?"

"Yes."

"Why?"

"Do I have to say?"

"Well, so far this conversation is voluntary, but that could change."

"They fired me because they said I sexually harassed a couple of women, but I swear, I didn't do it."

She nodded. "So why were you at the bank yesterday?"

"I went to ask my boss questions about unemployment insurance."

"And did you?"

"No."

"Why not?"

"I never saw him. I went to where his office is and started feeling uncomfortable about being there, so I decided that I would just leave and go ask the unemployment department."

"What happened at that point?"

"I was walking toward the front door when the two guys burst through the door and pushed me back inside." Chris had planned his explanation at great length. He certainly couldn't say he came in to shoot his former boss, or he would be spending the next five to ten years in jail. Chris was confident, knowing that the cameras would back him up, showing that he was trying to leave when the two robbers arrived. He had also carefully considered the fact that he never did see Hank Mercer, so the story worked. Being too embarrassed to talk to the boss who had fired him just made sense. If they accepted that, he was just one of the victims.

"Did you ever get a look at either of the two guys? See any distinguishing marks—anything that would help us identify them?"

"No. They were always masked."

"What did they do when they arrived?"

"They had us lay on the floor in a big conference room."

"Did they take anything from you? Money, cell phones, anything?"

"Nothing. They left everybody with their phones."

"What is the next thing that happened?"

"One of them came back and took three people out and took them somewhere else."

"You know where?"

"No."

"You know who?

"No, I didn't know anyone."

"Can you describe them?"

"One was an elderly woman—maybe early seventies. Another was an attractive woman, maybe late thirties. She was a looker. The third one was a guy. He was in his thirties, too. I think he had black hair, kind of short. And he had glasses."

"Did you see them again after they left the room?"

"Yeah. They were brought back about a half hour before we all left the room."

"Anyone do anything in the room while you were on the floor?"

"I think some people texted family. Most people were too scared to call or text anyone."

"After the three people came back, what happened next?"

"Like, I'd say, a half-hour later, one of the guys tells us all to follow him. He takes us to the waiting area near the front door, and then the two guys pull out beards, masks and hats just like the ones they were wearing and tell us all to put them on."

"Then what?"

"They had us wait there for a while, and then one of them told us to walk slowly out the front door and toward the police."

"He used the word police? As opposed to cops or something else?"

"Yeah, I think he did."

"Then you left the bank and made your way over to the police and paramedics?"

"Right."

Gray looked down at her notes for a moment and then added, "Is there anything else that you think I should know?"

There was a silence that was too short for Chris to reassess the course that he had chosen. He tried not to show any perceptible reaction and simply said, "No, I can't think of anything else."

* * *

An hour later, Kelly Parson was escorted into the same conference room. Stacey Gray walked into the room a few seconds later.

"Hi Dr. Parson, I'm Detective Gray."

"Pleased to meet you," Kelly said. "How can I help?"

"I want to get information about what happened at the bank. I'll get you out of here as quickly as possible."

"Sure," Kelly said.

"You are a doctor?"

"Yes."

"And you practice at Cedars-Sinai Medical Center?"

"Correct."

"What brought you to the bank yesterday?"

Kelly shook her head. "I was going to say bad timing, but I'm not altogether sure that's true. I stopped by to talk about setting up an IRA, something I that had been on my to-do list for a while."

Stacey reflected and asked, "So why do you think that this trip to the bank might not be bad timing? I'm not sure I know what you mean."

Kelly smiled. "When I first walked into the bank, I ran into a guy I hadn't seen since high school." She smiled and added, "A guy I might like to know better."

Stacey leaned back. "That is pretty good timing. Did this guy wind up one of the hostages?"

"Yep."

"Who is it? I won't let on that you might like to know him better."

Kelly grinned. "Kevin Roper, and no need to hide it from him. He took my number before the day got crazy. I hope to hear from him soon."

"How many people were involved in the robbery?"

"There were two men."

"You know they were both men?"

"Yeah, I think so."

"How?"

"Height and the way they moved. I'm pretty sure, even though I never saw a face."

"Where were you when it all started?'

"In the lobby area at one of those little tables where you prepare the paperwork for your transaction."

"Can you show me on this diagram we prepared depicting the bank layout?"

"Sure. Right there."

"Put your initials at that location."

"Okay." Kelly did so.

"So what happened after they walked into the bank?"

"They moved everyone into the big conference room over here and had us lay face-down on the floor."

"Did they take anything from you?"

"Nope."

"When did they next interact with you?"

"That would be when one of them came back and pulled three people out."

"Can you describe the three people?"

"Well, one of them was Kevin. Kevin Roper. The other two were women. One about forty and the other an older woman, maybe seventy-ish."

Stacey knew that the forty year old was Linda Caldwell and the seventyish woman was Margaret Pierce. "Do you know who these women are?"

"No."

"Do you know where they were taken?"

"No, ma'am."

"They came back at some point?" Stacey asked.

"Yeah. I think about twenty-five minutes, maybe half hour later, but I have to say, time is really hard to gauge. We were all pretty scared and the minutes seemed like hours on the one hand and ran together on the other. I'm not sure if that makes sense, but it was really anxiety provoking."

"Anything else happen before they came back?"

"Only when that guy pulled a gun."

"What? Someone pulled a gun?"

"Yeah. One of the hostages pulled a gun from somewhere and pointed it at one of the bank robbers. It was when he came in to get the three people I mentioned. As he was walking out, this guy pulls a gun."

"But he didn't fire?"

"No. Kevin knocked the gun away and yelled at the guy. Something like, "are you trying to get us all killed.""

Stacey reflected for a moment and then said, "I'm going to show you pictures that we took of all of the hostages. Can you point out the guy who pulled the gun for me?"

"Sure," Kelly said. It took just a moment before she said, "Here he is. This is the guy," and pointed to a picture of Chris Morgan.

"You're sure?" Stacey asked.

"Definitely. That's him."

"You have been a great deal of help. Thank you for your help, Dr. Parson."

"Sure. I hope you catch these guys."

"Okay if I call you back with any additional questions?"

"That's fine. Call me on my cell phone if you need me."

As Stacey followed Kelly out of the conference room, she saw Jeff Butler waiting for her in the hallway. She walked over to Jeff and said, "You aren't going to believe this one."

"What?" he asked.

"One of the hostages, Chris Morgan, pulled a gun on one of the robbers while they were all in the conference room."

"What?"

"Yeah. Morgan had been fired a few days before the robbery based upon sexual harassment allegations. Then he shows up the day of the robbery with a gun. Any thought about what he might have been up to?"

Butler shook his head. "But he never used the weapon?"

"Right. One of the other hostages knocked it away and said he was going to get them killed."

"Wow," Butler said. Then he added, "Well, if you think the day has been wild so far, get ready for some more news."

"What?" she asked.

"One of our hostages has just been reported missing."

* * *

Linda Caldwell checked out of the "Easy Rest," the roadside motel where she had spent the night, at 9:00 a.m. and drove north. She had no idea where she was going. Brad and the boys would have no idea where she was and they would be worried. But she had decided it was best that Brad had no information when he first spoke to the police about her. He would be convincing—he didn't know where she was and he couldn't help them find her.

She knew it would only be a few hours before police computers or one of the many people who saw her picture in the media made the connection. Linda Caldwell of today would soon be identified as Angela Bremmer, who had departed Columbus, Ohio, nineteen years ago after a manslaughter conviction that would have sent her to prison for three to five years. Angela Bremmer was only twenty the night of the accident. Everything on life's horizon looked promising and wonderful. She had her degree from UCLA and she was off to do great things with her life. After her first day at her new job, she went out for a couple of glasses of wine with two girlfriends. She was on her way home at 8:00 p.m., in the twilight of a summer night. She wasn't far from home when a young boy on a bicycle suddenly appeared in front of her car. She slammed on the brakes and then she heard that awful sound as the boy was thrown forward onto the pavement. She replayed the tape every day, and it was all still crystal clear: The boy lying in the street, her screaming to God to help the boy, the crowd gathering and then the paramedics working hard but unable to bring him back. She also clearly remembered the disappointment on the face of a fifty something judge who looked down on her from the bench. She had suddenly become the young woman who had so much going for her and who threw it all away by drinking and driving. Angela did not feel like she had been driving under the influence, but the prosecutor and ultimately the jury, after three days of deliberation, believed otherwise. For countless years since, she wondered about whether her second glass of wine had slowed her reflexes. Whether, if she had stopped after one glass, her reaction time would have been slightly better and the young boy would still be alive. It was a thought that still brought feelings of guilt a dozen times a day.

Then came the day after the guilty verdict. She just couldn't go to prison with people who were angry, cruel and lost. Surely, this wasn't the way her life was supposed to go. On impulse, she found herself packing a bag and then getting in the car and driving away. Nervously climbing onto the freeway with her heart racing, telling no one that she was going. She drove for fourteen hours without stopping to rest. Then, after a few hours of fitful sleep, continued on, still without destination. She pushed on and on, first stopping in St. Louis. Angela stayed low profile, finding a job as a shipping clerk in a warehouse. She changed her name and her appearance. After three months, she got nervous and moved on to Grand Junction, Colorado, where she worked as a data input clerk.

She took a year to make her way west to Los Angeles and become Linda Caldwell. She met a wonderful man named Brad and settled down to raise two boys. And the family she lived for had no knowledge of who she had been. They had no idea of the mistake that she had made that cost a life or how she had been living as a fugitive all these years.

Maybe Brad would be done with her for this big lie. Maybe he wouldn't be able to forgive her for inadvertently killing a teenager after two glasses of wine. Maybe he would feel that he had been defrauded and he didn't know the woman he had been with all these years. And maybe her boys, who were now old enough to understand all this, could not love a mother who had done these things. In an instant, her world had been destroyed. All it took was being a hostage and having the media circulate photographs and video for the world to see. Just like that, everything she valued was gone and she was living the life of a fugitive, all over again.

She had no idea where she would go or what she would do now. She would call Brad and tell him after he convinced the police he knew nothing of her whereabouts. When she told him, he would be hopelessly sad. He would be disappointed that the woman he built a life with was a fraud—and inevitably, he would leave her. She pushed tears from her eyes as she left Ventura and drove north on the 101 Freeway toward San Francisco.

* * *

Paul pushed buttons on a burner phone and waited. On the third ring, it was picked up. "Yeah?"

"Well, greetings to you, too."

"Any update?"

"Yep. Phase three now complete."

"Good news." Brian paused and then asked, "How are things in Coronado?"

"Nice place. Now that Phase three is complete, I'm going to have a margarita by the pool."

"Sounds nice."

"Anything on your end?"

"Nope. All quiet on the western front. I guess I'll talk to you Monday when we are both back in the office."

"Any word from number three—direct or indirect?"

"No, I assume we are staying on schedule. No conversation until next Wednesday."

"Okay. Take care buddy."

"Yep. Don't get sunburned."

* * *

Stacey checked her watch. It was 7:55 p.m. as she and Butler walked into Lieutenant Spencer's office. He gestured to chairs. They sat and waited. He looked up from his computer monitor and said, "So, what have you got?"

"A headache," Stacey said. "You got any aspirin?"

Spencer nodded. "Always." He opened his desk and tossed her a bottle.

She took two and made a face as she swallowed them without water. She tossed the bottle back to him, and then she said, "Forensics has nothing. No prints, no DNA, no clues left behind. Voices were electronically distorted. We have spoken with half of the hostages so far. No one got a look at the perps, but they called each other Mr. Abbott and Mr. Costello. The stories of the hostages are consistent. They all state that three of the hostages were taken away to different rooms. Those hostages were then given the money taken from the register in three separate bags. They were told to pull out dye packs, consecutively numbered bills and any GPS. They were returned to the bigger group in the conference room. So we have nothing that helps us ID the perps. We have no idea how they got over seven hundred and sixty thousand dollars plus three bags of register money out of the bank. And we have no idea how they got themselves out of the building because they were not among the bearded, ski masked people who walked out of the building, even though the hostages tell us that the two men were dressed that way. They seem to have found another exit that we can't locate. Oh, and the explosive devices used for diversion were made from household products everyone has, so there is nothing traceable.

"If all that isn't enough to justify my headache, one of the hostages was a former bank employee, fired a few days before the robbery for sexual harassment. He showed up with a gun on the day of the robbery, which he didn't mention during his interview. He may well have been there to exact some kind of revenge for his firing. So we will be speaking with him again tomorrow." She shook her head and then said, "And, one more thing. One of the hostages has been reported missing by her husband. Linda Caldwell never returned to her husband and kids after she left the police line last night. I talked to her husband an hour ago and he is extremely worried and has no idea where she might be or why she didn't come home. No sign of domestic violence, no argument between them, she just never came home."

"Jesus," Spencer said. "This is a bigger cluster fuck by the hour." He shook his head. "So what am I supposed to tell the Chief and the press? We have no leads on who did this and can't figure out how they did it? And as a bonus, one of the hostages had a gun and may have been there to shoot someone and another hostage has suddenly disappeared?" The room was quiet. "So where are you going from here?" Spencer asked.

Stacey said, "First we talk to the guy with the gun, then the rest of the witnesses. Then we check in with David Copperfield and find out how these guys made themselves disappear." She thought a moment and then said, "We have the techies checking out the device they used to kill the cameras. That might tell us something, too. Tomorrow after talking to the rest of the hostages, I'll also go back to the bank to see if I can figure out how they got themselves and the money out of there."

"All right. Get out of here and let me pretend we're making progress. Now I have a headache," he said. He opened the aspirin bottle and took three. "I want to know every new development. Check in with me every night, Gray." He paused and then added, "And bring me some good news."

"Yes, sir. It almost has to get better from here."

"One would think," he said, turning his attention back to his computer monitor and looking miserable as they left the office.

* * *

Linda Caldwell was in San Luis Obispo when she called home.

"Hello?"

It was Matt. "Hi, honey."

"Mom, where are you? Are you okay?"

"I'm fine, Matt."

"When are you coming home?"

"As soon as I can. Let me talk to Dad."

"Okay, hang on."

Linda waited nervously, trying to find words to say the unbelievable. Her hands were sweaty and her breathing was faster than normal. The adrenalin had been pumping ever since the robbery began and there was no sign of relaxation in sight.

"Linda, where are you? What's happening?" Brad asked, sounding extremely worried.

"I'm up north. Probably best if you don't know exactly where because you're going to be asked." She cleared her throat and said, "There's something I should have told you a long time ago."

"What? What is it?"

"Before we were together, I was Angela Bremmer. I lived in Columbus, Ohio. A couple of weeks after graduating from college, I went out for a drink with girlfriends after work. I had two glasses of wine over a couple of hours and then drove home. On the way home, I hit and killed a young boy on a bicycle. I was convicted of involuntary manslaughter and sentenced to three to five years for driving under the influence. I was given ten days to put things in order and I disappeared. I changed my appearance and slowly made my way to California over the next year."

There was a silence on the phone that seemed to go on forever, and then Brad said, "And now you're running again?" His comment was like a gut punch and left her without words. "You have to come home and face this, Linda. You can't run again."

"I know. The story about who I am will break soon and they will come looking for me. I have some information to trade about the robbery, so I am going to find a lawyer to try to make a deal for me." Silence. "Will you help me?"

"Yes, of course I'll help you." He said nothing more.

"Are you angry?"

"Yes, I'm angry. I'm also sad and I'm disappointed. I thought we were really close."

"We are, Brad, of course."

"You didn't trust me enough to confide in me, Linda. You didn't treat me like the guy you can trust with everything. So I guess we're not what I thought we were."

"I'm sorry."

"How long until you come back?"

"I'll look for a lawyer in the next day or two. I'll make a deal to turn myself in sometime during the next few days." She drew a breath. "I'm going to have to go to jail, Brad. Will you be around when I get out?"

"I would have done anything and everything for you, Linda."

"Does that mean now you won't?"

"I don't know what it means. I just got hit with all this, remember?"

"Okay. I love you, Brad, and I want to be with you." She fought tears. "I am sorry my love. I am so sorry."

Chapter Thirteen

Two Days After

"Okay, Mr. Morgan, do you know why you are back here?" Stacey Gray asked.

There was a delay while he assessed. "No."

"Anything important you forgot to tell me about yesterday? And before you answer, let me tell you that your decision to be honest can help you if charges are brought against you."

"Charges against me? I didn't rob the bank."

"Did you do anything?"

Chris looked down and softly said, "I brought a gun to the bank."

"Yes, so why were you dishonest about it? You didn't mention it at all when I let you tell your whole story of the day's events."

"I didn't want to get in trouble for having it. I mean I didn't use it. I never pulled it on anyone other than one of the robbers."

"What were you going to do with it?"

"I really don't know. I didn't have a plan."

"Were you thinking about shooting someone?"

"I don't know what I was thinking. Maybe that if they saw me with a gun they might treat me right. But I never did anything with it. I decided to walk away. I met the two guys coming in to rob the bank as I was trying to leave."

"You know that you could be charged with anything from carrying a concealed weapon without a license to attempted murder?"

"Attempted murder? I didn't want to kill anyone."

Stacey held his gaze and remained silent. She shook her head and then said, "The D.A. will likely think that the only reason you would hide a gun on you and return to the employer who fired you was to get even—to take a life."

"Am I going to be prosecuted?"

"When we are all done with the investigation, the D.A will make that decision." She paused and said. "So it's important that you fully cooperate now, you understand?"

"Yes, I understand."

"So where did you have the gun?"

"In the waist of my pants, covered by my pants and shirt."

"Where were you when you pulled it out?"

"I was on the floor of the conference room with everyone else."

"Tell me what happened."

"One of the robbers came in and pulled three people from the room. When he turned around, I pulled the gun and was going to aim it at him."

"And?"

"And one of the other hostages knocked it out of my hand."

"Who was that?"

"I don't know his name."

She showed him pictures of the hostages and Chris picked out Kevin Roper.

"You sure?"

"Yes."

"Did he say anything at the time?"

"Yeah, he said something like, 'you're going to get us all killed.' But I wasn't, I was going to stop this guy."

"Can you understand how he might be concerned that if you pull a weapon on one of these guys they might start shooting?"

"Yeah, I guess so."

"Anything thing else that you should tell me, Mr. Morgan?"

"No."

"Did you interact with any employee of the bank before the robbery?"

"Only to say hello to a couple of the employees."

"And you never pulled the gun out before the robbers arrived?"

"No ma'am, I swear."

"All right, Mr. Morgan." She looked at her notes and then back at his worried expression. "That's all I have for now. We'll be in touch."

He was quiet and then said, "Please Detective, don't bring any charges against me. I have three kids and another on the way and I have to find a new job. All I want to do is take care of them."

Stacey nodded. "I understand, Mr. Morgan. You stay level with me about whatever I ask you and I'll help minimize any charges. But know that the ultimate decision belongs to the D.A."

"I understand. Thank you, ma'am."

* * *

Stacey read her notes over as she walked to her desk. Butler was walking out of another conference room.

"Any other startling news that stands this thing on its head again?" she asked.

"Nope. Pretty consistent. They all tell the same story about the three taken out of the room and Morgan pulling the gun. About half of them sent texts to family sending love and thinking it could be a final opportunity to communicate. Two of them told relatives to contact 911. Nothing unusual, nothing that hostages wouldn't be likely to do. So, what have we got?" he asked, gesturing toward the notebook.

"Well, we have one techie and doctor romance blooming, a guy who showed up with a weapon, but according to everyone, flashed it only at the perps, and one hostage who has suddenly gone missing. Oh, and we still have no clue who did it, how they got the money out or how they got themselves out. I can hardly wait to update Lieutenant Spencer with today's insanity."

Valerie Wilson, who served as administrative assistant to both Gray and Butler walked over to her holding a couple of messages.

"Hey, Val. What have you got?" Butler asked.

"Two very interesting calls in the last five minutes. First, we got an ID on our missing hostage. Turns out Linda Caldwell is also Angela Bremmer, who has been an Ohio fugitive for about twenty-one years. Convicted of involuntary manslaughter and then disappeared during the ten days they gave her to put her life in order before serving three to five. Outstanding warrants in Ohio ever since."

"What?" Stacey looked at Butler. "Just when this investigation couldn't get any crazier."

"Unfuckingbelievable!" Butler said.

Stacey shook her head. "I can hardly wait to hear the other message."

"Curtis Lowell. He's a senior agent with the FBI. He said that he's been assigned to work on the bank robbery and wants to be brought up to speed."

"You know Lowell?' Stacey asked Butler.

"Nope. Until now our paths haven't crossed."

"Great," Stacey said. "Now we get to fight with the Bureau about who runs the investigation."

Butler shook his head. "Particularly annoying seeing as they usually win that battle where bank heists are concerned."

"Did you just say heist?"

"I did," Butler said grinning.

"Too many movies in your recent past."

"There can never be too many—Hollywood provides law enforcement with original ideas for catching and torturing B actors. Can't beat that."

"One day they are going to make a movie out of this case, Butler, and you and I are going to be the Keystone Cops if we don't make something happen soon."

"Good luck," Val said. "I'll go start putting together the framework for today's report for you guys to work over."

"Thanks, Val," Butler said, and she moved away from the desk.

"How did we get assigned to this again?" Stacey asked. "Did we piss someone off?"

"Your stellar track record got us into this mess. The more you do, the more they want you to do."

Val had been gone less than a minute when there was a buzz on the com line. "Hey, Val, long time no see," Stacey said.

She laughed and then said, "I have more news already. Mr. Caldwell called and said he located his wife and she is okay."

"Is he on the line?"

"No, he just said to pass the message along because he had to run. I thought that was an interesting choice of words given his wife's predicament."

"Yeah, that's for sure."

Val said, "I asked when she could be here to be interviewed. He said she is out of town."

"Out of town? Mr. Caldwell and I definitely need to talk."

* * *

Stacey glanced at the time on her phone. She was to meet and update Spencer in ten minutes.

She dialed the number and waited. It was answered on the second ring. "Hello?"

"Mr. Caldwell, this is Detective Gray."

"Yes, detective, how are you?"

"I'm good, sir. I was informed that your wife has been located. Is that accurate?"

He hesitated a moment and then said, "Yes, that's right."

"Let me talk to her please."

"She's out of town."

"Out of town where?"

"I don't know."

"Really? That didn't come up in your conversation?" He was silent. "Well, Mr. Caldwell, I really need to talk to her right away. If you can't give me information about how to talk to her, then we will have her picked up. We are going to bring her in one way or another." Stacey said nothing about the Ohio warrants.

"Hang on, Detective, please. She will get hold of you in the next twenty-four hours."

"Mr. Caldwell, do you know why she took off?" He was quiet. She added, "We know."

"Yes, ma'am, she told me. She is arranging for an attorney to negotiate her return."

"Not much to negotiate. There's a warrant out for her in Ohio, and if I don't hear from her in the next couple of hours, there will also be a California warrant. So you want to get her that message right away. We on the same page here, sir."

"Yes, Detective, I understand."

After she hung up, Stacey thought about the grim prospects of telling Lieutenant Spencer that they had no answers but more mysteries. She sat at her desk running through all of her notes and trying to figure out what they were missing. There were no other exits and the rooftop and back of the bank was watched by upwards of fifty cops. No one walked out carrying satchels or bags, so how did they get the money out? For that matter, how did they get themselves out? She scanned the notes of the interviews she and Butler did with all of the hostages. None of these guys look like they could have been the perps. Even the one who disappeared is a mom on the run from a prior conviction. There had to be something they were missing, but she had no idea what, and it was time to tell Spencer about all she didn't know. Another conversation she didn't want to have. Hopefully, he still had his aspirin handy.

Chapter Fourteen

Three Days After

Stacey dialed the number and waited.

"FBI."

"Curtis Lowell, please."

"Who can I tell Agent Lowell is calling?"

"Detective Stacey Gray, LAPD."

"Hold, please." Stacey shook her head. This was already a pain in the ass.

A male voice said, "Agent Lowell."

"Agent Lowell, this is LAPD Detective Stacey Gray. I understand that you have been assigned to work on the First California Bank robbery."

"Yeah, right. Why don't I meet you there and we can go over it all."

"How about 2:00 p.m.?"

"Can we make it 3:00?" Lowell asked.

"Yes."

"I need you to bring me up to speed on this one."

In an even voice, she said, "Bringing you up to speed. Like your assistant, maybe? Then what? You planning on taking over the investigation?" There was silence, so she added, "I'm good at what I do, Agent Lowell, and I am not relinquishing my role without resistance. And don't think that because I am a woman that I can't win a dick waving contest, got it?"

"Whoa, Detective Gray, you have me wrong here. I am not interested in just taking this thing over and I'm not interested in war with you or the LAPD. I envision us working as an inter-agency team on this. And call me Curt."

Immediately disarmed, Stacey said, "Okay. I'll see you at the bank at 3:00 p.m."

Lowell said, "My partner, Alicia Garcia, will be with me, too. I'm hoping your partner will be available so that we can get to know each other, find coffee and figure out how we want to share the duties. We are in the process of digesting all of the reports to date so that we can hit the ground running when we all get together."

"Sounds fine. My partner is Jeff Butler and we will see you at 3:00." She hung up, thinking that she had sounded more than a little defensive. The guy was pretty reasonable.

* * *

"Hello?" Kelly said, answering her cell phone.

"What time are you off tonight?"

She smiled. It was Kevin. "I'm working until 9:00 tonight."

"Perfect. Have a late dinner with me. The crowds will have gone home and I know a place with soft light, a creative chef, wonderful ambiance and enough privacy we can get to know each other."

"Sounds really nice," she said. "Where do I meet you?"

He recited an address and then said. "Maybe I shouldn't tell you this, but I have had you on my mind a lot since we re-met."

"Ditto," she said, finding herself grinning. "See you tonight."

* * *

Once their pictures were everywhere in the media and their se-cret romance was outed to the world, Josie and Don each knew that they were over. All of the intimacy was gone, and they struggled for words like strangers. Josie didn't stay for the three days of meetings Don Silver was to attend. And when they said goodbye, she meant it in the ultimate sense. She would see Don only at work.

She flew home feeling alone and foolish. How could she have been so blind? Tom was her guy—the one. She knew that once, but something had happened. When they were married she was over the moon about the guy. He lit her up whenever he walked into the room. Somehow, that seemed like another life. They had allowed themselves to drift away from the intimacy they shared and she had made a fool of herself. Fucking her boss, the ultimate cliché. Her perspective had returned and she now realized that Don Silver was no part of her future. He had been some crazy excitement she got caught up in. He knew his business, he had some power, he had money, and for some reason, she had wondered if he was what she really wanted. Now she knew better, but she may have lost everything she cared about in the process of figuring that out.

When the plane landed in Des Moines, she called Tom and got his voice mail. She told him she was back and wanted to see him right away. She told him she would be waiting for him when she got home from work and to please come and talk to her. She took an Uber from the airport wondering if the life she left behind a couple of days ago was already gone and unrecoverable. If Tom didn't want her anymore, she could hardly blame him. She would have to make a life alone. Could she even stay in this city and be reminded every day of what she had and managed to throw away? She looked out the window at a sunny day. Birds, flowers and beauty were all around her. It was so sad.

When the Uber stopped, she saw that the house was entirely in darkness. She thanked the driver and went inside, flicking on lights as she walked toward the kitchen. On the table was a note that said, 'Josie, I am staying at the Noble Rest Hotel for a while. I will call you when I am able to talk to you.'

* * *

Stacey Gray and Jeff Butler introduced themselves to Curtis Lowell and Alicia Garcia in the lobby of the bank. Lowell was a tall, thin man with big blue eyes and a friendly smile. He wore a gray suit and blue shirt with no tie. Garcia had long black hair and dark eyes. She had a classic Spanish beauty and a serious, all business, countenance. They took a silent walk around the bank building and then looked at the flow of the layout internally and all of the areas of the bank addressed in the reports.

"You have read the reports," Stacey said, "so share your initial impression."

"Baffling," Lowell said. "Invisible people with invisible money. Seems like that's the only way they get out of this building surrounded by cops."

Stacey nodded. "That's what I'm having trouble getting past. How do two people leave a building with big satchels and a hundred cops don't see the people or the satchels?"

"Good question," Garcia said. "You have a theory?"

"Yeah, maybe," she said, thoughtfully. "What if the money never left?"

"What?" Lowell asked.

"Yeah. Think about this. Bank employees looked for money in the vault and they came up short, right?"

"Then we all assumed the money got out with the perps, right?" They were watching her and considering. "What if the money is hidden somewhere else on the premises? Maybe it gets retrieved later or something?"

"Interesting," Garcia said. "What do you think about that?" Garcia asked Butler.

"Maybe," Butler replied. "If there was no way for the money to get out, maybe it stayed. The problem with the idea is that it wouldn't do the perps much good to leave the money."

"Unless," Stacey said, "there was an insider who could move the money the rest of the way out once it was out of the vault."

"I see," said Lowell. "And if that were the scheme, the task has probably already been completed."

"I agree," Butler said, nodding. "You would want to get the job completed and the money out of here as soon as possible."

"So that means we need to look at every bank employee as a likely suspect, even though our initial look at these guys didn't yield much."

"Yes," Lowell said. "And I say we revisit the one who just happened to be here with a gun at the time of the robbery. Chris Morgan."

"Good place to start," Stacey said. "And let's go on to the managers next."

Butler said, "I'll also talk to human resources to see if there is any employee who left the company in the last three days or who was new to this branch."

"Perfect," Garcia said. "We'll divide up the interviews and get them done by tomorrow."

Lowell added, "We will check to see if anyone had after-hours access to the bank to make the removal possible–bank employees, janitorial staff, repair and maintenance or security people. The electronic record should show the time of each access and whose key was used to enter."

* * *

"I don't do that," Kevin Roper said evenly.

"You understand who you are saying no to, right?"

"Yes. Look, I don't hunt personal indiscretions that can be used to blackmail a competitor of yours. If that's what you need, talk to someone else."

The voice responded quietly. "This could be a big paycheck for you and just the beginning of many opportunities to get really wealthy. You could spend a week or two on this and get mid six figures out of it, you know?"

"Yes, sir, I understand. And don't get me wrong, I'd love to work with your company. I'm just not going to figure out where a guy is getting blowjobs or what S&M he favors. Call me if you ever need help with someone's product or policies. I don't do fetishes."

"You're losing a big opportunity here, my friend. Blackstone International is not likely to call again when turned down once."

"Yes, sir. Thanks for the consideration, but no thanks."

Kevin hung up and shook his head. Some people are just too fucking pushy. The phone rang again. "Roper," Kevin said abruptly.

"Hi, Kevin."

"Greetings."

"The meeting is set. Wednesday night at 10:00 p.m."

"All good so far?"

"Yes."

"Okay, I will see you then." Roper hung up the phone and checked his watch. A smile crossed his lips. Time to meet Kelly.

* * *

The restaurant was quiet, the lighting soft and the tables located in private alcoves. Kevin and Kelly touched their pinot noir glasses together and Kevin said, "To our re-meeting."

She smiled and said, "I'll drink to that."

"So, what is your life like?" Kevin asked. "There's a twenty year hole in what I know about you."

"Well, I work too much. It became a habit in med school and my residency, then it just became normal."

"No one special right now?"

115

"No." She leaned toward him and said, "Well, maybe, but it's a first date, so I don't want to assume too much. How about you?"

"I didn't have anyone special before I re-met you. I want to assume that this is the beginning of something. Is that too much too quickly?"

"I hope not."

"So I know you're a doctor and that you work at Cedars-Sinai. What is your field?"

"Nuclear medicine."

"So you read every kind of scan and help other docs figure out what theirs mean?"

"That's a concise and accurate job description."

"As I recall, you were the girl voted most likely to succeed in our senior class."

"Yeah, it's amazing that you remember that."

Kevin smiled and said, "Of course. I remember a lot about you because I had a crush on you. You know, I wanted to ask you out back then."

"Really? Why didn't you?"

"I thought that you were already with John—I don't recall his last name. Smart guy, ASB president."

"John Stanton."

"That's right."

"He and I went together for a while, then we moved on. I chased my career and really didn't have time for dating and he chased other girls."

The waiter came and refilled wine glasses and delivered seafood linguini. "Anything else I can do for you?"

"No, this looks great," Kevin said, and the man gave a slight bow and moved away from the table.

They were quiet as they began eating. After a time, Kevin said, "I had a crush on you back then. Would you have gone out with me if I asked?"

"Yep. I actually hoped that you might ask me out. I thought you were a pretty classy guy. You were, well, really nice as well as attractive." She smiled as she recalled him in another time. "So, you got married?"

"Yeah, about ten years ago, a woman I met in college. It started out okay, but about seven years later she got bored, distant and then moved to someone else's bed without letting me know that was the plan."

"I'm sorry, that must have been hard."

"It was rough at the time. I mean, I knew we had problems, but I hadn't given up. Apparently, she had. I found out in the worst kind of way. I was walking down the street and saw her on the corner kissing some guy. I confronted her and she confessed that they had been seeing each other for about six months and was ready to move on."

"And that was three years ago?"

"A little more than that."

"And no one special since then?"

"Nope. I've dated, but I haven't found the one that I want to be with for more than a few dates." He grinned. "That may be changing even as we speak. Stay tuned." She smiled widely. Kevin asked, "You've been dating, too?"

"Yeah, when I find the time. I've tried it's just lunch, it's just coffee and it's just dessert, and that's all it ever was, thank goodness. I've also been set up by close friends and by my sister a couple of times and that's the worst. My family and friends have set me up with the weirdest people. It's like they selected from emotional mutants of some kind. It was genuinely awful. And the on-line dating was so bad, I just couldn't bring myself to keep doing it."

He nodded. "I get it. I've had some odd experiences with dating as well. I thought I was pretty jaded with all of it until I walked into a bank and saw this beautiful girl that I had known in a former life."

She smiled. "And maybe in your next life, too," she added.

"I sure hope so."

The waiter picked up empty dishes. "How was everything?"

"Wonderful," Kelly said.

"Thanks," Kevin added, and the man reprised his mini-bow and disappeared.

"How are you doing getting past the whole hostage thing?" he asked.

"Pretty good. It was a scary experience, but whenever I think about being a prisoner in a bank, I think about seeing you there and feel better."

"Yeah," he said. "I've been thinking more about tonight with you than I have about the robbery."

She paused and then said, "I get it. It gives us a chance to see what you and I might be, seeing as we never took that opportunity back then. It's the opportunity to see where a path not taken might lead."

Kevin said, "I like that perspective. Besides, I was too young back then and I might have screwed it up." He paused and then added, "I really appreciate you today."

Kelly smiled. "I understand that," she said. "I wasn't ready back then. I didn't know what role I wanted a guy to play in my life. A pretty limited one, because I was totally obsessed with getting through medical school."

Kevin pulled out a credit card and she reached for her purse. "This is mine," he said. "Maybe another night, you can take me out?"

"Okay," she said, "thank you, Kevin."

He paid the bill and they walked out of the restaurant. "Do you want to take a little walk," he asked.

"Sure," she said.

They strolled the late night streets looking in shop windows, talking about high school days and what became of friends and classmates that one or both of them long ago lost touch with.

They talked about what they saw in store windows and they talked about the beautiful stars lighting the skies above. As they walked on, he took her hand. They got lost in the moment, appreciating the night and the best date either of them could remember.

Even as Kevin drove her home, he didn't want the evening to end. "I really had a great time, tonight," he said. "I hope you will go out with me again."

She gave him a smile and said, "I will. Thank you for a wonderful evening."

Kevin walked Kelly to her front door and they kissed good-night. It was the perfect end to a wonderful evening.

Chapter Fifteen

Four Days After

Stacey left Chris Morgan sitting alone in the small conference room for about fifteen minutes. Then she walked into the room and sat down in the chair across a small table from his. He was visibly nervous, drops of sweat dotted his brow. He waited for her to speak first.

She looked at him with a stern gaze. "Mr. Morgan, I trust that you know why you are back in this room?"

"No ma'am, I don't." He looked mystified. "But I will help if I can."

She leaned back in her chair and let him sweat a little longer. Then she said, "We've concluded that this bank robbery was undertaken with an accomplice who had been an employee. You've already got a big problem bringing a gun to the bank, but it gets way worse if you don't tell us the truth about your involvement in the robbery." She watched him carefully.

"Not me," he said, without hesitation. "I had nothing to do with it."

"Well, let's see. The robbery involved a present or former employee. You are one of those. You also happened to be in the bank at exactly the right time. And, you were carrying a gun. Quite a number of coincidences at work there, wouldn't you agree, Mr. Morgan?"

He looked her straight in the eye. "Detective, I know that I fucked up bringing that gun to the bank, but I never used it. I never showed anyone I had it until I tried to protect the hostages with it." He drew a breath. "I have a family. I have no record and I had nothing to do with the robbery."

"Mr. Morgan, you are a former employee on site and with a weapon. What would you think, if you were the investigator?"

"I don't know, but I didn't do it. I wasn't involved in the robbery in any way. I swear."

"Anything else you'd like to tell me, Mr. Morgan?"

He looked directly at her with concerned eyes. "No, but I promise you, it wasn't me. I know I exercised bad judgment bringing a gun there and not telling you about that right away, but you have to believe me, I had nothing to do with the robbery."

Stacey was good at reading people, and her read on Morgan was that he was telling the truth. She nodded. "Okay, we're done for now. You have no plans to leave town in the next couple of weeks, correct?"

"Correct, ma'am. I am not going anywhere."

"If there is anything else you haven't told me, now is the time. If we find out anything else you're hiding, it gets worse from here."

"There is nothing else."

She nodded slowly. "Thanks for coming by, Mr. Morgan. We'll be in touch. If you think of anything we should know, you call us."

"Yes, ma'am. But you have to believe me, I was not involved with the robbery and I don't know who was."

As she watched Chris Morgan walk from the room, Stacey couldn't help believing that he was telling the truth. Bringing a gun to his former place of employment was pretty fucked up, and he may have intended to shoot someone, but he was probably not involved in the robbery.

* * *

Curt Lowell walked into Stacey's office. She hung up the phone and checked her watch. "Let's get out of here and get coffee," she said.

"I'm on board," Lowell replied. "I could use straight caffeine right about now. Set up an I.V. drip."

She smiled and they walked down the block to Bennigan's Coffee House. They ordered a cup and sat in cushioned seats by the window, looking out onto the street.

"I just heard from the bank," Curt said. "There was no key access to the bank after hours by anyone since the robbery. Janitorial has been limited to two long term employees with a manager present. We'll interview those three, but no other access by anyone at all except the manager and the acting assistant. So I guess that means if anyone moved the money out after the robbery, they did it during banking hours. Doesn't seem too likely, does it."

"No, damn it. If the three on the janitorial team check out, it sounds more like another dead end," Stacey said.

"So what is your professional assessment of Mr. Abbott and Mr. Costello?" Lowell asked?

She took a moment and then said, "I think that they are pretty damned good. No prints, no DNA, explosives that can't be traced and a disappearing act. Pretty impressive."

"I agree," Lowell said. "I heard one of my associates say that the only thing they missed was taking phones from the hostages, but I don't think that was a screw-up either. These guys knew the cops were coming. In fact, waiting for cops was planned, so they didn't care if the hostages notified anyone and didn't waste time collecting phones."

"I agree. The fact that we have no clue who these guys are speaks for the quality of their work."

He chuckled. "It's funny how cops can appreciate good work on the other side."

Stacey smiled. "We can acknowledge good work, but I'm glad most perps are dumb or our stats wouldn't look as good. Seems to me that these guys haven't tripped over themselves at all yet."

Lowell's phone rang. He looked down at the read-out. "This is Lowell."

"Really? Okay, we're on it, thanks." He turned off the phone and looked at Stacey with a grin. "They found something in the bank."

* * *

Throughout the morning, convention attendees asked Don Silver if he was okay. They said it must have been a harrowing experience to be a hostage in a bank robbery. They wanted to know if they could help him in any way. Lots of support on site, but home was different. His home life was in total disarray. Naomi knew he was with another woman and his marriage was terminal. His anxiety over the fact that he had been caught with another woman far exceeded that resulting from having been a hostage for a few hours. During the lunch break, he walked outside to the hotel's garden area and placed his fourth call home this morning. He had left three prior lengthy voice mails, telling Naomi that he was sorry for a big mistake and he wanted to make it right. She had not returned any of the calls.

This time she answered on the fourth ring. "I got your messages, Don. I don't want to talk right now."

"Please, we have to talk this out."

"What is it that you think you need to say to me?"

He was momentarily speechless, groping for words that might break through. "I want you to know that I love you."

"Okay, is that it?"

"And I want to be with you forever."

Her turn to be quiet. When she spoke, it was in angry tones. "You want to be with me forever, and to show me how much you mean that, you've been fucking your young coworker, is that right?"

He replied, knowing he sounded desperate, "It was just a fling. It didn't mean anything."

She was quiet for a moment and when she spoke, it was in a clam, controlled voice. "Fucking a woman is not shaking hands, Don. Being intimate is a choice, one that you made. And you are so wrong about it meaning nothing. It means everything. It means your vows don't matter. It means you didn't love me as I loved you." She paused and then added, "And it means that I won't live my life with someone who cares so little about the most important promises he ever made. I think that you and I are done."

"Please, don't give up," he pleaded, but the line had gone dead.

* * *

"Hi, Kelly. This is me, hoping that you will recognize the voice. I called to tell you that I had a wonderful time last night and I can hardly wait to see you again. How about a movie in the next two or three days, or a beach walk, or something else. Call me and let me know when you are available so I can stop rambling before you think I'm too weird to go out with." He paused and added, "And now I've done it, I ended that last sentence with a preposition." Kevin hung up and shook his head. Calling a woman in the middle of the day to leave an incoherent message had never been his style before, but then again, it had been a long time since he felt so taken by anyone.

* * *

When Stacey Gray and Curt Lowell walked into the bank, the manager and three cops were there to greet them.

"So what have you got?"

"We found three money bags that are the same type as the bags used to move the money between the tellers and the vault," the cop in charge of the search said. "The type of bags that two of the hostages described they were given to inspect for serial bills, dye packs and GPS devices."

"Okay," Lowell replied, "but doesn't the bank have a number of those kinds of bags?"

The uniformed officer nodded. "They do, they have a lot of them. The significance of these bags is that they were found wadded up in the back of a file cabinet that contains only closed file material."

"That's right," Hal Mercer said. We keep these in a specific location in the assistant's office. It looks like these three were hidden. My people all say that they have never put any bags in this location."

"Are they untouched? Still where you found them?" Stacy asked.

"Yes, ma'am," the officer said. "Okay, show us," she said, and they followed the officers to where the bags were stuffed down at the back of the third drawer of a four drawer file cabinet in the bank's supply room. "Okay, get forensics out here. I doubt these guys left us anything we can trace on these bags, but just in case, let's give it a shot."

"Yes, ma'am."

Stacey and Lowell searched the four drawer cabinet while Mercer looked on. "Nothing but closed files," Stacey said.

"What you found is exactly what I would expect," Mercer said.

"And you have never found things like that in this file cabinet before, right?" Stacey asked, pointing at the sacks.

"No, never. It's an odd place for money bags."

Stacey and Curt Lowell walked away and Lowell asked, "What do you think?"

"I don't know. If these are the same bags that were used during the robbery, then it could be important. I mean, if the bags were left here, maybe the money was placed on the bodies of the disappearing perps. It's hard to figure."

"I had the same thought. Maybe these guys filled their underwear and t-shirts with money and left the containers behind. The problem is, that would only account for a few thousand from the tellers' drawers, but they certainly didn't strap seven hundred and sixty grand to their bodies. It has to mean something else." He considered a moment and then said, "I don't think an employee could have moved that much money out of here during working hours. You can't make ten trips out the door with money and not have another employee or the cameras notice. We also know that no one has accessed the bank after hours since the robbery, so they had to devise another way to get the money out. It's almost like they had an underground tunnel."

Stacey gave a nod. "I agree. I had the same notion, so I had our team take another lap around the premises, inside and out, looking for any way out of here other than the front and back doors. They found nothing, so I ordered a copy of the original plans and the as-built drawings for the bank building. I was thinking that maybe there was some way to connect with underground utilities from inside the building. We should have the plans sometime today. It's a long shot, but I thought it was worth a try."

Lowell nodded. "Sure can't hurt. And whoever these guys were, it's not hard to believe that they did their homework enough to have pulled the plans themselves." He shook his head. "I wouldn't tell this to very many people," Lowell said, "but you have to admire the work these guys did. I don't believe in the perfect crime, but these guys found a way to be here without leaving any trace. And we can't even figure out how the hell they got out of the building."

Stacey shook her head. "Impressive for sure, but you and I have got to get to the bottom of this or our agencies get skewered by the media. They're already having a field day pointing out all we don't know." She looked directly at Lowell and asked, "I'm still trying to figure out if this assignment was a reward or a punishment. How did you draw this gig? Were you awarded this prime assignment as a reward for great work today or because your director thinks you need a poke in the eye?"

Lowell chuckled. "I like you, Detective Gray. You are good people. In my case, we are given assignments on a rotational basis, so I think it was all timing. Of course, if someone up the chain wanted to poke me in the eye, they could make it happen in more ways than I can count."

Her turn to laugh. "I think we live in similar worlds," Stacey replied. "I'll call you as soon as I get a look at the drawings."

"Great," Lowell said. "I hope they teach us something because I'm tired of feeling like I have no clue about this case."

"Yep. You and me both."

* * *

Kevin's phone rang at 10:30 p.m. He grabbed it quickly, hoping it was Kelly and not someone selling timeshares. "Hello?"

"Hi, Kevin. I just got off work. Is it too late to call?" Kelly asked.

"No, I was just looking at a file and hoping you'd call. How was your day at work?"

"It was a good day. I was able to assist a couple of other physicians and had the pleasure of reviewing diagnostics that showed shrinkage of a big tumor in a twelve year old girl who has stage four cancer. It feels so good when they are making progress. I think she could be on her way to remission, which is incredible."

"That is wonderful news. You have a really rewarding job."

"Yeah, it's either really uplifting or really depressing depending on the day. But I think breakthroughs are coming soon. We are going to get control of this disease, just like we have for polio and AIDS in the past."

"That is really awesome, Kelly."

"Now that I have been so over the top, how was your day?" she asked.

"A little annoying. I turned down a potential client who was unhappy that I passed. He became kind of a jerk. But if I don't like a job, I pass."

"Nice position to be in, Kevin. I'm glad you can do that." There was a moment of quiet and then she said, "Your message made me smile," she said. "I had a great time last night as well. And yes, I'd love to do a movie with you–or something else. Tomorrow night would work for me if you can make it."

"Can I pick you up at 5:30 so we have time for dinner first?"

"Works for me," she said. "Do you remember how to get to my place?"

"I do."

"What kind of movies do you like?" she asked.

"Mysteries, thrillers, comedies, dramas, independent films and foreign films," he said. "Oh, yeah, and documentaries, too."

"Shouldn't be hard to find something that works within those parameters," she said. She paused and added softly, "I'm really glad we re-met."

He could feel his heart pounding. "Yeah, me too. I'm walking around grinning like an idiot thinking about you."

"Sleep well, Kevin. See you tomorrow."

"Good night," he said softly.

Part 4
Hostage Fallout

Chapter Sixteen

Five Days After

Stacey grabbed her second cup of coffee and walked back to her desk. It was only 8:30 and she'd already been at work for two hours. The phone buzzed and Stacey picked up her com line. "Good morning, Val."

"Morning Stacey. On line three is a lawyer named Johnson who wants to talk about Linda Caldwell," Val replied.

Stacey grabbed the phone and pushed a button. "Detective Gray," she said.

"Hi, Detective, this is Arthur Johnson. I'm calling you on behalf of Linda Caldwell."

"Good morning, Mr. Johnson," Stacey said. "You have consulted with Ms. Caldwell?"

"Yes, and I'm calling to see if we can reach some kind of agreement."

"What did you have in mind?" Stacey asked.

"Well, are you aware that Ms. Caldwell has an issue in her past?"

'An issue,' Stacey thought. This was apparently a euphemism for negligently killing a child and running from the sentence. "Yes, I'm aware of Ms. Caldwell's prior life as Angela Bremmer, and that she has been a fugitive for way too long."

He took a moment and then said, "Detective, she has a husband and two kids, and she just wants to be able to come home to them."

"I understand, but there is the matter of the warrants for fleeing a conviction."

"Right." He paused. "So she would like to make a deal to give you information in exchange for dealing with her other problem."

"You're aware, Mr. Johnson that her conviction is in Ohio and the California district attorney and attorney general have no authority to do anything about it?"

"Right. But you can make recommendations to the Ohio authorities, right? If you value the information and cooperation provided by Ms. Caldwell and strongly urged the Ohio D.A. to make a deal so that you can have the information, then it could all come together."

"Where do you practice, Mr. Johnson?"

"San Diego. But Ms. Caldwell is not here. We did not meet in person."

"I see." Stacey thought for a moment and then asked, "So what information does your client have that she believes will make us want to persuade the Ohio authorities to give her a break on her sentence?"

"We were thinking more of making the sentence go away," Johnson clarified.

"What information does she have?"

"She saw a third person with Mr. Abbott and Mr. Costello at the robbery. A third person she can identify."

Stacey was quiet. If true, that was indeed a newsflash and could be worthy of some kind of deal. "You know that Ohio is already back on the trail. They have the name she has been living under and they have law enforcement on alert across the country," Stacey said.

"I understand," Johnson said.

"The upshot is that she is likely to be picked up sooner rather than later. She will likely come out ahead if she comes in voluntarily."

"I get it," Johnson said. "That's why we are reaching out to you. She will come in as soon as we can make a deal."

Stacey smiled across her desk at her waiting partner. "I will talk to the Ohio prosecutor. I assume that you can reach your client in the event we are able to talk about some kind of a deal?"

"Yes. She is available to me."

"I'll call you at the number you called on later today."

When she hung up, Jeff Butler asked, "What have you got?"

"The missing hostage, Linda Caldwell aka Angela Bremmer, wants to sell us some information for a reduced sentence."

"What information?"

"She says there was a third man with Abbott and Costello and that she can identify him."

"Holy shit!" Butler said. "You got any pull in Cuyahoga County, Ohio?"

"I guess we're about to find out," Stacey said.

* * *

Paul and Brian sat in the large conference room between their offices. "You have the final list of recipients?" Brian asked.

"Right. I show twenty-two," Paul replied.

"Agreed."

"And we all agree that this is strictly 'Robin Hood,' correct?"

"Yep. I think it's the only way," Brian said. "If this ever surfaces, we don't want to have taken any of it. Not even enough to reimburse our out-of-pocket expenses."

"I agree. That's critical."

"So when do we trigger the distribution?"

Paul thought for a moment and then said, "I've been watching the news and listening to word around here. There are a couple of agents working with LAPD, but that's the Agency's only involvement. And so far as I can tell, no one has connected any of the dots. I think maybe we do it right after our meeting on Tuesday unless something happens to make us delay."

"I'll look forward to Wednesday morning," Brian said. "It's going to be a great day."

* * *

Josie stood in the hallway outside of Tom's hotel room. She took a deep breath and knocked. She heard footsteps and then the door opened. His expression was so sad and distraught that she was momentarily stunned. "Hi Tom," she said, lamely. She wanted to hug him; to hold him and not let go, but she didn't. She waited through a moment of silence.

"Hi, Josie," he said. The voice sounded friendly, but then he spoke again. "What do you want?"

She searched for words and finally said, "I want to be with you."

He nodded quietly and then he said, "I knew that we had problems to fix, Josie, but I wasn't the one who gave up on us."

She pushed a tear from her eye. "Can I come in?" He was quiet and did not move to let her pass. "Please, Tom, just so that we can talk a little more."

He took a moment and then moved aside. They sat down at the small, circular table between the bed and the window-mounted air conditioner. She touched his hand and he pulled back. "Tom, I know I screwed up. I really do. But now I know it was a mistake and I also know that we belong together."

He shook his head. "When did you realize it was a mistake? Was it before or after you knew that your picture would be in the paper next to Don Silver's in Los Angeles when you were supposed to be visiting your sister in Minneapolis?"

"I wish I could take it back, Tom. I promise you." She took a deep breath. "My life is with you. Not him and not anyone else."

"Josie, I'm angry. How long were you fucking this guy?"

"Do we have to do this?"

"No, we don't have to do this. We can just go on with our separate lives from here."

She nodded. "About four months," she said softly. "The biggest mistake of my life."

He started to cry. "Josie, I really loved you. And now I feel like I can never trust you again. I can't even look at you without thinking about you fucking him."

"I know. I get it. It will take a while, but I will earn your trust again." She reached for him and hugged him while they were both still seated. He didn't hug her, but he didn't pull away either. After a moment, he sat back in his chair and she moved back into her own.

"Come home, Tom. Come home and let me love you."

"You gave up, dammit, Josie. You were loving someone else so you stopped working to make us better."

"I did. I did that. Please forgive me, love. Then give me the time to show you that I will never stray again." She took his hands and began to cry. He began to cry and took her in his arms. "God dammit Josie," he said through tears.

She stood and pulled him to his feet. She threw her arms around him and said, "It will never happen again." She held him tighter than she ever had. "I love you so much. Please don't leave me."

* * *

Linda dialed Brad and waited. On the third ring he picked it up. "Brad Caldwell."

"Hi, Brad, it's me."

"Hi," he said in tones that were decidedly cold.

"Are you all right?" she asked.

"Under the circumstances, I'm okay."

"You're mad?"

"I'm angry, I'm disappointed and I'm sad. Turns out my wife of many years didn't trust me with an important secret. Turns out she is someone else that I never knew. Makes me feel like my whole life raising two kids with her is a sham."

"I know that I really screwed up. I came close to telling you a number of times, but I just couldn't do it. It was such a risk. And part of me wanted to just forget the old life. I wanted to leave behind that big mistake made by a young girl named Angela and begin a new life with a husband and kids I adore." She paused a moment and then said, "I know that this is crazy, but I didn't want to let that old life back in to ruin my new one. I thought I might never have to deal with it, and that was clearly another big mistake." She paused and then added, "And I know that it's something I need to face."

He took a moment and sounded less angry when he spoke again. "So what will happen now?" he asked.

"I found an attorney to reach out to the police on my behalf. I understand the detectives at LAPD are connecting with Ohio prosecutors to get the authority to make some kind of a deal. If that happens, I will be back in Los Angeles within the next day or two." She paused and said, "Will you be there to meet me at the police station?"

"Yes," Brad said without hesitation, "but I have one condition. You have to come back whether a deal is made or not. It's time to stop running and own this with your family. I am not okay with you or any of us living on the run. So you need to come back and deal with it." She was quiet. "You still there?" he asked.

"I'm here."

"And?"

"Okay, I'll come back either way. Will you wait if I serve time in prison?"

There was a brief silence and then Brad said, "I think so. There was that whole better or worse thing in our vows, right?" She chuckled through tears. "But there was also a sharing and honesty component to those vows, Linda."

"I know."

"And you let us down."

"I'm so sorry, Brad. I'm so sorry," she replied.

After a moment, he said, "I hear Ohio is a nice state. They have the Rock and Roll Hall of Fame. So, if you serve time in Ohio, I will find a job there so the boys and I can visit you and it."

"Thank you, Brad. I'm so sorry and I love you."

"I love you too."

"I'll call you as soon as I know more. You're an amazing man and I will thank you forever."

* * *

It was a beautiful evening as Kelly and Kevin left the restaurant and decided to walk to the theater. They held hands and talked about some of the people they knew in high school in a game of 'whatever became of.'

After they had discussed all of their friends and what they are doing now, they talked about the weirder, more daring and more troubled members of the class. They both knew of someone who landed in jail. They had no idea what became of a number of these people.

"So tell me your favorite things," Kelly asked.

"Like whiskers on kittens?" He asked.

"Yeah, maybe."

"This evening is one of my favorite things at this moment. I don't ever want it to end."

She smiled. "Yeah, me too." She reflected and then said, "I want to know all about you. Tell me about your work."

"Well," he said, "I research and analyze products and services in an attempt to help the company that is my client outperform competitors."

"Sounds interesting. How do you do that?"

"A lot of ways, really. I look at strengths and weaknesses of products and marketing opportunities. I look for the other guy's vulnerabilities and I advise my clients to focus on their competitor's weaknesses."

"You have a degree?"

"Yeah, and a doctorate in computer science."

"Interesting. And what do you do when you are not working?" She grinned at him and asked, "Date a lot of women?"

"Not really. Like I said, my experience with dating hasn't been great. Dating is like," he paused and then said, "throwing darts in the dark. There are just so many who are not the right person and I find it tiring." He grinned. "So now I am so glad that I'm only dating one woman and she just might be the right one."

The marquis of the theater came into view and Kevin stopped. Kelly looked up at him and said, "You okay?"

He nodded, putting his arms around her and, on impulse, kissed her compelling lips. When he pulled back, her eyes were still partially closed. "That is my new favorite thing," he said.

"Yeah, definitely something I could get used to," Kelly said as they walked toward the theater with arms around each other.

Chapter Seventeen

Six Days After

Stacey was in the office at 6:00 a.m. and Butler twenty minutes later. She checked her notes and made plans for the day and put calls in to people who weren't yet in the office, including Linda Caldwell's attorney, Arthur Johnson. At 8:15 a.m., she and Jeff Butler were reviewing the big board that they had been building along one wall in one of the conference rooms. On the far left, the word "Suspects" was written and underneath were pictures of all of the hostages, all of whom had been suspects initially. Then the lead suspect became Chris Morgan, a former employee with a gun he initially didn't disclose and now there was no one. There was a line from Linda Caldwell's picture to Angela Bremmer on one side and a big question mark on the other, representing the third man she had yet to identify.

There were a whole series of questions on the board, including the identity of Mr. Abbott and Mr. Costello, their means of escape, how the money was removed from the building, and all possible witnesses. All had question marks beside them, none had answers or even good theories. Stacey shook her head as she considered the dearth of information they had been able to gather. Her meetings with Lieutenant Spencer had become sessions she did not want to attend. He would complain about press portrayals of the event and the police, take too many aspirin for his perpetual headache, and send her back out to make something break. So far he had not lost confidence in her or threatened to reassign the case, but she was feeling the pressure. Between her and Butler and the FBI team, they had to break something quickly.

Val walked to the door and said, "Good morning you obsessed people. Stacey, Arthur Johnson is returning your call. Line two."

"Thanks, Val, and good morning." She walked over to the phone in the conference room and said, "Detective Gray."

"Good morning, Detective. You called me, so I'm hoping you have some news?"

"I spoke with the D.A. for Franklin County, Ohio, at some length, and the good news is that they are prepared to work with us. First of all, your client is going to have to do some time. There is no way that she can walk from her sentence of three to five and the additional time that would come from her years of flight." There was quiet while he waited for the bottom line, so Stacey continued. "They are willing to allow her to serve eighteen months including the original three to five term and the likely additional two years that would be added based on her flight. With an eighteen month sentence, and good behavior credits, they say that would mean she would likely serve less than a year."

He was silent a moment longer and this time Stacey waited. "I will have to check with her."

"That's fine. Just know that this is a good deal. Otherwise law enforcement finds her and she serves at least five to seven years. Fleeing a conviction doesn't get much sympathy from most judges. And you know that we are going to find her, so this is her one and only chance to come in and take the deal."

"Let me contact her and I will get back to you."

"Wait. There is more to this deal," Stacey said. "We are only prepared to make this deal if your client can actually identify this third person she saw and testifies to it at any trial or other hearing. She must sign a written agreement to answer all of our questions truthfully and without withholding information. She doesn't come through on any of this and the deal is off. Understood?"

"I will convey it all to her," Johnson said. "I should be able to get back to you within a couple of hours."

* * *

Don Silver arrived home shortly after noon. He had received nothing but support and empathy for his role as a hostage and having the courage to stay and make his presentation. There would be new business from well-wishers and admirers. But Naomi wasn't talking to him. His next three voice mail messages and four texts to her brought no response.

Her car was gone. He studied the house from the driveway and saw no movement. Don unlocked the door and walked into the house. He looked around but found no note. He went directly to the bedroom and looked in the closet. All of her clothes were gone. He felt a rising panic. He raced to her bureau drawers and opened them one by one to find each empty. She was gone. He tried to make himself think rationally. It was likely she went to her sister Jean's place in Cedar Rapids. There is no one closer to her and no one else she would turn to when she needed to talk about something important.

He dialed Jean's number, but his call went directly to voice mail. He left a message saying that he was home and asking that Naomi call him. Then Don sat down on the floor next to the empty closet that his wife's dresses and shoes used to occupy. He thought frantically about what actions he might take to calm Naomi and save his marriage. Nothing came to mind. He stared into the empty closet and wondered if he should drive to Cedar Rapids. He had no idea of what to do next.

Detective Stacey Gray was driving between meetings and de-cided to use the time to catch up with Curt Lowell. She hit a button and dialed his cell phone.

"This is Agent Lowell," he said evenly.

"Curt, this is Stacey. I wanted to give you an update. The D.A. is going to charge Chris Morgan with unlawfully carrying a con-cealed and unregistered weapon. They are considering whether they can make a case for assault or attempted murder, but I don't think it's likely and I'm recommending against it so long as he continues to cooperate and we don't find out he's lying to us. I mean, he never pulled the gun on anybody other than two guys in the process of committing an armed robbery, and who's going to convict him for that?"

Curt Lowell considered for a moment and said, "I think you're right, but it's possible that they may be able to make a case for attempted murder or attempted battery because he went as far as showing up at the site with a weapon. They would have to prove it was his intent to do harm to someone in the bank and that evidence is all surmise based on the presence of the gun." He paused and added, "They can't get him for assault because you can't put someone in fear of imminent injury based on a gun you never show them."

"We are on the same page," Stacey replied, and then added, "I asked the D.A. not to do anything at all yet, because I don't want this all over the press. Not only will it make Morgan a robbery suspect in the media, it will have everyone seeing this investigation in the wrong way and may interfere with our work on the ground."

"Good. This is already a clusterfuck without the media shin-ing lights in the wrong direction." There was a pause and then Lowell asked, "Any further word from Caldwell's lawyer?"

"Not yet."

"Okay. Let me know what you hear."

As they hung up, Stacey was pulling into the LAPD parking lot. She walked into the office and Val met her near the elevator. "Stacey, I have Arthur Johnson on line two."

Stacey raced back to her desk and picked up the phone.

"Mr. Johnson?"

"Yes, hello, Detective Gray."

"Any news concerning Ms. Caldwell?"

"Yes. My client agrees to the terms of the deal."

Stacey made a fist and pumped the air in front of her. "I think that's a good decision for her. When can she be here?"

"Tomorrow morning about 11:00 a.m. Does that work for you?"

"Yes, that will work."

"Will you accompany her?"

"Yes, ma'am."

"Okay, I will see you both tomorrow morning."

* * *

It took Don Silver two and a half hours to make the one hundred twenty-seven mile trip from Des Moines to Cedar Rapids. Naomi's car was parked on the street in front of the house. He walked slowly from the car to the front door, still searching for the right words—the words that might make her forgive him and come back home.

He knocked and waited. There were footsteps and Jean opened the door. He knew instantly that she was aware of what had happened. She gave him a look that said it all; betrayal, disappointment and sadness. Unlike prior visits, there was no hug, no greeting and no invite inside.

"Hi, Jean. Can I see Naomi?" he asked weakly.

Jean's hesitation to let him in was painful. Finally, she said, "She's in the living room." She stepped aside and let him walk into the house.

As he turned left from the hallway into the living room, he saw her sitting on the couch, looking at him as she might a stranger. She didn't speak. He sat down in the armchair next to her and said, "I am so sorry." She said nothing. "It was a mistake, that's all. Please, come home."

Naomi's eyes flashed anger. "Why don't you go live with her? She's the one you wanted until all of it went public, right? When it was all your choice, when no one was looking, you made a decision. So now that it's all out in the light, you can live with the decision you made in the shadows."

"Naomi, please. You're the one I love." The words sounded hollow, even to him and he was getting more desperate. "We all make mistakes, right?"

"Yeah, we all make mistakes. This is different. You made a choice." She was quiet for a few moments and then said, "Don, I can't trust you. You made a decision that fucking some younger woman at work was more important than us."

He looked at her with pleading eyes. "I can make this right."

She looked at him coldly. "Don," she said in a soft and pained voice, "I know this is not the first time."

"It is," he said, "I swear it is."

She shook her head and looked at him with sadness and disappointment. "Don't make a fool of yourself. The time for lying is all done."

"Naomi, you have to believe me…"

Her eyes cut into him. "Really? How about the fact that your former secretary Nicky wrote me a letter after she broke up with you. You slept with her for six months and she stopped it because she felt guilty about your marriage. Apparently, she was the only one who felt guilty about what you were doing to your marriage." She leaned back and her expression moved to sadness. "But when it was over you got closer to me and I thought we could make it, so I never confronted you. Obviously, that was a mistake. I should have known it was just a matter of time until you did it all over again."

"We can work this out," he said.

She shook her head and said, "No more. I won't be treated like that anymore." She let out a breath and said, "You probably saw that I have my clothing with me. Tomorrow, I'm going to look for an apartment here in Cedar Rapids and start over. We'll put the house up for sale and divide the furniture and our financial assets and we will move on."

Don grabbed for anything that might make a difference—anything that might sway her to give him another chance. "I planned to end it on that trip and I did. It was all over."

She had a sad, hurt expression. She said, "Thanks for coming by Don. We'll talk about how we divide the furniture and the accounts, and setting the right price for the house when we get a realtor. Good night." She stood and walked from the room and left him there on his sister-in-law's couch, to show himself out. He sat for five minutes trying to think of something else he could do, but nothing came to mind and no one came back to the living room. He walked from the house with tear-filled eyes into a clear, starry night. As he walked toward his car, he thought about calling Josie in hopes of salvaging one of his relationships.

Chapter Eighteen

Seven Days After

At 11:00 a.m., Linda Caldwell and a painfully thin man in his late sixties with wisps of white hair pointing in all directions sat at a conference room table at LAPD. Brad Caldwell waited in the lobby to take his wife home.

"That's her lawyer, Arthur Johnson," Stacey told Curt Lowell as they looked into the room through a one-way mirror.

Stacey and Curt Lowell walked into the room, while Jeff Butler and Alicia Garcia watched through the mirrored window and took notes. Upon entering, Stacey said, "I'm Detective Gray with LAPD. This is Agent Lowell with the FBI." They shook hands briefly, and then as she sat down, Stacey added, "I want to go over the terms that have been agreed for this meeting. First of all, Ohio prosecutors have agreed that they will agree to you serving eighteen months, inclusive of your three to five conviction and all additional time you might suffer for having fled the jurisdiction and having been a fugitive all these years. I have email confirmation from the prosecutor." She handed Johnson and Linda a copy of the email, and then she said, "This is expressly conditioned on you providing us with the identity of the third person you saw working with Mr. Abbott and Mr. Costello in the bank, you testifying to what you observed at all necessary trials and hearings; and finally, you answering all questions put to you fully and truthfully, which means no partial answers and no misleading answers, no omission of any material facts." She looked at Linda and at Johnson and then said, "Are we in agreement to each of these terms?"

"Yes," Linda said.

Johnson nodded, and then added, "We are."

"So, Ms. Caldwell, take me to the point where you were when you saw this third man with Mr. Abbott and Mr. Costello."

Linda nodded. "Okay. You recall that I was one of the three taken out of the conference room and I was taken to the manager's office." Stacey nodded and waited. "The one called Costello gave me one of the bags of teller cash and told me to find dye packs, consecutive bills and any GPS. Then they closed the door and walked out."

"Okay," Stacey said, "then what happened?"

"I was panicked. I knew that I couldn't be a hostage because even if I survived the day, I would be discovered and arrested. I would lose my family and they mean everything to me." She drew a deep breath and then said, "So, I wanted a way out. After a few minutes in that office, I opened the door very slightly to look for an exit. I didn't see any way out at all. Any exit would take me out to where everyone would see me. But what I did see is one of the other hostages making his way to where Mr. Abbott was seated."

"Did you get a look at his face?" Stacey asked.

"Yes. At one point he looked back in my direction. Then I saw him walk to Mr. Abbott, who was sitting at one of the banker's desks, and I saw them have a conversation."

"Could you hear anything that was said?" Stacey asked.

"No, I saw them talk, but I couldn't hear the conversation. Then I ducked back into the manager's office to finish my assignment before someone saw me."

"So he could have been asking a question about the assignment or sharing what he found in the money bags?"

Linda reflected a moment. "I suppose, but I don't think so."

"Why not?"

"They seemed too cordial and familiar. And he didn't look nervous at all."

Linda looked over at Curt Lowell, who gave her a raised eyelid and a slight nod. Then Stacey asked, "This hostage was on the floor in the conference room with you?"

"Yes."

"So you remember seeing him before you saw him approach Mr. Abbott?"

"Yes, and he was one of the three of us pulled out of the conference room and given one of the money bags to go through for dye packs, consecutive bills and hidden GPS devices," Linda said.

"You saw and heard him get the same instructions you did about going through the cash bags?"

"Yes. He was directed into the room right next to the office I was ordered to enter. Costello told him to get into that room and then took me to the next office along the hallway"

Stacey produced a book of photos and handed it to Linda Caldwell. "These are all twenty-six of the hostages from the bank, Ms. Caldwell. You are on page seven. You'll find two hostages on each page. Please locate the man you're telling us about."

Linda studied faces and turned pages. Everyone waited silently, until she said, "Here he is, right here on page eight. The picture at the top of the page."

Linda pushed the book back to Stacey who studied it and then asked, "Are you absolutely certain about this?"

"Yes, Detective, I'm certain," Linda said, as Stacey looked back to the picture of Kevin Roper.

"Can you find the third person who was given the assignment of going through one of the teller bags?"

"Sure," Linda said. She took the book and went through it page by page. "Here she is," Linda said, and showed Stacey the picture of the woman on the bottom of page eleven. She was accurate. This was the elderly woman Stacey knew was Ms. Pierce, the third of the hostages given that assignment.

Stacey looked at Curt and then back at Linda. "Give us a couple of minutes," she said, and she and Curt walked out of the room. Jeff Butler and Alicia Garcia walked with them to a conference room down the hall. They took seats inside and Stacey said, "Curt?"

"Yeah, I buy it. She's credible."

"Jeff?"

"Me too. She's got the motivation and she's got the facts right."

"Alicia?"

"Yes, I'm convinced. She's for real."

"One thing that occurred to me," Curt Lowell said. "She identified Kevin Roper." He looked around the room and then added, "Roper was the one who knocked the gun away from Morgan, right? In the name of protecting the group from harm?"

"Yeah," Stacey said. "In light of this new insight, it seems like he might have been more interested in protecting Mr. Abbott and Mr. Costello."

Butler shook his head and said, "Shit, these guys are really good. They call themselves Abbott and Costello, right? They could have picked anything, so why those names?"

Stacey smiled. "Because Abbott and Costello was a duo. It quietly reinforces what they want us to believe–that there were just two of them involved."

"That's right," Butler said, nodding.

Curt Lowell gave a soft whistle. He said, "We have our first big break and it's only because one of the hostages was a fugitive when all this went down. Without Ms. Caldwell, how do we ever get to the fact that they may have had a third man embedded in the hostage group?" The group was quiet as that settled on the room.

Stacey said, "I'm going to kick her loose. She goes home, doesn't leave town, and remains available to us on two hours' notice, and she keeps quiet about all of this. Agreed?"

Lowell nodded. "Yep. She wants to be with her family and she wants her deal to work. I don't think she is a flight risk any longer."

Butler said, "An amazing morning. I'll get Kevin Roper in here. Let's get to him before he figures out we have any information."

Stacey said, "Definitely. Let's get him in here today."

* * *

"I found the connection," Kevin Roper said.

"What? Are you kidding?" Kent Barkley, the chairman of North American Dynamics replied. "Not kidding. We have it. I can show you what I have and how I got there."

"Can we meet today?"

"Yes. I can be there at three o'clock. Does that work for you?"

"I'll be waiting for you," Barkley said, sounding excited.

When they hung up, Kevin sat back in his chair. Work was always fun, but more and more he found himself counting the hours until he could be with Kelly. He dialed her number and got voice mail. "This is Kelly. Tell me something I don't know and then I'll call you back and return the favor." Then came the beep.

"You may already know this, but I miss you and want to be with you. I've been thinking about that kiss last night and I can hardly wait for the next one. I hope you feel the same and I hope you're having a great day. See you tomorrow night, which seems too far away." He paused. "I'm thinking about you a lot." Then he hung up.

Kevin checked email and then poured a cup of coffee. His phone rang, but this time not one of the secure lines in his office. This time it was his cell.

He hit a button and said, "Kevin Roper."

"Hello, Mr. Roper, this is Detective Jeff Butler with LAPD."

"Hello, Detective."

"Mr. Roper we need you to come talk with us this afternoon."

"Sorry, I have an important business appointment this afternoon. How about tomorrow morning? I can make it then."

"We really need to see you today, sir. It's important."

Kevin took a breath. This didn't sound good. "Okay. My meeting should be over by four o'clock and it's not too far from you so I should be able to get there around 5:30. Will that work?"

"Yes, sir, that will be fine. See you then"

When they hung up, Kevin considered what this meeting might be about. They had stumbled onto something, some fact that has them curious about him. He had no idea what they had discovered, but he was already a little nervous.

* * *

Linda and Brad picked the kids up from school together. Jason came running out and hugged Linda with all his might. "Are you okay, Mom?"

"Yeah, sweetheart, I'm fine. I just had to make a trip unexpectedly."

"To Las Vegas, right?"

"No, buddy, I had to postpone that one."

"Do you have to go away again?" he asked with serious eyes. Linda glanced at Brad. "I may have a longer trip at some point, but you guys will know all about it before it happens, okay?'

"Yeah, I guess so."

They drove down the street to the high school and tried to be inconspicuous while they waited for Matt to emerge. For some reason, teenagers were always embarrassed to acknowledge that they had parents. Linda could remember feeling that way herself back in high school. Some things never changed.

Matt came out of the school's massive front door with his arm around Claire. He walked down the sidewalk to the curb and then glanced in their direction. He said something to Claire and came over to Linda. He gave her a hug and said, "What's wrong, mom? Why did you leave?"

Linda looked at Brad and began to tear up. She said, "I guess we should have a family meeting tonight."

* * *

A busty blonde woman with a gorgeous smile showed Kevin into Kent Barkley's private conference room on the thirty-seventh floor of the North American Dynamics building. Barkley stood and offered a smile and a hand.

"Kevin, you are amazing. What is this, the fourth time you've cracked something for us?"

"Yes, sir, I believe it is."

"Call me Kent."

"Okay, Kent."

"So take me through it—what have you got?"

"Well, Parnell Corporation's lawyer wrote in his letter to you that their inventor was the first person to invent the product, and that you were pirating their ideas and must cease and desist, right?"

"Yes, that's right."

"He also said that their inventor is Dominic Marshall. Before you tell them what you've got, have your lawyer take the deposition of Dominic Marshall and have him tell you under oath that he, Dominic Marshall, was the inventor of the product and that he was first in time. Then depose someone further up the chain and have him adopt the same lies under oath. I'm sure that they'd love to pitch exactly that story, so it should be easy. After they testify under oath, they will be locked into that story, which is what you want."

Barkley poured two glasses of brandy from a crystal decanter and handed Kevin one of them. "Why?"

Kevin grinned. "Because I've been through their internal email chains. What they have, they stole from your firm." He took a sip. "Wow, good stuff," Kevin said, lifting the glass. He continued, "On February 18, 2014, there is a transmittal from John Ortiz. That transmittal is to Dominic Marshall telling him that the attachment came from inside North American Dynamics and is their latest project." He stopped and smiled.

"And?" Barkley asked with anticipation.

"And Ortiz is a non-existent person. He doesn't work for Parnell Corporation, so you would never normally learn of him and never seek any communication chains from him. You would have no idea what to ask for under usual circumstances, and that is the intent." He took one more sip. "Like I say, Ortiz doesn't exist, but John Ortiz is a pseudonym used by Lucas Grossmont, one of their product VP's."

"Unbelievable," Barkley said, assembling the information in his mind.

"So Marshall never responds to this email, but another non-existent employee, Tim Wilmer does. And non-existent Tim acknowledges the email from non-existent Ortiz and says that Marshall will start working on a similar product immediately." Barkley looked stunned. "Yes, Parnell uses a network of non-existent, fake people who talk to each other to convey sensitive stuff that their human counterparts don't want to acknowledge ever discussing. It is like a parallel world of communications to and from people who don't exist." Kevin laid his twenty-two page report on the table.

Barkley picked it up and began reading. After a few quiet moments, he turned to Kevin and said, "This is incredible."

"I'm glad you're pleased. The only thing I ask, other than the fee we agreed, is that I stay anonymous. No one can discover your source for this information."

"Agreed."

"Thanks for the brandy," Kevin said, raising the glass, "it was excellent." Kevin shook Barkley's hand and headed out of the suite. The attractive blonde walked him to the executive elevator and put a key in it. She told him to have a great day. He smiled and wished her a good day, but he was already focused on his appointment with the LAPD and trying to anticipate what they might have discovered.

* * *

Stacey Gray walked into the small conference room to see Kevin Roper seated at the small conference table. He stood and extended a hand.

"Hello, Mr. Roper. I'm not sure if you remember me, I'm Detective Gray." Stacey wanted him to feel at ease, but also wanted a witness to the interview, so Butler watched the interview through the one way mirror from the adjoining room.

"Yes, Detective, I remember you from our first meeting."

As Stacey sat down across from Kevin, she said, "You okay if we record this conversation?"

He shrugged. "Yes, sure."

"What did you not tell me the first time we met, Mr. Roper?" Stacey said, watching his expression as this kind of an open question forced him to consider what they might already know.

He thought a moment and then said, "I can't think of anything. Maybe you can remind me of what it is you're thinking about."

"Well, I'm thinking about truth, Mr. Roper. I'm thinking about you telling the whole story."

"I don't follow," Kevin said, looking her directly in the eyes.

"I'm thinking about you being acquainted with Mr. Abbott and Mr. Costello," she said and watched for the impact of the statement.

His expression was one of surprise. "What?" Kevin replied, furrowing his brow. "Are you kidding?"

"No, sir, no joke. We have information that tells us you are involved with these gentlemen. You want to tell us about that?"

"I have no idea what you're talking about. I was a hostage, remember?"

"We thought so originally, yes. Now we know better."

Kevin shook his head. "I don't know what you're talking about. Let me in on what you're thinking and I will be happy to tell you what I know."

Stacey thought for a moment. If this guy was lying, he was good. "You told us that you were taken to an office and given a bag of money."

"Yes."

"And you were told to look for dye packs, consecutively numbered bills and GPS devices, right?

"Yes, ma'am, that's right."

"And you did that?"

"Yes."

"You forgot to tell us about the part where you left the room and went out into the bank to see Mr. Abbott and Mr. Costello."

Kevin shook his head. "Not me," he said. "I never left the room until they came back for the bag and took me back to the conference room."

"Did you at any point open the door to the room you were in?"

"Nope. I wasn't going to mess with those guys."

Stacey considered this. "Would you take a lie detector test concerning all of this?"

"Probably not. I have been told by several lawyers that they are not reliable and that false readings aren't uncommon." He looked her directly in the eye and said, "But I have no idea what you are talking about." He shook his head. "Someone's giving you bad information here, Detective."

Stacey said, "Did you know one of the other hostages?"

Kevin involuntarily smiled. "Yes, Kelly Parson. Actually, I hadn't seen her since high school, but we ran into each other in the bank that day."

"Is there anything else you'd like to tell me now, before I find out some other way and it all gets worse for you?"

"No, I'm a little confused. I don't know what you mean." He shook his head and added, "I can't think of anything I haven't told you."

"Okay, Mr. Roper. Let us know if you think of anything else or if there is anything you decide is in your own best interest to reveal."

"Detective, I don't have more information. But if I think of anything, I will certainly call you."

"You have any travel coming up in the next couple of months, Mr. Roper."

"Nothing extended. Periodically I have to go to San Francisco or Sacramento for business, usually just a day or two at a time."

"Thanks for your time, Mr. Roper. We'll be in touch."

"Sure, anytime," Kevin said, shaking Stacey's hand before walking out of the room.

After Kevin Roper left the room, Jeff Butler, who had watched from the other side of the one-way mirror walked in and sat down. "Well, what do you think?" Stacey asked.

"The guy is either telling the truth or he is one great fucking actor."

Stacey nodded. "Yeah, he was credible. And so was Linda Caldwell, but one of them is lying to us."

Butler nodded. "Let's find out more about Roper, like who he associates with and what he's doing."

"Agreed," Stacey said. "The guy is hard to read. He looked me in the eye and didn't act like he had anything to hide. Maybe he doesn't."

"Or maybe he's just that good," Butler replied.

Part 5
The Missing Money

Chapter Nineteen

Ten Days After

Josie took a couple of vacation days and then nervously appeared for work for the first time since the robbery in California. Family and friends had been supportive of her and the hostage ordeal she had been through. She was working to make amends to Tom and recover her life. The night before he had kissed her for the first time since all this had happened, and she could feel his forgiveness on the horizon.

She grabbed coffee at eight o'clock and within three minutes, Don called her into his office. "Close the door," he directed. She did so.

He stood and walked over to her. "Josie," he said softly, "I want to be with you, just you. I am prepared to leave Naomi for you—for us."

He put his arms around her. For a moment she froze, but then she pulled back slowly. She looked at him and said, "Thank you for caring about me. I really mean that." She drew a breath. "But we don't belong together as a couple. We can work together professionally, but that's where it has to end."

His face became red. He was silent for a moment and then he said, "No, that's not okay. We belong together. He put his hands on her cheeks and pulled her close to him."

"No." Josie said. "Don't, Don."

"Josie, please." He grabbed at her and she moved away. There was a ripping sound and her blouse was torn open. "Oh, my God," he said. "I didn't mean to do that."

Her expression was surprise and then anger. She took a breath and said, "I understand," she said. "Now help me think of a way to get out of your office so that I can go change." He just stood there. "I know, hand me those files." He handed her three files and she pushed her blouse back together and held the files against her chest. She started toward the door.

"Josie, you can't leave me," he called out too loudly. Without turning around, she could tell that he had moved toward the doorway. She continued walking, checking her peripheral vision to see if anyone in the office was watching this. Things were now in proper perspective. She wanted the affair behind her. She wanted Tom and she wanted her job. And now she feared that Don might do something to mess up her career and her home life.

* * *

Stacey and Jeff Butler sat outside the Hotdog Shack with coffee and linguica dogs. The place could have been called the cop-dog shack, because cops from all agencies tended to gather here for conversation and indigestion. Stacey considered the fact that you could tell a cop hangout pretty easily. Everyone there had a kind of a cop presence, whatever that was, and they were constantly looking around and assessing the environment and the people; always anticipating that something might happen.

"This morning I got a response on our request for known associations of Roper," Butler said. "Nothing. No associations with any known criminal."

"Of course," Stacey replied. "Why would we expect this case to get any easier?" She took a bite of her hot dog as her phone began ringing. She hit a button and said, "Detective Gray," doing her best to be audible around a mouthful of hot dog. She listened a moment and then said, "We can be there in fifteen minutes." She hung up and said, "Hank Mercer just discovered something he wants us to look at in his bank. You okay to eat while we roll?"

"Let's do it," Butler said, grabbing his soda and hot dog.

When they arrived at the bank, Hank Mercer was waiting. He said, "Detectives, thanks for coming. This may not turn out to be anything, but I wanted you to get a look just in case."

"Yes, sir." Stacey said. "What are we looking at?"

Mercer led the way to the big storage room, in which there were several file cabinets and two shelves two and four feet off the ground. He pointed up to where there was a third shelf about seven feet off the ground. A ladder was in place to allow access.

"This area was all inspected by officers before, wasn't it?" Stacey asked.

"It was. And like I said, I'm not sure we have anything. We moved everything off the shelf to make it a little easier to see."

Stacey climbed the ladder behind Mercer. They crouched on the upper shelves, where their heads were just a couple of feet below ceiling level.

"Look over here," Mercer said, pointing to an area at the level of the highest shelf.

Stacey looked, but nothing really registered. She looked at him questioningly.

"If you look real close, this piece of wall tile looks newer than the rest," he said.

She looked at it and saw that it was a slightly different, cleaner color. She tugged all around the large tile, but it was secure. "Has anyone cleaned up here recently, or worked on this area?" she asked.

Mercer said, "No. I checked with the entire staff. It hasn't been cleaned nor has any part of the wall been repaired or replaced."

"You have some tools?" she asked. "Large screwdrivers, maybe a crowbar?"

Mercer instructed one of the employees standing below to get the tools from the locked box in the Operations Manager's office. As that employee disappeared, Stacey tugged at the tile. "Good observation on your part, Mr. Mercer. This tile is clearly not as old as the surrounding tiles, although it is pretty secure."

The employee returned with a hammer, a crowbar, a drill and some pliers. The tools were passed up the ladder. Stacey asked Mercer, "Okay with you if I damage this tile?"

"Yeah, sure."

She started the drill and began to work on the grout that surrounded the tile. As she got into it, she realized that the grout wasn't particularly old either. She was becoming more convinced that Mercer might have something here. It jammed periodically and Butler whacked at it with the hammer and the crowbar. Then Stacey continued to drill. Once they made their way around the entire tile they were able to break the last connections and pull the tile off of the wall. As she looked inside, Stacey couldn't believe what she was seeing.

They all looked into the newly created hole in the wall. "Holy shit," Butler murmured.

"Yeah," Mercer agreed.

"All right," Stacey said. "Let's get it down."

* * *

Lowell and Garcia joined Stacey and Butler in the bank's big conference room—the same one that had held twenty-six hostages ten days before. On the table in front of them were bags and piles of money that the team had just finished counting. The count had revealed that all seven hundred sixty eight thousand dollars, plus the money taken from the three tellers' drawers, was there. They sat around the table staring at the treasure in stunned silence.

Stacey hit a preset on her phone to set a meeting with Lieutenant Spencer. She would meet with him in forty-five minutes. She put the phone away and said, "This is the strangest thing I've ever seen. A robbery with the money not only left behind, but hidden. These guys take hostages, hide money, let the hostages go, and then somehow disappear."

"So why does someone hide money in the place it was taken from?"

"I've got it," Alicia Garcia said thoughtfully. "They want us to believe that the money is gone. We stop looking in the bank and the money waits in that wall until someone comes back to get it."

Lowell nodded. "That could be right. It is a great hiding place. Who's going to look for stolen money in the place it was stolen from?"

"Right," Butler added, "and they avoided moving the money while the street was full of cops. Ingenious, really."

"Okay," Stacey said thoughtfully, "if the money was hidden for future collection, how are they planning to get it out of here?"

Alicia said, "Well, we know they know how to kill the cameras and come and go without a trace. So they plan to do it again to retrieve the money when the heat is off, we just don't know the timetable."

The room was silent for a moment and then Lowell said, "So we can't release word that we recovered the money. This has to stay our secret."

Stacey nodded. "I agree. If word gets out that the money has been found, they will never return. So we say nothing. We surveil the bank and we catch them when they return. We need eyes on the bank around the clock until they return." She glanced at the time. "I have to go brief Lieutenant Spencer. Curt, can you assemble Mercer and the other bank personnel who know what we found and tell them how critical it is that we keep a lid on this?"

Lowell nodded. "Yes." He paused and then added, "Tell your boss that we will agree to share surveillance expenses with him. Teams of two, twelve hour shifts."

"That works," Stacey said. "I'll recommend that we start within the next two hours."

* * *

Kevin drove toward Kelly's place to pick her up for dinner. He dialed a burner phone and waited. On the third ring, it was answered by a male voice.

"Something happen?"

"Yeah, Detective Gray called me back in today."

"What did she have?"

"Apparently one of the other hostages saw me walk from my assigned task of looking for dye packs and sit down next to you."

"What did you tell her?"

"I told her it never happened. I had no choice, I was locked in by the interview I gave them after the hostage release."

"Did she believe you?"

"Probably." He paused. "I don't know. Maybe the cops don't know who to believe."

"You know who the hostage is—the one who saw you exit your assignment."

"No, but I'm guessing it had to be one of the other two. Margaret Pierce, the older lady, or Linda Caldwell, who was stationed in the manager's office and would have had a better view of me leaving the room. My guess is that it was Caldwell. Pierce seemed too nervous to go near the door."

"I'll see what we can find out about Caldwell and Pierce and we'll talk about it at Tuesday's meeting."

"Okay, see you then," Kevin said as he hung up. He was feeling a little shaken. This was not a good development.

* * *

Kevin and Kelly walked down a narrow street in old Pasadena, holding hands as they gazed in store windows. The ornamental street lights had just come on, and it was the beginning of twilight. Shadows were long and the tree-lined streets spoke of quieter downtowns of the 1950s. They made a left turn to find a literal 'mom and pop shop.' It was 'Mama's And Papa's Fine Pizzeria,' with broad windows on the street and a big wooden door.

As they walked into the restaurant, a woman waited at the hostess desk. She spoke warmly and with an Italian accent. "Mr. Kevin, how are you tonight? I'm glad you have a new friend with you. Please, sit in your favorite seat by the window." She was about sixty-five and rotund. She had many wrinkles and a smile that filled her eyes when she spoke.

"My friend is Kelly. And actually, I hope she is more than my friend."

"Yes, she is a pretty, pretty girl. You would have good babies with her," she said matter-of-factly.

Kevin and Kelly grinned at each other, then Kelly said, "I'm Kelly. Good to meet you, Mama."

"And you, my dear. You take good care of this one, eh? This one, he needs a good woman around him."

"Okay," Kelly said, "I will."

"How are you, Mama?" Kevin asked.

"Excellente! We have a new pizza for you to try. A surprise. Yes?"

"Yes. I love your surprises."

"And we have red wine. New Chianti that is..." she hesitated and put her fingers and thumb to her lips and opened them widely in a gesture to convey just how good this wine is, "fantastic. You will try it, yes?"

"Yes," he said.

"I'll be right back. Don't move." She moved away from the table and Kevin said, "I told you she's a character."

"She's perfectly charming," Kelly said.

She immediately delivered full wine glasses and they toasted another wonderful evening together. Ten minutes later she delivered a pizza large enough to cover most of the round table.

The tablecloths were red and white checkered vinyl, the music was accordion, and the pizza was thick and delicious, with cheese melting everywhere.

"This is one of my favorite hole-in-the-wall places," Kevin said. "I've been coming here a couple of times a month for about five years."

"You okay?" Kevin asked. "You seemed a little down when I picked you up."

"Yeah, I guess so. Today was one of those days that I like least about my job." Kelly replied.

"What happened?" Kevin asked, touching her hand.

"I consulted on a scan today that revealed stage four cancer in a darling, six year old boy; beautiful, smiling kid with a loving family. There are some things you can't get used to, you know? It's all just so unfair sometimes."

"I'm so sorry. That had to be really hard," Kevin replied.

Kelly forced a slight smile. "You're a pretty supportive guy," she said. "Why did we let twenty years go by before we started spending time together?"

"I have no idea. I would have liked a lot more days like the ones I'm spending with you now."

"How about nights?"

"What?"

She leaned across the small table and kissed him softly. "How about spending the night with me at my place?" she said, and then kissed him again.

"Definitely," he said. "Can we go now or do we need to eat first?"

Chapter Twenty

Fourteen Days After

"Why do you think that you are back in this conference room today, Ms. Caldwell?" Stacey asked.

"I really have no idea," Linda Caldwell replied, "It is a little alarming."

"You remember the terms of our deal, right?" Stacey asked.

"I remember."

"Truth and full disclosure, right?" Stacey recited.

"Yes."

"And that means that you don't make things up in order to buy a shorter sentence for your past conviction."

"Yes, I know that. What are you suggesting?"

"That you may want to recant what you said you saw. This is really your best opportunity to be entirely forthcoming," Stacey said.

"I don't need to recant anything. I told you what I saw."

"Will you take a lie detector?"

She hesitates. "Legal counsel I have spoken to in the past says that they are not reliable, so I don't think that's a good idea."

"You realize that you are betting everything on the accuracy of your testimony?"

"Yes," Linda Caldwell said, looking directly at Stacey.

"And there is nothing that you would like to change?"

"Nothing."

"You are prepared to testify to everything you've told me without hesitation?" Stacey persisted.

"Yes, ma'am. All of it."

"And you're sure that the person you saw approach Mr. Abbott and Mr. Costello was the hostage that you identified? Any doubt? If so, this is the time to say so."

"No doubt, Detective. He is the one."

Stacey checked her notes and said, "That's all I have for now, Ms. Caldwell. You're free to go." She paused and then added, "You will stay available to us in case we need you further?"

"Yes, ma'am. I will."

Stacey watched Linda Caldwell leave the room and then she walked into the adjoining room where Butler, Lowell and Garcia waited. "What's the verdict?" she asked.

"She looks honest to me," Butler replied. "Manner of delivery, confidence, direct eye contact all says she's telling the truth."

"I agree," Lowell said.

"Unanimous," Garcia added.

"Perfect," Stacey offered. "We have two people providing grossly inconsistent accounts of the same events, and we all want to believe both of them."

* * *

"Josie, can you come in for a minute, please," Don Silver asked through the intercom speaker.

"Okay, but I have a meeting in five minutes," she replied.

"It won't take long," he said.

"On my way."

Josie opened the door and walked in as Don continued to focus on the document in front of him. She waited. "Sit," he said, abruptly. She sat in one of his visitor chairs, smoothed her skirt and waited. "How are things going on the Haber presentation?"

"Going well. I expect to be done and ready to present in the next couple of days."

"Good," he said, nodding. He was quiet a moment and then said, "Josie, you and I should be together again."

"Don, please. Let's not do this."

"Not do what? A couple of weeks ago you were fucking my brains out and now you shut me off. I thought you wanted to know what I want from the relationship. Well, I want you. I want us to be together all the time."

Josie was quiet a moment and then said, "I'd like it if we could continue to work together in a cordial way. And I'd like it if we could remain friends. I hope that you are open to those things as well." She looked at him. "Please, Don, we can still be there to support one another."

"I feel like you're just throwing me away, Josie. I'm trying not to be upset, but I love you."

She shook her head. "You don't love me, Don, that's why you never wanted to move away from your relationship with Naomi. And that's okay. You wanted to be with her and that's okay. And I want to be with Tom," she said. "I also want a good working environment."

"I left Naomi for you, Josie. I've changed my life so that I can be with you."

"What?' She shook her head. "No, you didn't. That is total bullshit. You had no idea what you wanted from the relationship we had, remember?"

"Yes, but I came to realize you are the one for me, so I ended it."

"Then go back to her, Don. We are going to be co-workers and friends if that's possible, but nothing more."

He leaned back in his chair and anger flashed in his eyes. "I don't know that this will work, Josie. We'll think about it, but it may be necessary for you to find another job."

Josie was stunned. "What? I've been with this company for more than seven years. And I'm doing a good job, right?"

He shrugged. "Yeah, but you have to have a good relationship with your boss."

"Define good relationship," she asked.

"We have to be able to work together well. We have to be close," Don said.

"Close? Does that mean intimate?" Don said nothing. "I have to go to my meeting," she said. "I'm already late."

"Okay. Well, we'll both give it some thought and talk again later."

Josie was suppressing anger. She took a breath and said, "There is nothing more to think about."

He was quiet and then said, "Go to your meeting."

* * *

"I have to go to work," Kelly said.

"Does that mean you have to put clothes on and leave this bed?"

"Yeah, I think so."

"I don't want to let go of you," Kevin whispered.

"I noticed that and I really like it." She paused. "How come you don't have to go to work?"

"Well, I'm self-employed, so I have really flexible hours." He shook his head. "And it's hard to get motivated to go back to work when the alternative is being naked with you."

"I know what you mean," she said, smiling widely.

"I guess I may as well go to work as well," he said. "Let's meet back here, naked again, in twelve hours and twenty minutes."

"We better get some nourishment first if we're doing this again," she said.

"True," he replied, "I want you energetic." He grinned and then said, "I really do want you in my arms all the time. We fit together so well."

"Save that thought and we'll both think about it all day." She walked naked toward the shower and he smiled at the pleasure of watching her walk away.

Chapter Twenty-One

Fifteen Days After

"I know it's unusual for me to insist on an early morning meeting, Detective Gray, but it's important."

"Yes, Lieutenant, I understand."

"So what has the surveillance yielded so far?" he asked.

"Nothing," Stacey said. "Four days and nights and no one has attempted access to the bank after hours."

"It's puzzling," Spencer said. "They hide a hundred and sixty eight grand and then don't come back to it." He reflected a moment. "Do you think something happened to these two guys—Abbott and Costello, so that they couldn't come back?"

"I don't know. It is puzzling that no one is coming after the hidden money after all that effort to steal it. Since Linda Caldwell gave us the story about the hostage Kevin Roper meeting with the perps during the robbery, we've been watching him, too."

"And?" Spencer asked.

She shook her head. "Romantic date with his girlfriend and journeys to and from his office. Nothing else at all." She paused and then said, "Butler and I are meeting with the FBI team this morning to cover all the evidence."

"Here's the problem I have. The investigation has yielded nothing we can release to the press until now. Politics is now playing a role. The chief is getting his ass chewed for lack of progress and he's chewing out mine in turn. You know, shit rolls downhill." He drew a breath. "I'm getting pressure to tell the press that we have recovered the money. I know that doesn't help the investigation any, but I'm not going to be able to sit on it much longer. I can get you about forty-eight hours and then the world is going to know that we have the money."

"I understand, Lieutenant. I appreciate you buying us as much time as you can before this gets out."

"Good. Go figure something out. If you give me something else to release, maybe I can drag the money thing out a little further."

"Yes, sir," Stacey said, wondering what else she might be able to get him in the next forty-eight hours.

* * *

The next morning, Kevin Roper had a big smile on his face when he woke up with a hand on Kelly's breast. He was instantly aroused. He pressed himself against her buttocks and she said, "Good morning," and started to move. He threw the blankets off and she turned on her back. He ran a hand down her midsection and between her legs, feeling her wetness. He scooted towards the bottom on the bed, slowly moved her legs apart and began to kiss her. Then he began moving his tongue in distinctive ways that had her groaning and him extremely hard. She tasted wonderful. As he moved his tongue to caress her, she began to writhe and then to scream as she thrust forward. He moved upward and kissed her, and then he was inside her and they were moving together and moaning, the rest of the world entirely shut out. She climbed on top of him and began to move more quickly, thrusting him deeply into her. They moved faster and grew louder until the moment of complete release. He held her cheeks and kissed her hard as he came. She moaned through the kiss and then they fell into an embrace and drifted into that peaceful world that comes after lovemaking, where there are no worries, just total tranquility as they held each other tightly.

"I want this moment to last forever," Kevin said.

"I like that idea," she said, looking up at him and smiling. "You know, it already feels like we belong together."

"Yeah," he replied, grinning. "I'm still pinching myself. That is whenever I'm not pinching you."

"Want breakfast?" she asked.

"Coffee."

She stood and walked to the bathroom and he stared as she walked. She turned and said, "I see you looking. Didn't you get enough?"

"I will never get enough of you," he said. "Not ever."

As they drank coffee, Kelly asked, "Will I see you tonight?" She picked up her purse and kissed him before heading off to work.

"I have a meeting tonight," Kevin said. "It's probably going to keep me tied up until 10:30 or 11:00."

"So tomorrow?"

"How about tonight? Will you come to my place tonight?"

She smiled. "Yes, okay."

Kevin wrote down the address and gave her a key. "The security alarm is out of view. When you walk in the front door, turn left down the hall and open the second door on the left. There's a security pad on the wall just inside." He wrote down the sixteen digit code on the note that contained the address and handed it to her.

She glanced at it and said, "A sixteen digit code? How long do I have to get the alarm turned off?"

"Two minutes. It's really plenty of time."

"Unless I'm so nervous that I keep getting the code wrong."

He grinned. "If it goes off, call the phone number I wrote at the bottom and give them the code words, which are "Live every moment.""

"I like that code," she said, smiling.

"And I like the idea of finding you at home when I get there."

"Anything else I need to know?" she asked.

"Just that I can hardly wait to see you there." Kevin kissed her and said, "I can't remember the last time I was this happy."

She nodded. "Me too. I'm grinning like an idiot all day long." She touched his cheek. "See you tonight. Have a really good day and a good meeting tonight."

* * *

The four investigators of the joint task force sat in the LAPD conference room with coffee in their hands and diagrams all around them.

"First, the update," Stacey said. "Lieutenant Spencer told me that he is getting a lot of heat because there is no information to release to the public. He says that he can't hold off the political brass for more than forty-eight hours before the Department is going to release the fact that we have recovered the money, which makes for good press."

"I get it," Curt Lowell said, "we're getting similar heat. So a byline that the joint task force has recovered the money is what our people want, too."

The room was quiet for a few moments and then Stacey said, "I've been working on what might be a wild theory that I want to try out on you guys, okay?"

"Fire away," Lowell said.

"We need as many theories as we can get at this point," Garcia added.

"Well," Stacey said, "we all agree that these guys are pretty smart, right?" There were nods around the room. "Let's just suppose that they never really intended to take the money. Maybe they just wanted us to think that they took the money and direct our energies figuring out how they got the money out."

"Some form of misdirection or diversion," Butler said. "Like the explosions at the time the hostages were about to be released."

"Right," Lowell said. "The money wasn't just left behind, it was well hidden, right?"

"Yes," Stacey said. So maybe they wanted us to spend all of our time looking for money that never left the premises."

Garcia made a questioning face. "Why would they do that?"

"Let's take it one step further," Curt Lowell said. "We just spent four days having teams and cameras surveilling the bank, waiting for someone to come and get the money and there has been nothing. No one has even come close. Maybe they are not coming. Maybe, they don't want that money."

"What?" Butler asked. "We're talking about people who rob a bank but don't want the money?"

"I don't know," Lowell replied. "I'm shooting in the dark here."

"Don't stop," Stacey said. "We've been missing something big. There has to be some reason that they hid the money, which I think is so that we spend our time chasing ourselves down rabbit holes. Time is our most important asset and they have figured out how to distract us by having us chase what we are not going to find." She leaned forward in her chair and said, "So maybe they hid the money just to distract us and make us keep chasing our tails. And maybe they never intended to come back for the money."

Butler shook his head. "So we're back to bank robbers who don't want money."

"Right, there's that," Stacey said. "I haven't got that part figured out, so this line of reasoning has more than a few holes in it. There are other possibilities, of course. I mean, maybe they came back for the money and discovered the surveillance, so they aborted. Or something might have happened to them between the robbery and today. Maybe they drove off a cliff or had heart attacks, although we've been checking hospitals and mortuaries and haven't found any unknowns that meet the descriptions."

Lowell said, "So we keep working on this and unless we get some major breakthrough, in forty-eight hours the joint task force puts out a statement that we recovered the money taken in the robbery. We say we are not giving out more at this time because this is an ongoing investigation. Politicians get relief and we get credited with some good work—that doesn't sound too bad to me."

Jeff Butler said, "Makes sense." He paused and said, "I think the fact that they didn't carry any money out of here may tell us how they got out of the bank though."

There were nods around the table. Lowell said. "I think so, too. It was something that didn't make sense before, when we thought they carried out a shitload of money, but now..." he let the words trail off.

Stacey smiled. "They walked out of the bank as cops in the middle of a hundred cops."

Alicia was smiling, too. She shook her head and said, "Damn. At the time the hostages were released, they were all given the same beards, masks and hats that the perps wore into the bank, so we naturally assumed that they were hiding among the hostages. More misdirection."

"That's right," Stacey said. "And when we thought they had walked out with almost seven hundred thousand dollars, it wasn't plausible that they came out disguised as cops, but now that we know they left the money behind, and none of the hostages are the perps, it all fits."

Butler said, "We had SWAT and then three other police agencies running around inside the bank. If they came with the right uniforms..." he let the words trail off.

"Holy shit," Lowell said. "These ballsy bastards left the money in the bank and walked out dressed as cops, with cops all around them."

"We can't prove it and it doesn't bring us any closer to knowing who these guys are, but it sounds right," Stacey said. "We can check police and media video to see if there are unaccounted for cops; any faces that don't belong." Heads nodded agreement around the table. Stacey let that thought settle on the room and then added, "The bank advises that none of its customers have suggested there was any tampering with their accounts. I asked that bank personnel determine whether there were any transactions initiated by any computers in the bank during those two hours that the hostages were held. They said that each branch has daily reports on all transactions. The report for this branch shows that there were no transactions during the robbery."

"So, this team we call Abbott and Costello went to great lengths to take over a bank, take hostages, hide money and then exit in a creative way for no apparent reason?" Butler asked.

"Right," Lowell replied. "All of which makes no sense at all."

* * *

At 7:00 p.m., Kelly's shift ended and she followed her GPS to Kevin's address. She checked the address again as she pulled up. Could this be right? The property was a two story mansion; a giant colonial that sprawled across the midsection of two or three acres. It had massive, white columns on each side of the front walkway. The front door was double width and about sixteen feet high. She used the electronic key and walked into a two story entry with stunning tile and an enormous chandelier. There was a circular staircase to the right and a magnificent marbled entry piece in the foyer. She was so consumed by what she was witnessing that she momentarily forgot about the alarm, which was sending out beeps every three or four seconds. She walked quickly down the hall and found the doorway and then the numerical key pad inside. She typed in the sixteen digit number and the alarm stopped.

Kelly walked back to the entryway and then past the stairs into a sitting room. There were two couches and four big, comfortable looking armchairs that sat as a conversation grouping around an enormous cherry wood, hand-carved fireplace. The other side of the room opened into a large kitchen with granite countertops that followed the semi-circular shape of the kitchen. There were two marbled islands, one with a second sink. Off the kitchen in one direction was a large pantry. On the other was a morning room that was all glass, overlooking a forested rear yard. The place was staggering. Down the hall there was a theater room with a screen that covered a wall and eight theater-like seats. Kevin hadn't mentioned any of this and that made her a little nervous.

She walked up the stairs to find one wing that was all master suite and an office the size of a library. The other wing contained a man-cave room with pool table and couches and three other bedrooms with their own bathrooms. There were massive upstairs windows that overlooked all parts of the estate, including an enormous pool and a tennis court.

She looked around and shook her head. How could this be? Had Kevin failed to mention that he was a member of the Kennedy family? For the first time since they re-met at the bank she had questions and she was a little nervous about Kevin.

* * *

Kevin Roper walked into the Ritz-Carlton at five minutes to seven. He went to the sixth floor and then down the hall to the boardroom that had been reserved under the name of some non-existent enterprise.

Brian Gallagher and Paul Mason stood to meet Kevin as he entered the room.

"Been a while, buddy," Brian said.

"It has. Good to see you guys," Kevin said. "There just aren't that many people you get close to in our line of work."

They sat and Brian poured coffee. "That's for sure," Brian said. "You can seldom put your guard down, let alone confide in someone."

Paul adjusted his wire-rimmed glasses and smiled at Kevin. "It seems that so far they have not connected the dots, but this case will get ongoing national attention after tomorrow. Until then our only issue is the woman who saw you in the bank—Linda Caldwell, right?"

"Right. For the last few days I've been surveilled. I had to engage in an hour of misdirection to get here tonight."

"No problem with that?" Paul asked.

"None. Three cars in three cities, and a train in between. By the time I had done the first half hour, I had shaken any possible followers."

"Good," Paul said.

Brian said, "So, we checked out Linda Caldwell. Seems that she is also one Angela Bremmer, who has a negligent homicide conviction in Ohio. She's been on the run for a long time and so she's offering you up as part of a deal to limit her jail time for the vehicular homicide and the flight."

"There's always something impossible to foresee," Kevin said. "So any ideas about how we handle her?" he asked.

Paul said, "It's all a credibility contest between the two of you, right?"

"Yeah, that's right," Kevin agreed.

Paul added, "And we can't let her win that battle. If they find you responsible, it's an easy connect to us as well. We worked with you frequently on Agency business, so it's not hard. So in the public eye, you have to be made to appear more credible. The rest of it will play out behind the scenes."

"So for the part of this that plays out in the public eye, we just have to make you more credible than Ms. Caldwell," Brian said.

"Don't we already have that in place if she's on the run from a conviction?"

"Maybe, but I think she might be making a deal to testify in exchange for some relief on her sentence. We should eliminate all doubt about who will be most credible."

"Okay," Kevin said. "I don't know what you are contemplating, but I favor some kind of misdirection over any kind of family pressure."

Paul nodded. "I agree. Let's not test the strength of her character, let's just provide some additional facts that challenge the credibility of her testimony."

"How do we do it?" Kevin asked.

"Let's get her to a meeting with us," Brian said. "We'll give her some new information to take back to the task force."

"We can make this happen in the next couple of days. We will have to be careful with her because she's likely being followed as well," Brian said.

Paul nodded. "I agree."

"None of this should affect the release of news tomorrow, right?" Brian asked.

"I don't see any reason to adjust the timetable," Paul said, then added, "We have to expect that the covert investigation will be off and running within a few hours after the release tomorrow. So keep your eyes open for anything and everything." He looked at Kevin. "You're going to be emotionally ready for FBI visits, right? We told you how that is likely to go. You just need to be an innocent guy who doesn't appreciate the intrusion, but stays professional."

"Yeah, I got it. I'm ready," Kevin replied, hoping his nervousness didn't show.

"If you're questioned any further by the police, stick with your story. You don't know anything, you had no involvement and none of it makes any sense, right?"

"Right."

"As soon as we can get it set, we will impact Ms. Caldwell's credibility and close that loop."

"Well, you make it sound easy enough," Kevin said.

Brian gave him a nod. "It really is. Stay confident and you will be fine."

* * *

It was 10:30 p.m. when Kevin got back home. He saw Kelly's car in the driveway and it brought an instant smile. As he approached the front door, she opened it and stood dressed in a robe. She gave him a questioning look and said, "You never told me about the Rockefeller estate."

"Yeah, I guess I forgot to mention that," he said.

She put her arms around him and he could tell that she wore nothing under the silk robe. "Wow," he said. He kissed her and said, "Can we talk about the house later?"

"Uh-huh," she said, not breaking away from the kiss.

"Wow," he said, "coming home never felt like this before."

She took him by the hand and they made their way to the master bedroom. She dropped the robe to the floor and put her arms around him. "Welcome home," she said.

Part 6
Other Money

Chapter Twenty-Two

Sixteen Days After

Kelly got dressed for work and met Kevin downstairs in the enormous kitchen. She poured coffee and gave him a smile. "Good morning."

He sat on a bar stool around the immense countertop and pulled out the stool next to his so she could sit down. "I really like seeing you first thing in the morning," he said.

She sat and raised her coffee cup. "Cheers," she said. He clinked cups with her. She looked around the room and said, "So, you never mentioned the estate here. How big is this place anyway?"

"About 8,600 square feet."

"Do other people live here and you just never run into them?" She asked.

He chuckled, "Nope, just me."

"It's beautiful," she said. "I had no idea that you were…"

"Rich?" he asked.

"Yeah, I guess so."

"I've done okay. Does it matter?" he asked.

"I don't know. I never expected to fall for a rich guy. Is it your business that got you here or is Warren Buffet your grandpa?"

He laughed. "You are too funny. I'd have to say its work because I don't have any rich relatives."

"So do you have a staff that cleans this place?"

"I have a maid service that comes once a week. But I have one wing of four bedrooms and bathrooms that seldom get used, so that area doesn't require much."

She furrowed her brow. "What do you do again?"

"Research."

"Hmm. I had a research job in med school. It paid all of twelve bucks an hour."

Kevin smiled. "It depends what you research. If you come up with important information that other people don't, it can pay pretty well." He hesitated. "You'd be more comfortable if I wasn't so comfortable?"

"It wouldn't matter if you didn't have anything, so I guess it shouldn't matter that you're doing okay." She leaned toward him and kissed him softly. "Thanks for inviting me over."

"My pleasure." He took a moment and said, "You know, I am falling for you in a big way."

"Good," she said. "I must be too, because being with you feels wonderful."

* * *

Paul and Brian watched the CNN breaking news in a large conference room down the hall from their offices.

"We have some remarkable news to report," Dana Bash told the world. "First, one hundred fifty million dollars has been donated to assist Syrian refugees and the humanitarian crisis in Syria. Who made the donation? We don't know. The money was delivered anonymously." She grinned and added, "But that's just the beginning. There has been a fifty million dollar donation to aid Crimean and Ukrainian refugees and another fifty million to the Ukrainians resisting Russian influence and control. Interesting, right? But we're not done yet. There has also been a fifty million dollar donation to NATO and finally, a fifty million dollar donation to two candidates who will oppose Vladimir Putin in next year's Russian election. Whoever the donor is, seems to be someone or some group pushing back against Russian interests. Thanks to the nameless philanthropists behind these masked donations, thousands who are without homes will be aided."

Brian grinned and looked over at Paul. "We did it."

Paul raised his hand and they high fived. "Best money we ever spent," Paul said.

"So, predictions from here?" Brian asked.

"My guess is that they pull the robbery investigation and place it in the hands of the FBI Director. His elite will dissect this one," Paul said.

"And they are going to question everyone who might have pulled this off. They will see the way this was done and at some point they will look at some of us inside the Agency on that list," Brian reflected.

"Yeah," Paul said. "I think that they will consider the possibility of Agency insiders within a few days. But I hope I'm wrong."

* * *

Curt Lowell sat back in his chair, thoughtfully scratching his chin and shaking his head when he wordlessly arrived at a missing puzzle piece. He reflected a moment longer and then said, "We know that Kevin Roper does corporate research and investigation for a number of clients. We also know that he lives well and is dating one of the hostages. Aside from that, there's not much to find. The guy hasn't gone anywhere unusual or done anything suspicious and we certainly can't tie him to the robbery or to Abbott or Costello," Curt Lowell said to the other three cops in the room. "Still no move to pick up the money hidden in the bank." He shook his head. "So they got scared away, something happened to them or, like Stacey suggested, maybe the money was one more diversion and that's not what they were after."

Stacey's phone rang. She glanced at the caller ID and hit a button. "Detective Gray," she said evenly.

The cops in the room watched her eyes widen and then she asked, "I thought you said there were none. What happened?" After a moment, she murmured, "I see. Okay, thanks for the update." She put the phone down and shook her head as she considered the new information. There were waiting eyes around the room anticipating an update.

"They're not coming back for the money," Stacey said. "That was never the point."

"What? What have you got?" Lowell asked, excitedly.

"Brace yourselves for this one. The daily transaction reports that the bank relied on were inaccurate. The bank has now gone through all individual transactions that took place on each of the branch's computers during the period of the robbery. There were fifteen transactions from the bank's computers during the critical two hours." She shook her head in disbelief. "About three hundred million dollars was withdrawn from fifteen accounts. That money was first disbursed to sixty-two different accounts."

"Holy shit," Lowell said, his eyes wide. "Why didn't they pick that up before?"

"Until now, the bank had relied on the daily transaction reports, which do not show any activity at the branch during the robbery. Those reports were hacked."

"Shit," Lowell said. "You mean these guys cleaned up after themselves by altering the transaction reports so that their work didn't show?"

Stacey nodded. "They broke into bank computers while they were here to redirect millions and then broke into the bank computers when they were done to cover their tracks. The branch reports showed no transactions because they were sanitized by these guys."

Butler reflected and then said, "Every step of the way, these guys anticipated what had to be done to keep us from figuring out what happened. Masters of misdirection, don't you think?"

There were nods around the table. "Unbelievable," Lowell said.

Butler added, "And now that we know what they did, we still have no clue who pulled this off."

Stacey said, "The bank wants FBI assistance in tracking the funds to identify what entities are behind account holder names and to find out where the money went."

Curt Lowell punched a number into his phone and after a moment said, "We have a big break in the case and I'm going to need to expand the team."

"I better meet with Lieutenant Spencer to update him on this now," Stacey said. "Want to come, Jeff?"

"Sounds like too much fun for words," Butler said. "Sure, I'll go."

Chapter Twenty-Three

Seventeen Days After

At 7:00 a.m., Stacey and Jeff Butler were in the office working through the detail on each of the transactions that occurred during the robbery. They charted each amount by account name from which the funds were taken and by accounts into which they were delivered. A whole series of individual transactions. All of the initial recipient accounts had been opened within two weeks. All of them were opened in the names of entities at various banks. The funds deposited into each of these accounts on the day of the robbery had been electronically moved out of each of those recipient accounts to other accounts within three hours. The FBI was now trying to find the endpoint for all of the funds taken out of these accounts and repeatedly bounced from one account to another, through a variety of financial institutions.

Stacey's phone then rang. "Detective Gray," she said perfunctorily. A moment later she said, "Yes, Butler is with me. We'll be right up." She hung up and looked at Butler. "It seems that we also have an emergency meeting to attend. Probably something political. Maybe the need to release information to the press again."

* * *

Stacey Gray and Jeff Butler occupied Lieutenant Spencer's visitor chairs and waited for him to walk into the room. Spencer walked into the room and sat down in his chair. He wore a look that said he was unhappy. "Anything new since we learned of the doctored transaction reports?" he asked.

"New, but not helpful," Stacey replied. "After a review of all of the video, it seems that there were two Sheriff's officers who are unidentified. They came out of the bank looking down at the ground and never looked up. Then they disappeared in the confusion. All members of the Sheriff's team were accounted for, so we know it's them. One is about six feet tall and the other about six-two. That's all we've got."

He shook his head and then he was quiet. After a moment, he looked at Stacey and said, "The FBI is ending the task force and pulling the investigation up their chain of command. This is now world news and we have been cleared to reveal that all of the money has been recovered by the joint task force. At this point, we take a bow. After that, it's up to the FBI to decide what to do with this." He drew a breath and said, "Whatever they do, you two are to be commended for your work on the task force and your files will reflect exceptional service in that regard."

"What?" Stacey asked, indignantly. "That's it? We are dumped from the case after all the work we've put in? We've earned the right to chase this to the end without having it pulled for some political reason."

Spencer frowned. "I don't disagree, but the politics surrounding this are a little intense and the truth is, these guys have the right to pull the case." He shook his head. "I know how you feel, Gray. I've been there. But, I can't do anything about it, so just accept the Department's acknowledgment that you did great work."

"Thank you, sir," Butler said.

Stacey just nodded, not happy and unconvinced that it had to go this way.

"Thank you, detectives," Spencer said, signifying that the meeting was over and they needed to exit. Stacey was still frowning.

As they walked out of Spencer's office, Butler asked, "What the fuck do you think is going on?"

"It got so big they want it to be purely within their arena now. They suddenly decide to push us out. I hate this bullshit," Stacey said. "This sucks."

"So I guess we accept a commendation and work on the other cases awaiting our attention," Butler said.

"Hmm," Stacey said. "I want to see this one through. This is the most amazing case I've ever worked on and we are making progress for the first time."

Butler said, "I agree. You have to appreciate the quality of the crimes here. These guys are worthwhile adversaries."

"That's for sure," Stacey replied. "Hank Mercer told me that daily reports are generated for every branch, transaction by transaction, throughout the day and that the branch reports were clean for the day of the robbery. These guys were so damn good that they even anticipated the bank's reporting system and doctored the daily transaction record for the branch to assure that no alarms went off when the reports were reviewed. Incredible preparation. Each of their transactions were removed from the bank's internal daily reports, like they didn't exist. When the report was issued the next day, there was nothing to find and nothing suspicious. These guys either knew or learned banking operations."

"Yep," Butler replied, "and it's pretty fucking anti-climactic to be pulled off the case now."

"It is," Stacey said thoughtfully. "We have to keep our hand in somehow."

"What? Gray, don't get us into a world of shit," Butler said with concern.

Stacey smiled and said, "Maybe we can operate behind the scenes. When people don't know you're in the game, you can move through the shadows."

"I'm not sure I like the sound of that," Butler said, but Stacey was already deep in thought.

Chapter Twenty-Four

Eighteen Days After

Assistant FBI Director Mitch Tanner walked into the room and stood at the head of a walnut conference table that seated twenty-four. All of the seats were taken. He wasted no time with greetings. "You've all got a copy of pertinent case information. The tables contain data on the accounts from which each of the amounts were taken. Your job is to follow the money from the initial deposit through its arrival at each of the organizations that received these big gifts. I need this in the next twenty-four hours. Questions?"

"Yeah," Senior Agent Clark responded. "I looked at the data. Every one of the accounts from which money was taken belongs to Russian Oligarchs or Russian corporations controlled by or close to Vladimir Putin, is that right?"

"Seems that way," Tanner said.

"Most of these guys are personally sanctioned by US policy."

"Yes," Tanner again replied.

"And all of the money was given to charities that do public good in times of crises. Do I have that right also?"

"We think so, yes," Tanner said, impatiently, sensing what was coming. "Is there a question here?"

"Yeah. The question is, why do we want to mess with any of this? Why are we investigating people who did good things with money taken from bad guys? I mean, isn't this consistent with some of our own Agency objectives?"

"Bank robbery and hostage taking is not a part of our protocol last time I checked," Tanner said, sounding annoyed. He took a breath and then added, "We are going to conduct the investigation and get to the bottom line. Any other questions?" The room was silent. "Okay, let's get to it."

* * *

Josie walked into Don Silver's office and said, "Any questions on the Mintner proposal I emailed before I go for the day?"

He stared at her and smiled. "Not so much of a question as a request."

"Sure. What?"

"Take your top off. I really miss those gorgeous tits."

Josie was instantly angry. She turned and walked to the door. Before walking out she turned back. "We are done, Don. There's no more relationship between us." She hesitated and then added, "And you didn't leave Naomi for me. She left you for fucking around. I know it and you know it. I know that because she called me to tell me that I had helped ruin her marriage." He looked surprised and then angry, but he remained quiet. She said, "By the way, I recorded this conversation and the next time you say anything about my body I go to human resources with the recording. I don't want to do that Don. I want us to end as friends. But I will." She turned and walked out. The conversation left her shaken. As she left the office, she could feel her pulse racing. She hadn't recorded anything, but she had considered it, and the fact that he didn't know one way or the other was fine with her. She also had no intention of going to human resources to complain of sexual harassment and end up describing the history of consensual sex she had with Don Silver. As far as coworkers are concerned, men who fuck their assistants are having an affair, but women who fuck their bosses are sluts, and revealing all of that would likely end her career as well as her marriage. There was no chance she would go public with any of this, she just hoped that Don would believe she might.

* * *

Kevin was sitting behind his desk and on the phone when four agents walked into his office. He donned a look of concern and then said, "I have to go. I'll call you back later." He put down the phone and said, "Can I help you gentlemen?"

The tall man closest to him said, "FBI. I'm agent Murray." He pulled an envelope out of his pocket and handed it to Kevin. Here's a search warrant. He looked up and said to the others, "Okay, get to it."

Kevin said, "Agent Murray, why would you be searching my office?"

"Part of the investigation," he said abruptly. Agents were opening drawers and peering into files. "We'll be taking your computer, as well."

"What? I need my computer. I have a business to run here. Come on, guys, you can't take my livelihood."

"We'll get it back to you as soon as we can."

"This is unbelievable," Kevin said. "You've got to be kidding. I was a hostage, remember?"

"Yes, sir. Just doing our jobs."

"Right," Kevin said, sounding annoyed. "What are you looking for?"

"The description is right there on the warrant."

Thirty minutes later, they had looked through his desk, in all file cabinets and drawers and under the couch and between the cushions. They had searched the reception area and every nook and cranny in the office. As they disconnected and picked up the only computer now in the office and Kevin's iPad, one of the agents handed him two folded sheets of paper. "One is an identification and claim sheet identifying your computer and iPad, and the other document reflects these files we are taking. Thank you, sir, have a good day." Without waiting for a response, they turned and marched out satisfied that there was nothing in the office they hadn't logged or taken.

Kevin sat back in the chair and grinned. That was easy enough. He had always kept one of his three computers for just this purpose—the decoy in case anyone came after him with a warrant or in case someone at a corporation he went after came after him. He didn't use it for work, except occasionally to pull down information that he or anyone else could access on the internet. That computer was pure as the driven snow. He had readied for this FBI visit by making his other two computers disappear; the ones that he used for more sensitive activities, like looking behind corporate security protection and accessing confidential and proprietary material not available to the public. Kevin was satisfied that the visit had gone exactly as scripted. He picked up his jacket and walked out of the office, locking it behind him.

* * *

Linda Caldwell carried a laundry basket filled with clothes that had been scattered all over the boys' rooms. She walked down the stairs and then toward the laundry room. She was not sleeping well and obsessed by the threat that hung over her head now that her real identity had been discovered. She felt some relief now that Brad finally knew of her past, but she knew it had shaken him to the core. He seemed to be coping on the outside, but some part of him was wondering who he had married and how such dark secrets could be kept for so long. She feared that his knowledge of who she was might wind up ending them. And then there was the daunting reality that she would be going to jail.

As she made her way through the kitchen, the phone began to ring. She got to it after the second ring.

"Hello?"

"Ms. Caldwell?"

"Yes."

"This is Mr. Abbott." There was complete silence for a moment, and then he added, "First, you should know that this call is untraceable."

"Okay," she said with hesitation.

"We need to meet, Ms. Caldwell." He waited and then added, "Or should I say Ms. Bremmer?"

"Why would I want to meet with you?"

"You'll want to meet with us because we can help you. We can help make things better for you."

She was quiet and then asked, "How do I know that I won't be harmed?"

"You won't be harmed because we have no reason to harm you. You don't have any idea who we are and you still won't know after we meet." He paused and then added, "You'll remember that none of the hostages were harmed, right?"

"How can you help me?"

"We know some folks who can say good things about you and get your sentence reduced. That's what counts, right?"

Linda thought hard. How could a bank robber help reduce her sentence? It didn't make sense. "I don't get it."

"What don't you get?"

She decided to ask her real question. "How can bank robbers assist me with my years old conviction? It doesn't make any sense."

Paul drew a breath. She made a good point that he couldn't counter without giving out too much information. This strategy was going nowhere, so he decided to change direction. "Ms. Caldwell, does Brad know that you were once detained while you were on the run and that the cop didn't realize that you were Angela Bremmer until after he let you go? You remember that questioning in Tucson?"

She sat in stunned silence. How could this guy possibly know that?

"I point that out because it was something else that you could have shared with Brad about who you were and what you had done. I'm guessing you never did, right? I suppose that now that all of this is out in the open, you could tell him. But you elected not to tell him about Angela Bremmer for so many years that it became hard to talk about. Now your husband feels deceived and hurt because you never trusted him with this critical part of your past. Even after all that, there is still more he doesn't know." He paused and added, "We've done our research, Ms. Caldwell. We want to talk to you in a public place where you can be sure that you are in no danger, that's all. Alternatively, I have a good deal of information that I could share with Brad that you could have shared with him some time ago. That would create even greater distance between you, don't you think?"

She was shaking and felt cornered. "Okay, I'll meet with you. When and where?"

"The Sheraton Agoura Hills in two hours. There is a conference room reserved for the Piedmont Society. You come alone and tell no one or the meeting simply won't happen, but other undesirable things will be disclosed to Brad. Understood?"

"I understand," she said, feeling scared and cornered.

* * *

Linda Caldwell pulled into the parking lot of the Sheraton at 6:45 p.m. She found herself scanning the parking lot for anyone who might be Mr. Abbott or Mr. Costello. Some people were pulling suitcases from cars, while others talked on cell phones and paced. It was just like the parking lot of any hotel. She made her way up three stairs and through massive glass doors that opened as she approached. Ahead on the left she saw the registration desk. Straight ahead was a large stone fireplace that separated the cocktail lounge from the rest of the lobby.

She momentarily considered turning and walking out of the hotel, but knew that there was too much at stake. She walked tentatively toward the front desk and waited for the guest ahead of her to complete his transaction and wheel his bag toward the elevator. It was a typical evening at a busy hotel. Nothing out of the ordinary.

"Do you have a conference room reserved for the Piedmont Society?" Linda asked.

The forty something woman at the desk smiled and flipped pages on a clipboard in front of her and announced, 'The Cartwright Room.' Take the elevator to the second floor, turn right out of the elevator and walk toward the end of the hall. You can't miss it."

"Thank you," Linda said, and began walking toward the elevator. She again considered walking away and calling Mr. Abbott's bluff, but part of her wanted to know why this guy wanted to talk, so she kept moving forward. She climbed into the elevator and rode up one floor alone. She began the walk down the hall, past guest rooms, past a vending area and near the end of the hall, saw a sign that said, 'Cartwright Room.' She moved forward slowly, until she could see the front door was open. She peered into the room, where two bearded men sat at a conference room table configured for eight. The beards were long and they both wore hats from right above their eyes. They sat next to one another on the other side of the conference table, looking directly at the front door and now, directly at her. Neither moved. "Come in, Ms. Caldwell. Please, close the door and have a seat."

Linda stepped inside. She looked at the door and hesitated. "Ms. Caldwell, you're in a hotel. You're perfectly safe."

She closed the door and took a seat across from the men.

Abbott said, "We have no desire to do you harm, Ms. Caldwell. In fact, we'd like to help you. But we'd like you to help us as well." She was quiet, nervously chewing her lower lip. "We just want you to forget that you saw someone approaching us during the robbery; be unsure about what you saw. That's it."

"But I'm not unsure," she said, "and I already told the police that."

"Well, uncertainty is not unusual. You don't have to..."

At that moment, the door flew open and Kevin Roper came in. Linda turned to see his angry expression. Costello sounded surprised, saying, "What are you doing here. You're not supposed to be here."

Roper blurted out angrily, "I can't take this anymore. I know who you are and I'm going to tell them. I'm going to tell the cops."

"No. No, you're not, Mr. Roper. Sit down."

Roper stared a moment and then yelled, "No, I won't." He turned and moved to the door.

Costello yelled, "Stop!" and Linda stared in horror as he drew a gun and fired. The gun made a spitting sound and the bullet struck Roper in the back. There was a thud as Roper hit the floor in the doorway and a pool of blood began pouring from his body and onto the surrounding floor.

With wide eyes, Linda looked at the two men without speaking.

"Get out of here. Get out, quick," Abbott screamed at Linda. She hesitated and then stood and moved to the door. She stepped over a widening pool of blood and began to run down the hall. She glanced back to see the body being dragged into the room and then ran down the emergency stairs. Linda's heart was pounding as she ran into the parking lot and then to the area where she left her car. She glanced back again to make sure no one was following and then she climbed into her car and raced from the parking lot, shaking so hard she could barely hold the wheel. She hit button number one, where Brad's cell number was stored, and it began to ring. "Please be there," she said to the empty car.

He answered on the second ring. "Hi, Sweetheart." There was a feeling of relief, but no words would come. She began to weep loudly. "Linda, what's wrong?"

She pulled to the side of the road, still shaking and through tears told him, "I just witnessed a murder."

* * *

As soon as Linda had disappeared down the stairwell, Brian said, "Okay, you can get up."

Kevin stood and looked at Paul and Brian. "Jesus, what's with the outfits? You guys look like two thirds of ZZ Top." Kevin looked down at himself. "And what's with this fake blood. Look at the floor—there's more blood here than there is in the human body. Were you trying to emulate the shooting of a rhino?"

Paul smiled at him. "Yeah," he said, "I think it went well, too."

Brian said, "We better get this place cleaned up before the cops get here. It's a damned good thing we made sure we got a room with a tiled floor."

They pulled material from under the table and began to clean up. Within six minutes the place was spotless and they were walking from the room.

As they moved toward the emergency stairwell, Kevin asked, "You really think that this will get us somewhere?"

"Well, it should do some interesting things for her credibility," Paul replied. "Don't forget, as of right now you have to disappear for three or four days and then suddenly emerge unscathed. Does your girlfriend know anything?"

"No, and that's the part of this that disturbs me most. She's great and I don't want to lose her."

"I know, but the local cops will contact her looking for you. If she knows that you're fine and walking around, the whole ruse goes down the drain."

"All right, but three days, that's all."

Brian smiled at him. "I think you've been bitten by the love bug, my friend."

"Yeah, I think so, too. She's the best thing that ever happened to me and I don't want to fuck it up."

Chapter Twenty-Five

Nineteen Days After

The New York Times headline was an eye-catcher. "**The FBI and LAPD task force has recovered all of the money stolen in the California Bank robbery.**" The Washington Post said, "**The task force got back every dollar.**" The cable news shows praised law enforcement for the fine investigative work and crews began seeking interviews with members of the task force.

Stacey didn't answer calls for an interview, but that didn't slow anyone down. CNN's crew followed Stacey as she left work for the day and approached her when she stopped at a grocery store. In an instant, there was a tall woman with perfect hair holding a microphone and a man hidden by a large camera standing behind her.

"Detective Gray, please, Detective Gray," the woman said getting louder. "Just give us a moment."

Stacey stopped and looked at her. "Can you tell us about it?" The woman asked, thrusting her microphone forward. "How did the task force do it?"

Stacey gave her pleasant camera smile and said, "Yes, all of the money taken from the bank has been recovered and returned. I want to thank the FBI who worked with us on this task force.

Resources were pooled and it got the LAPD and the FBI a good result."

"Have you identified the alleged perpetrators?"

"No, not yet."

"Can you give us any more information about the investigation?"

"I'm sorry, that's all I can say at this point as it is an ongoing investigation. Naturally, all leads are being followed to bring the perpetrators to justice. Thank you," Stacey said and turned to go.

As she walked away, she heard the woman say, "There you have it, the impressive latest update from the joint task force that recovered the money taken from the bank. We will keep you in the loop as further developments occur. This is Jackie Dawson, CNN. Now back to you in the studio, Jake."

"Thank you, Jackie. So there it is. The FBI-LAPD task force gets all the money back, but what they haven't told us is how they did it or who took it. We'll keep a close eye on this one."

Stacey knew that she should have acknowledged that the case is now entirely in the hands of the FBI, but she wasn't prepared to publicly acknowledge her exclusion from the project. There was more that she wanted to do, and the public perception that she had the authority, at least until the FBI said otherwise, would help her get it done.

* * *

FBI Director Michael Sayer sat in his executive conference room with Deputy Director Mitch Tanner. After eight years as the FBI's Director, Sayer was seen as a force to be reckoned with by both sides of the political aisle. The deep partisan divide that had consumed Washington stopped at Sayer, who had repeatedly proven that he will call any matter as he sees it regardless of politics.

Senators and members of Congress of both parties respected him for standing firmly for what he believed and catering to no one. Sayer thought it was strange that politicians never seemed to consider that they would be better served by doing more of the same, rather than rigidly adhering to party talking points and dogma.

Sayer had straight, black hair that he wore combed back over his head. He dressed immaculately and wore glasses over penetrating eyes that always seemed to be assessing, but never gave away what he was thinking.

"Mitch, what have you got?" Sayer asked. "From the tone of your call, I figure it's something significant."

Mitch Tanner was forty-five, bald and good looking. His looks were Vin Diesel meets Yul Brynner in Westworld. He was the tough guy agent who was also smart enough to make his way to the top over the past twenty years. "As you already know, during the hostage taking specific accounts were targeted from inside the bank. Sixteen accounts were the subject of withdrawals within the period of two hours."

"And we know whose accounts they were," Sayer replied.

"Right. All sixteen accounts track back to Russian politicians and oligarchs."

"So the whole bank robbery, hostage taking thing was a ruse?" questioned Sayer.

"Yeah. This was an amazing plan. They made it look like money was stolen from the bank to throw us off the track, then they hit specific accounts using the bank's computers. The team was too busy looking for what they thought was missing cash. The robbery was cover to hit these accounts from inside the bank using bank computers. It was a sophisticated piece of work."

"I see," Sayer said, thoughtfully.

Tanner added, "In most of our cases, cyber investigations can take us to the IP address of the perp. This time the IP addresses take us right back to the bank and can't be used to identify anyone. They sent the money to sixty-two different accounts.

Within a short time, all of that money is fanned out to four hundred accounts, then moved again and again through many institutions and around the world. The money moved eighteen times in the next two days." He paused and then added, "You know what happened right after that, right?"

"Yes," Sayer said, running a hand through his hair. "The massive donations to refugee relief and anti-Russian causes." He shook his head. "They used Russian money to attack Russian causes."

"Yeah, and they took no more than twenty percent of the money in the accounts of each of their targets."

"Mitch, do you see this the way I do? I mean, as we consider suspects, we know who we have to look at, don't we?"

"Yes, sir. We have been looking at it hard and I think it's one of our own."

"Maybe. We have people who have the talent and the connections to get it done, that's for sure."

"And I think it's political. You know how some of our people feel about a president who rejects reality and won't take on the Russians. I think we have agents who took it upon themselves to go after the Russians for their election hacking because the administration won't do anything about it."

Sayer looked thoughtful and then said, "It has to be someone senior, someone with the skills and resources to do this quietly and someone willing to accept the fact that they would go to jail if things went south."

"We have a list of eighteen possibles inside the Agency, and we're looking at a few known hackers, terrorists and thieves that might have the ability to pull this off, but no connections so far."

"Start the lie detector tests in-house, and do everything right. I'm going to wind up testifying before Congress about this."

"Okay," Tanner said, with hesitance.

"What is it, Mitch?"

"This is going to fuck the Agency. If you wind up having to testify that one of our people did this, then we will never see any funding again. Especially from an administration that doesn't want to listen to what we know in the first place."

Sayer was quiet a moment and then said, "Good point. I assume that you've checked alibis of everyone on the list?"

"Sure, but you know how good these guys are. Whoever's in on it will have a great alibi that includes ten people who saw them in a faraway place."

"Okay. Before we test, you and I are going to meet with everyone on the list individually. Set it up starting tomorrow morning at 7:00 a.m."

"Yes, sir. See you in the morning," Tanner said, standing and walking to the door. He turned back and said, "I fear that this is one of ours, boss. It just seems right." Sayer remained silent as Tanner walked from the office.

Sayer stared out his window into the darkness. He shook his head and said "Unfuckingbelievable" to the empty room. Sayer thought about the implications of this for his Agency. Would a president who protected the Russians from sanctions after their election hacking approve of the fact that someone, maybe someone within the Agency, had turned the tables on the Russians? Probably not. He was all too friendly with the adversaries and all too ready to attack his own intelligence community. There was only one possible conclusion. If his people had done this, it was going to be a shit storm. His Agency would be burned big time: Money taken away, all top management ousted and an uncertain future for an Agency that did amazing work protecting this country. He had spent years avoiding being dragged into politics and now his Agency was about to land squarely in a political quagmire. This was not going be good for anyone.

Part 7
Your Own Back Yard

Chapter Twenty-Six

Twenty Days After

There was no scheduling of a meeting and no warning of any kind. That's the way the FBI did things, even with its own employees. It was 3:00 p.m. when Paul Mason was told to report for meeting with the Director and the Deputy Director. He walked to the designated conference room and knocked.

"Come in."

Director Michael Sayer spoke as he entered the conference room. "Good afternoon, Paul. Take a seat."

"Good afternoon, sir."

"Hi, Paul," Deputy Director Mitch Tanner said.

"Hello, Mr. Tanner."

These were top managers that Paul knew well from group presentations and policy discussions that involved numerous agents, but he didn't know them well and had spent no time with them one on one. Paul sat and waited for what came next.

There was a few moments of silence while they simply watched him. Everything in interrogation was about a psychological edge and these guys were already working it. Then Tanner said, "Paul, is there anything that you would like to tell us?"

Paul reflected a moment and then said, "No sir, not that I can think of."

"Have you been working on anything other than your assigned cases?"

"You mean do I have another job on the side?" Paul asked, as if he really believed that might be the question.

"No. Have you been working on any projects that the Bureau did not assign?"

Paul made a point of looking perplexed and then said, "No, sir."

"You used freelancer Kevin Roper for Bureau business a number of times, right?"

"Yes. Kevin is bright and good at what he does. I've called on him about half a dozen times over the past five years."

"He a friend of yours?"

"Well, I don't know. We get along well, but we don't socialize."

"You know that Kevin was one of the hostages at the California Bank robbery, right?"

"Yeah, talk about bad timing. I had heard that, although I haven't had a chance to talk to him about it."

Sayer and Tanner exchanged glances and Sayer nodded subtly. "You think it's bad timing, do you? We think you know better than that." He paused and looked into Paul's eyes assessing—it's what the Bureau did, always assessing, looking for a read or a "tell" in the eyes, expressions and demeanor. After a moment, he asked, "So, Paul, were you there?"

The question was out there, just like that. "Was I where?"

"Were you at the bank robbery?"

"What? No."

"If you were, this is the time to tell us."

"No, I had nothing to do with it."

"You know how the robbery went down, right" Sayer asked.

"Yes, sir, I've heard that withdrawals were made on the bank computers."

"Right. Very selectively." He paused and said, "You know that too, right?"

"Not sure I know what you mean, sir."

"Three hundred million dollars was withdrawn from sixteen accounts. All from Russian oligarchs and friends of Vladimir Putin. People that you speak out against rather strongly, right?"

"Yes, sir." He added, "I think all Americans should be speaking out against them."

"And another big coincidence is that the money was taken very close in time to massive donations to causes that you favor, right? I mean one hundred fifty million dollars was donated to Syrian refugees, another fifty million dollar donation to aid Crimean and Ukrainian refugees and another fifty million to the Russian resistance in the Ukraine, fifty million dollars to NATO, and a fifty million dollar donation to two candidates who will oppose Vladimir Putin in next year's election." He paused and studied Paul. "All causes that you strongly favor, right Paul? All causes that you are pretty outspoken about."

"Yes, sir. I think all of those are great causes."

"And that money taken was initially disbursed to sixty-two different accounts, Paul. Kevin Roper is capable of moving money like that, right?"

"I don't know. He's a smart guy, but we haven't done that kind of work together. And I certainly don't have reason to think that he was involved."

"You know how serious this would be? If it were proven that someone from the Agency was involved in this?"

"Of course."

"You know that the Agency is not in the business of determining worthy causes and redistributing the wealth of foreign citizens, right?"

"Yes, sir."

"It is obvious to us that the causes that were selected to receive donations from these Russian oligarchs seem to be the same causes you might have selected, Paul. And they are aimed at sending a message to an administration that you perceive is too Russia friendly in the wake of election interference in 2016. It all seems to fit you, you know what I mean?"

"I guess I can understand why you would think so, sir, but there are a lot of us in the Bureau that feel that way."

Sayer leaned forward in his chair and narrowed his eyes, locking onto Paul's eyes. He held silent for a moment and then said, "You know that we are going to prosecute this when we identify the perpetrator?" It was not really a question.

"I would assume so, yes, sir. We usually do."

"So, do you have anything you want to tell us, Paul?"

"Not that I can think of, sir."

"See Westfall this afternoon at 5:00 and he'll administer a polygraph."

"Yes, sir."

"Okay, that's all," Sayer said. "Thanks, Paul."

"Yes, sir," Paul said, rising and walking from the room. He knew that Brian was going to have a similar experience. They clearly saw an agent's fingerprints on this, and apparently, they were already looking closely at him in particular. The polygraph would be no problem, but they would keep coming. All he could do was play out the hand.

After Paul walked from the room, Sayer asked Tanner, "Is that our guy?"

Sayer was thoughtful and then said, "Maybe. I mean it fits, but I'm not sure. These guys know how to use what we taught them even when they work outside the lines. We've created a group of agents who are capable of setting up alibis that are hard to break. And you know that the polygraph won't get him even if he's the guy. I mean we have to go through the process to dot the 'i's' and cross the 't's', but these guys often beat the machine and the polygraph reader."

"Yep," Sayer said, nodding. He reflected a moment and then said, "If Mason was in on it, I bet his partner Brian Gallagher was, too."

"He's in next," Tanner said, "but I think we'll need to legalize torture to get anything from him. That son of bitch has nerves of steel."

"All right. Bring him in and let's do this," Sayer said. He studied the look on his Deputy Director's face and asked, "What is it?"

Tanner said, "Off the record for a moment, don't you think that this enterprise was pretty fucking well done? I mean, I know we have to act on this, but it was a good piece of work."

Sayer gave him a sideways glance and then said, "I can't have this conversation, Mitch. This Agency doesn't make policy regardless of whether we agree with policy that comes from the White House. Now, let's talk to Brian Gallagher."

* * *

Stacey Gray walked into the coffee shop. She looked around at the patrons sitting and sipping until she spotted Linda Caldwell sitting by herself in the back of the coffee shop, with eyes locked on the door. She signaled Stacey with a wave.

Stacey made her way through the tables and sat down across from Caldwell. She could see that the woman was shaking. "What's wrong?" Stacey asked. "What's the emergency?"

"I don't know what to do," Caldwell said, fighting back tears. "I am so scared."

"It's okay," Stacey said, touching her hand. She could feel that Linda was shaking. "Tell me what happened."

Linda swallowed hard and glanced around the room, clearly nervous, seemingly expecting something bad to happen. "They shot him," Linda said, stopping as if that told the story.

"Who shot whom?" Stacey asked.

"Mr. Abbott and Mr. Costello. They shot Kevin Roper."

"What?"

"Yeah. I got a call telling me to meet them. They said they could help me and kind of threatened me if I didn't show. So

I met them at a Sheraton conference room. They were wearing beards and hats so I couldn't see their faces. They started talking to me and then Roper walked in and they had this argument. Then one of them pulled a gun and shot him." She started crying again and through tears said, "He fell to the floor and there was blood everywhere. It was a nightmare. Then they told me to get out, so I ran away."

Stacey pulled out her phone and hit a button.

"Hi, Jeff. We have a situation."

"What's up?" Butler asked.

"Linda Caldwell is with me. She just witnessed Mr. Abbott and Mr. Costello shoot Kevin Roper."

"What? Where?"

"At the Sheraton, Agoura Hills."

"Holy shit!"

"Linda says that there was blood everywhere and they told her to get out. See if you can find Roper, will you? And check with his girlfriend, Kelly Parson. She might know what is going on."

"Yeah, okay."

"Get a team out to the Sheraton in Agoura Hills. There was a conference room." Stacey looked over at Linda and moved the phone away from her ear. "You know who had the room reserved?" she asked.

"Yeah, something called the Piedmont Society," Linda replied.

Stacey put the phone back to her ear and said, "The conference room was reserved by something called the Piedmont Society. Probably a bullshit organization, but have someone check it out, okay?"

"I didn't think this case could get any crazier. I'm on it, partner. I'll go see Ms. Parson myself."

"Thanks," Stacey replied. "I'm headed out to the Sheraton. I'll talk to you later."

Brian Gallagher was ushered into the conference room and took a seat. Deputy Director Mitch Tanner, whom he knew reasonably well from contacts over the years, sat to his left. Director Michael Sayer sat across the table from him and waited, although Brian wasn't sure what he was waiting for. After a long while, Tanner said, "Brian, we have a problem."

"Oh?" Brian replied with a tone of surprise.

"Yes, it seems that a couple of our own, and in particular you and Paul Mason, were involved in the California Bank theft."

Tanner was watching him closely as Brian put on his indignant expression. "No, sir. I think someone has given you bad information."

Tanner shook his head. "You and Mason, with the help of Kevin Roper stole three hundred million dollars from sixteen accounts. That money was disbursed to sixty-two different accounts. And after some movement, one hundred fifty million dollars has been donated to assist Syrian refugees and the humanitarian crisis in Syria, fifty million dollars was donated to aid Crimean and Ukrainian refugees and another fifty million to the Russian resistance in the Ukraine. And, oh yeah, fifty million dollars donated to NATO and fifty million to two candidates who will oppose Vladimir Putin in next year's election. Right up your alley, right?"

Brian waited, saying nothing.

"The only problem is, Brian, you can't donate money that isn't yours." He was getting louder. "You and your buddy are undermining this Agency and I consider it treasonous." He drew a breath and forced himself back to a calm voice. "What do you want to tell me, Brian?"

"Nothing, sir," Brian responded softly. "I really don't have any information about this."

There was a deafening silence while Sayer stared at Brian, studying his eyes. Then Sayer said, "Kevin Roper was at the scene, Brian."

"Yes, sir. He's a good guy and I was sorry to hear that he got caught up in all of this."

"He was not there by accident, Brian. You and I both know that you and Mason arranged all of this."

Brian gave him a look of concern. "Not sure why you would think that, sir."

Tanner shook his head. "I am really disappointed, Brian. And we are going to get to the bottom of all this and then you and Mason are going to have some hard truths to face."

Brian gave a nod. "Well, sir, I hope you find out who did this. Please let me know if I can do anything to be of assistance."

"You can. You'll start with a polygraph."

"Yes, sir."

"That's all, Brian."

"Yes, sir." Brian stood and walked from the room without expression.

After he was gone, Sayer asked, "What do you think?"

Tanner shook his head. "I don't know. Hard to read."

"Yeah, I guess we train them to make this difficult."

* * *

Stacey arrived at the Sheraton and walked quickly into the hotel. She flipped open her badge and identified herself to the clerk at the front desk, who gave her a nod. After getting quick directions, she made her way to the conference room that had been reserved for the Piedmont Society. At the door she found two uniformed officers and a tall man of about forty, who wore a tie and a white shirt. He was greying just slightly and handsome in a Robert Downey, Jr. kind of way.

"Detective Gray, this is Marc Foster, the Hotel Manager."

"Mr. Foster," Stacey said, extending a hand. Foster shook her hand and gave her a warm smile. She couldn't help noticing he had big blue eyes and a great smile.

"What have we got?" Stacey asked the first responding team.

Bob Mitchell, the senior of the two officers said, "We have got nothing. Take a look."

Stacey looked around to see the conference room in perfect order. Nothing damaged, no blood and no sign of any commotion. She walked into the room and looked carefully around her. Not so much as a drop of spilled coffee. Stacey shrugged and said, "I don't see anything out of whack, but the lab team should be here any minute." She turned her attention to Marc Foster. "Did you see anything out of order?"

He shook his head. "Nope. When I got here, right before these officers arrived, it looked just like this."

"Not exactly a text book murder scene," Stacey said.

The forensics team arrived and walked to the doorway. Stacey looked over and said, "Hi, Carlos. Give it a good going over. We were advised there was a shooting here and a lot of blood."

Carlos Morton looked at her blankly. "Are you sure it was in this room? Maybe the hotel staff cleaned up before we got here."

Foster said, "No, we haven't touched the room."

"Well, someone sure worked it over." Carlos shrugged and added, "We'll see what we can find, but this place looks like it has been sanitized."

"Yes, it does," Stacey said. "Call me as soon as you have some results, will you guys?"

"You got it."

Stacey and Marc Foster walked from the room and down the hall. Foster said, "Nice work by the way."

"What?" Stacey asked.

"You were involved in finding the missing money from the bank robbery."

"Yes," she said grinning. "Thanks."

"I'd love to hear the story sometime," he said.

"There's only parts of it I can tell," she said.

"Well, I'd love to hear what you can tell me." He hesitated and their eyes met. He exchanged a smile and both held their gaze for a little longer than they should have. "Maybe sometime we can talk about it further, Detective."

"Yes," she said. "Maybe we can." She was struck by the fact that he was both attractive and extremely nice. She was also getting the sense that he thought something similar about her.

Stacey smiled at him as they stopped near the front desk. "Can you check around and see if any of your people noticed anything unusual in the condition of that room or if they saw the people who occupied it in the last couple of hours. If so, I will come and interview them."

"Shall do," he said. He started to say something else and then stopped.

Stacey handed him a card and said, "My office and my cell numbers are both on here." As she spoke, she noticed those blue eyes again.

"I'll get back with you as soon as I check with hotel staff."

She smiled and said, "Thanks, I appreciate it."

* * *

Jeff Butler saw only one car as he pulled into the driveway. He walked to the garage door and stood on his toes to get a distorted view of an empty garage through the mirrored window at the top of the garage door. He walked to the front door, rang the bell and waited. Kelly Parson opened the door to find the detective examining her expression.

"Hello, Detective."

"Good evening, Ms. Parson. Sorry to bother you at home. Is Mr. Roper here?"

"No, he's out of town for a couple of days."

Butler paused and then asked, "Do you know how to reach Mr. Roper?"

"Yeah, sure. I have his number."

"Any contact info for the period he is gone other than his cell?

She looked concerned. "Is there something wrong?"

Butler said, "We'd like to talk to him and make sure that he is all right."

There was instant concern on her face. "What? Did something happen to Kevin?"

"I don't know, ma'am. We had a report and want to check it out. Can you see if you can get him on the line for me?"

"Of course." Kelly hit a speed dial number and waited. The line rang four times and then she got the recorded message. "This is Kevin Roper. Leave me a message and I will call you as soon as I can. Thanks, and have a good day."

Hearing his recorded voice, Kelly was even more worried. "What report did you get," she asked, looking at him steadily.

Butler hesitated, and then said, "We got a report that he had been shot in a hotel meeting room."

"What?" she cried out, covering her mouth as her eyes grew wide.

Butler said, "We checked out the hotel site and he's not there. There is no victim to be found and no sign of any struggle or shooting. We are double-checking all possible sources of information. We just want to assure that he is okay."

She nodded and managed to say, "I understand."

Butler could see that this was news to her and that she was shaken. "Will you call me if you should hear from Mr. Roper?"

"Yes, Detective. I will. Please call me as soon as you get any information. I will be worried until I know that he is okay."

Her face reflected deep concern and he found himself saying. "It could be that he's perfectly fine, but we just need to confirm that, Ms. Parson."

She nodded and mumbled, "I understand," her expression fearful.

"Call me if you are able to reach him," Butler said, handing her a card. He turned and walked towards the unmarked car at the curb.

Kelly was already redialing Kevin's number as Butler drove away. The call went straight to voice mail. His voice announced his unavailability and then came the beep. "Kevin, it's me. I need to know that you are okay. The police were just here. Someone reported that you were shot at a hotel. Please call me as soon as you can. Maybe this is not the right way to say this for the first time, but I love you. Please call me right away."

* * *

Kevin played the message over and over again. The fear and worry in her voice tore at him. Her unanticipated confession that she loved him filled him with joy. The plan required him to stay gone and talk to no one while Linda Caldwell reported his death. But he just couldn't do it. After an hour of listening to Kelly's message, he called her.

"Hello"

"Hi Kelly. It's Kevin."

"Oh, my God. I was so scared. I was going crazy. That detective was here and he told me that you might have been shot in a hotel room."

"I'm really okay."

"I was worried," she said. She blurted out, "Kevin, I love you." She drew a breath and then added, "I should have told you already."

"I love you, too, Kelly. I should have told you, too." He searched for the right way to say what he had to tell her, but couldn't think of anything. He said, "I need to keep the fact that we spoke quiet for now."

"What?" Kelly asked, confused.

"You can't tell anyone that you talked to me. I'll explain it all when we are together again."

"Not even the police?"

"Especially not the police. I promise I will explain it all when I return in two more days. Just don't tell them that we spoke."

"Kevin, are you wanted by the police? What's this all about?" she asked, alarmed.

"I promise to explain it all. Just trust me for now."

She was quiet and then said, "Okay, but this doesn't feel right."

He couldn't think of anything better, so he replied, "I understand."

"This isn't your phone that you're calling me on."

"Yeah, this is a throw away."

More quiet and then, "You really are hiding."

"I'll be home the day after tomorrow."

"Kevin, I need to know what's going on. I love you, but I don't want to be in a relationship with a fugitive."

He was quiet for a long moment and then replied, "You know the person I am. And you know that I'd never hurt anyone, right?"

"Yes," she responded, although there was doubt in the way it was delivered.

"Please, hang on until Thursday night and I'll explain. I should be there around seven, okay?"

"Okay, I'll be waiting." There was a caution in her voice that he had never heard before. But why shouldn't there be? And how was he ever going to explain this to her? Could he tell her the truth? That possibility would never have occurred to him except for the fact that he had allowed himself to say it out loud—he really did love her.

Chapter Twenty-Seven

Twenty-Two Days After

Stacey Gray readied herself for her first coffee date in four months. She couldn't believe that she had signed up to try this again, as she had neither the time nor the desire to be matched with one more jerk. What was this guy's name? Oh yeah, Alan Milner. She wore clothing to avoid accentuating her figure; conservatively attractive. A blouse that showed no cleavage and slacks, a blue sweater and limited make-up. She hated these social experiments and she knew she was a little jaded by past experience. Most of the men she met were boring, egocentric or just horny. Most of these guys weren't worth spending an evening with, let alone a lifetime. The last one had grabbed her ass as they walked from the restaurant and she had almost taken him down on the sidewalk. Thinking about the panicked look on his face as she grabbed his arm and twisted, made her smile with amusement. Maybe the son of a bitch would respect the next woman he dated. Even as she got ready, she wondered if all of this was worthwhile. It would be nice to have someone to care about—something other than the job as a focus. But the likelihood of finding the right guy, or even a decent guy, seemed remote based upon past experience. Her thoughts strayed to

Marc Foster momentarily. He was a nice guy. He was also great looking. Probably married with six kids.

Stacey checked herself in the hallway mirror and gave a nod. Then, she returned to thoughts of the job. She was convinced something was not right with the investigation, starting with the fact that the FBI/LAPD task force had been abruptly dismantled. She had been informed by Curt Lowell that the accounts accessed by the bank computers during the hostage taking were best described as the friends of Vladimir Putin, but the press, and the world, had no idea. The only public reports were that the FBI/LAPD joint task force recovered the money that had been taken. It was all under wraps while the top of the FBI pyramid sought the perps.

She thought again about Linda Caldwell's statement that Kevin Roper had been shot. There was no trace of a body or even a scuffle in the hotel conference room where the shooting took place. Stacey's gut told her that Linda Caldwell was telling the truth, or at least she believed that she was telling the truth. Caldwell had seen a shooting, so maybe whoever pulled off the robbery shot Roper to stop him from cleansing a guilty conscience. Butler told her that Kelly Parson said Roper was out of town for a couple of days. He also said that she had been genuinely surprised to hear that he may have been shot. Parson said she would call them when she reached Roper, but there had been no call so far.

She walked the four blocks to Pirate's Cove Coffee and walked inside. She didn't see anyone meeting the description of her date, so she stood in line and ordered a latte. She took a seat at a table near the window, where she could enjoy watching the lights and movements of the well-lit street. A man she could only describe as a lounge-lizard walked directly towards her table. "Hi, honey, I'm Alan," he said, grinning ear to ear.

'This is why I hate this stuff,' she thought. "Well, Alan, I'm not 'honey.' My name is Stacey as I think you know."

He raised his hands and stepped back. "Whoa, coming out of the gate hostile. I got a feminist this time."

"Good-bye, Alan. Have a wonderful life," Stacey said. She moved toward the door and as she did, she saw a man seated at a table near the door smiling her way.

"Classy guy," he said as she passed his way.

"Yep, I think that completes a trifecta of my recent date experiences."

The man had short black hair and wore glasses. He was good looking in a studious kind of a way. As she gave him an amused smile, Paul Mason stood and extended a hand. "My name is Paul."

"Hi Paul, I'm Stacey."

"I know. I saw you on television. Very impressive how you and the feds recaptured the missing money."

"Thanks," she said. "You're married, aren't you?"

"I am."

"Seems like the ones with a little class are the ones that are off the market." She smiled. "Good to meet you though, Paul. And thanks for that nice smile, it made this a little more bearable."

"Thank you, Stacey. I can assure you that if I weren't off the market, I would love to have coffee with you. You have a great smile and you're even prettier than on television."

She grinned one more time and walked out of the door, her thoughts returning to Linda Caldwell and Kevin Roper.

Her phone rang and she answered, "Detective Gray."

"Detective Gray, this is Marc Foster; you know, the Sheraton Manager."

"Hi, Mr. Foster. I remember you."

"Please call me Marc," he said.

"Okay, Marc."

After a moment he said, "I wanted to let you know that we have checked with all staff. No one cleaned that room and no one remembers seeing the occupants or anything out of the ordinary about the condition of the room."

"Interesting," she said thoughtfully. She would have liked to talk to Marc Foster some more, but she couldn't think of a reason. She could also see another call coming in and said, "I have to take another call, but thanks for checking that out for us, Marc. I appreciate it."

She hit a button. "Detective Gray," she said.

"We found nothing. Not so much as a fiber or a hair of any use. No traces of blood or any other substances."

Another brick wall, Stacey thought. "Okay, thanks for giving it your best, Carlos."

"All I can say is that if someone was shot in that room a short time before we got there, they have a clean-up squad as good as ours."

"Doesn't surprise me on this case. There doesn't seem to be much they aren't good at."

* * *

On Thursday evening, Kevin Roper pulled into Kelly's driveway just before 7:00 p.m. He walked to the front door and was about to knock when it opened. Kelly gave him a quick, awkward kiss and took his hand. She sat him down on the couch and took the chair across the coffee table. "Okay," she said, "Tell me what's going on."

Kevin was perceptibly nervous. He had decided to tell her the truth, contrary to the plan that had been formulated with Paul and Brian. He felt he had no choice. He loved this woman and did not want to lose her. He had also spent the last forty-eight hours racking his brain and could think of no credible explanation for the shooting. He either had to tell her he knew nothing about it, and it was clearly too late for that, or tell her the truth and hope she wouldn't throw him out the door or call the cops.

He took her hands and began by telling her that he worked frequently with FBI agents over the past several years and had come to know a couple of them very well. Without naming them, he laid out the emergence of the plan to provide donations to those with the greatest need at the expense of oligarchs and criminals who had far too much money and were using American investments to launder it.

He quickly added, "We did not take a dime for ourselves. It was money distributed to those with the greatest need around the world. To aid the Syrian refugee crisis by providing food and shelter and to support political candidates who would stand against Vladimir Putin in Russia." He paused, finding it hard to get air. Everything he cared about was on the line here and he was extremely nervous. "I love you with all my heart, Kelly. I have never been so happy and I want us to be together more than anything."

She looked at him for a moment and then said, "So you are a fugitive. The FBI doesn't know who they are looking for, but they're looking for you." She looked overwhelmed but she did not let go of his hands. "So that day at the bank, you weren't there like the rest of us, victims of something terrifying. You were part of the scheme." There was concern in her voice with that realization. He simply nodded. After a moment, she said, "And when you kicked the gun away from Chris Morgan, it was to protect them, not us."

"I knew that we would all be safe. I knew that no one would get hurt and that the two of them and all of us would simply walk out without injury at the right moment."

"But what if something had gone wrong? Someone could have been shot."

"Not by us—no loaded weapons."

"So if there had been a cop or someone else who pulled a weapon—someone like Chris Morgan, none of you could fire back?"

"Correct. We were going to make sure no one was hurt."

She was thoughtful for a few moments and then asked, "So is that how your morality works, Kevin? Doing wrong is okay if you have a good reason? I mean, what you're saying is that it's okay to steal if the cause is good enough, right?"

"I believe that's true."

She shook her head. "Have you thought about us at all? About our future together?"

"Every day," he said softly.

"They are going to figure this out, right? And you are going to spend twenty years in some prison?"

"The people who donated to our good cause were very carefully selected."

"Meaning?" she asked pointedly.

"Meaning two things. First, they have so much money that what they lost barely makes a difference. And secondly, the FBI has money laundering cases that can be made against each of these guys. If they came after the bank for their losses, they would be risking a great deal. Not to mention the fact that what was taken was less than twenty percent of their account balances."

She gave him an indignant gaze, and then said, "So they are off the hook for international crimes if they remain quiet?"

"No, I don't think that they're off the hook. They just aren't in a position to start drawing attention to themselves."

"So you have the FBI tracking you and maybe some of these Russian oligarchs are looking for you too? All with an agenda to put you in jail or worse?"

Kevin was quiet a moment and then said, "When you put it that way it doesn't sound too good, but this money did great things for some of the people who have been most hurt by war and displacement, people who are starving and have nowhere to go. A lot of people who now have food on the table; some who even have a table with this help."

226

She considered him and said, "Kevin, I don't doubt your motives, just your methods." She leaned toward him and kissed him softly. Then she said, "I don't want to spend my life without you because you went to jail for some international good deeds that happen to be illegal or because some Russian hit man got to you."

He said, "I understand." He drew a breath and took her hands. "Kelly, since I met you, I've been happy like never before and I don't want to spend a single day without you." He got down on one knee and said, "I love you, Kelly Parson. Please say that you will marry me."

She shook her head. "This is a bad time to ask, Kevin. I love you, but I think I need to know if this commitment involves every day or just visiting days."

* * *

Stacey sat in her car and waited, watching the Parson residence. At 7:00 p.m. she watched Kevin Roper pull into Kelly Parson's driveway and walk to the door. He knocked, the door opened and he went inside. The first thing that she noticed was that he didn't look very dead.

Stacey waited in her car for three hours and it was getting pretty clear he wasn't coming out before morning. She started the car and drove away, thinking that the reports of Kevin Roper's demise had been greatly exaggerated. Yet, Linda Caldwell had seen him shot and bleeding on a conference room floor.

She considered what Lowell had shared with her the last time they spoke. Kevin Roper's computer was clean. Nothing unlawful, no improper access to proprietary materials, nothing out of the ordinary. So how did a guy who traded in corporate secrets have a computer that reflected innocuous word processing and visits to Amazon, Goodreads and Facebook, and nothing more nefarious? He obviously hadn't turned over all of his work tools as required by the FBI search warrant.

And, they set Linda Caldwell up to see a shooting that didn't really happen. In that instant, all the dots connected and Stacey knew that she had the big picture. Linda Caldwell was going to credibly testify that Roper had been on the robbery team; that he had walked over to the disguised robbers and freely associated with them as one of the team. She was far too credible, so the team had to do something to turn that around. She shook her head as she considered how they had figured out a way to undermine Linda's credibility. On the witness stand, she would have to admit that she witnessed and reported the shooting and murder of Kevin Roper, the murder of a guy still alive. Roper would then walk into the courtroom and testify that he was never shot, let alone killed, and he knows nothing about any events at the Sheraton Hotel. At that point, Linda Caldwell's credibility as a witness is hopelessly compromised. She is a liar or just crazy. Wow, these guys are good; it was a mantra that she found herself repeating too often. A pretend murder to destroy the credibility of the only witness who can tie Roper to the crime. And, Linda Caldwell becomes collateral damage. Linda's credibility goes up in smoke, probably destroying her plea deal and she goes to jail for a long time.

Stacey drove home thinking about the fact that she was the first to know that Roper was alive and well. It wasn't her case anymore, but she decided that she would talk to Mr. Roper tomorrow morning. If she could take him by surprise, maybe some critical information could be obtained.

Chapter Twenty-Eight

Twenty-Three Days After

At 5:30 the next morning, Stacey Gray was parked in front of the Parson house again. Roper's car was still there. Stacey drank coffee and waited until 7:00 a.m., watching nothing in particular and seeing no movement from the house. At 7:15 she knocked on the door. Kelly Parson answered and her eyes filled with surprise and then, nervousness. She appeared ready for work, wearing her blue physician's attire. All that was missing was a surgical mask.

"Good morning, Ms. Parson, may I come in?"

There was hesitancy. Kelly glanced quickly over her shoulder before saying, "Okay, sure." She walked into the living room and Stacey followed.

"What can I do for you, Detective?" Kelly asked, regaining composure.

"Ms. Parson, you never called Detective Butler when you learned that Mr. Roper was okay. Why was that?"

"I guess it didn't seem important once I knew he was okay. Everything was just fine."

"Right, but you knew that we didn't have that information." Kelly was silent, out of words that would assist. "I need to talk to Kevin Roper," Stacey said.

She could see Kelly evaluating before the response came. "Okay, I'll get him." She stood and left the room. Two minutes later, Kevin Roper walked in dressed in jeans and a polo shirt.

"Good morning, Detective Gray," he offered. Neither Stacey nor Roper offered to shake hands with the other.

Stacey looked at him coldly and asked, "Mr. Roper, tell me about what happened at the Sheraton Agoura Hills." She watched his eyes, but he gave away nothing.

"Not sure what you mean," he responded.

"I mean tell me about the little skit you and your co-felons pulled to convince Linda Caldwell that you had been shot. Tell me about that."

He delivered an uncomprehending expression. "I don't have any idea what you mean, Detective."

"Were you at the Sheraton three nights ago?"

"No."

"You're not telling me the truth, Mr. Roper. Is there anything about what you've told me that you'd like to fix, while you still can?"

"I can't think of anything."

"We'll have to arrange for you and Ms. Parson to come in for further questioning. I'm convinced that you're not telling the truth and she's covering for you. You want to put Ms. Parson through extended inquiry rather than just telling me the truth now?"

There was a moment when the words hit home, but he recovered quickly. "I just don't have any more information, Detective." He reflected a moment and added, "I heard the FBI had taken over this investigation. I didn't know you were still working on this."

"Oh, I'm still on it. Mr. Roper. I'm still interested in the truth and I will be pursuing it as long as you're attempting to hide it."

"Thank you for stopping by Detective. If there is nothing further, I have to get ready to go to work."

"There is one other thing I should mention." He watched her silently. "We know the type of work you do and we know the depth of, shall we say 'research' it takes." She paused.

"Yes," he said, sounding a little impatient.

"Did you use the computer that the FBI took with their warrant for that purpose?"

He drew a breath. "Yes."

"Did you use any others?"

Kevin looked at her, momentarily assessing, and then he said, "I've had others in the past," he said evasively.

"Sure. Did you use any others within the last year?"

"Not that I recall."

"And you'll be prepared to testify to that?"

"Yes, ma'am."

Stacey stood and smiled. She had him in a lie and they both knew it. She extended a hand and he shook it. "Well, I'll let you get ready for work. Do call me if you should recall that there were other computers you used for business, will you?" He was silent. "Oh, and I assume that you aren't planning on any more trips away over the next week or two in case we need to talk again?"

"I have no other trips scheduled in the next couple of weeks."

"And this trip you just took, it was scheduled?"

"Yes."

"You have a calendar that would lay out your meetings and business trips for the past year?"

"Well, sort of. Some of my meetings and events can be spontaneous and don't make the calendar."

She nodded and said, "I can only imagine. Well, have a great day and we'll talk soon." Stacey left him standing in the living room and walked from the house. She had shaken him a little and he was a guy not too easy to shake.

* * *

Paul Mason walked into the Director's private conference room at 9:00 a.m. Michael Sayer and Mitch Tanner were already seated and waiting.

"Good morning, Paul," Sayer offered.

"Good morning, sir."

"You know why you're here, Paul?"

"No, sir."

"Well, it turns out that you weren't entirely honest with us before."

"I don't know what you mean, sir."

"Any part of your previous statement that you need to change?"

"Not that I can think of, sir."

"You were involved in the robbery, Mason." A statement, not a question.

"No, sir."

"I see. Well, let me play something for you." He hit a button on the machine in front of him and conversation sprang to life:

"So, are we going through with this?"

"I'm not talking here. Let's go outside and take a walk."

He stopped the recording. "You recognize those voices, Paul?"

"Yes, sir," Paul responded quickly, careful not to show surprise that he had been caught on tape.

"Who is speaking?"

"That would be Brian Gallagher and me."

"Yes, it would."

"When was that conversation?"

"I don't recall it, sir."

"Really? Well, let me refresh your recollection. It was May 18. Just twenty-eight days before you, Gallagher and Roper did your thing at the bank." Paul said nothing. "Ready to change or amplify your statement yet, Paul?"

"No, sir. I really don't have any more information."

"What were you and Gallagher talking about doing? What were you going to go through with that you couldn't talk about in the building?"

"I don't recall, sir."

Sayer knew that he wasn't going to remember because he wasn't going to give an explanation that would allow inconsistency of testimony between himself and Gallagher. Sayer already knew that Gallagher's answer would be the same. The Agency had trained these guys well. Sayer added, "We have additional recordings of your conversations, Paul."

"Okay, that may help me recall," he offered.

"The problem, Paul, is that we know that you already recall. We have other tapes and you are going to find yourself caught between what you've told us and what the tapes reveal. The time to fix the discrepancies is now."

Paul almost laughed at this blatant gotcha routine. It might work on the average perp on the street, but not on trained FBI agents. Paul put a considered expression on his face and said, "I think I've told you all I know."

"The tapes say otherwise, don't they?"

Sayer was giving him a challenging look. Paul reflected a moment and then said, "No," sounding a little impatient. "You and I both know that if such tapes did exist, you would tell me that to test how I would respond, and if they didn't you would still tell me you had them to see if I could be pressured into supplying what you need." He waited a moment and then said, "I can shortcut all of that for you. There can't be more tapes because there weren't any incriminating conversations."

Sayer turned beat red. "Who do you think you're fucking with? I am not putting up with any bullshit." Paul looked at him impassively, but said nothing. Sayer's anger seemed to increase with the silence. "You are suspended as of right now and until you hear further from this office."

"Thank you, sir," Paul said evenly and walked from the room.

Tanner looked at his boss and shook his head. "We don't have enough to put him out."

"You know that and I know that..." he let the words trail off.

"I think he does, too." Sayer said. "The guy is impenetrable. Makes him a great agent but a challenging perp." Sayer rubbed a hand through his hair and asked, "So what's the plan from here?"

"Let's put Gallagher on leave, too. Maybe they think we have enough to do them in. Maybe each one thinks the other decided to sell out."

"The former, maybe. The latter, no way. These guys know that neither would turn on the other."

"Let's just play out the hand," Sayer said. "I think we'll get to them. Put surveillance teams on these guys once they leave here. Let's see what they do with time on their hands."

* * *

Stacey set up a meeting with Linda Caldwell at 3:00 p.m. They found a distant corner table at Starbucks and sipped lattes as they spoke.

"Thanks for meeting with me, Linda."

"Of course. Did you learn something?"

"I did. I learned that Kevin Roper is perfectly fine. Walking around as healthy as ever."

"What?"

"Yep. And he says that he knows nothing of a shooting at the Agoura Hills Sheraton."

Linda looked alarmed. She said, "Detective Gray, I was telling you the truth about what I saw. I promise you..."

Stacey raised a hand. "Oh, I don't doubt you. I'm here to tell you that you were set up."

Linda looked puzzled. "I was set up?"

"Yep. What you witnessed was a production put on for your benefit; to make you think that Roper had been killed."

"Why would anyone want to do that?" Linda asked.

Stacey took a sip of her latte and then said, "Because you are the witness that links Roper to all of this. Without you, that link is gone. So, they make you report that he has been shot and killed. Then, it turns out that he is just fine and he testifies that none of what you say you witnessed ever happened." Linda was listening intently. "Then everything's fine except your credibility—the person who reported a murder that never took place is either lying or crazy."

"Wow," Linda whispered.

"It's a pretty elaborate way to do away with the only witness that makes a difference."

"So, what do I do now that my credibility has been tubed? Am I going to lose the deal that I made for leniency?" Linda asked.

"I hope not," Stacey said, supportively. "We have to find a way to see that doesn't happen."

"Do you know how we do that?" Linda asked.

"Nope. No idea yet," Stacey replied. Linda allowed silence to settle in and her expression said that she was thinking something she wasn't saying. "What?" Stacey asked.

Linda drew a deep breath and then blew it out, carefully choosing her words. "What if I could prove it really happened?"

Stacey stared at her wide-eyed. "Can you?"

"I think so, yeah."

"How can you prove it?" Stacey pushed.

"I was really nervous going to a meeting with Mr. Abbott and Mr. Costello. I mean, I thought I had no choice, but I thought they might decide to hurt me, you know?"

She paused and Stacey jumped in, "Yes, and so?" Stacey waited with an impatient expression.

"So I wore a recording device to the meeting."

"Why didn't you tell me that?"

"I wasn't sure that it was needed until you told me they set me up. And I don't know how good it is. I haven't even listened to it yet. But there should be some conversation from the meeting on the device." She paused and added. "And a gunshot."

* * *

Atlantis Seaboard was the kind of restaurant that was made up for the movies and serviced special occasions. It featured dark mahogany walls, crystal chandeliers and private tables where powerful business and political forces came together to discuss the investment of staggering amounts of money in limitless projects. The menu was extraordinary and prices were astounding. Kevin and Kelly sat in an isolated booth with shrimp salads and crab casserole.

Kelly wore a blue blouse that hung off her shoulders, a black skirt and gold earrings that shined in the reflection of the chandelier overhead. "You look wonderful tonight," Kevin said, smiling at her.

"Thanks," she said in a distant voice. After a moment she added, "My confidence in us is shaken, Kevin."

He stopped dead, fork half way to his mouth. "What do you mean?"

"You joined a gang and stole more money than I can conceive of. You think it's odd that I see that as a morality issue?"

He nodded. "I understand that you are concerned, Kelly, but all the money went to help the world's most needy people."

"Well, some of it did. I doubt politicians in a runoff with Putin are the world's neediest people."

"Maybe not, but many of the Russian people who have leadership like Putin are." He wore a worried look and added, "And you know that I didn't make a dime from this."

Kelly looked mystified. "I don't know what to take from that. I don't agree that stealing is okay if you don't personally profit. Seems to me that it is still stealing."

Kevin was quiet for a moment, and then said, "I feel bad that you are disappointed. For me, it was a public service. I helped people all around the world and I did some bad things to some bad guys."

Kelly nodded. "Okay, I acknowledge that there are some good effects of what you did. But can't we help the world by going on a mission or donating to the world foundations?" She touched his hand and said, "I just don't want the guy I hoped to spend the rest of my life with doing prison time for what he thinks are good deeds. I don't want to spend my life thinking that you're on the run from the FBI because you're redistributing wealth at someone else's expense. You can see how having a fugitive husband would be unappealing, right?"

"Yeah, I see that." Kevin said with a tentative grin. "How about if I agree I don't get involved in any similar good deeds without discussing them with you first?"

"It's a start. How about you don't do it at all?" Kelly asked. "To me, stealing is stealing, even if you attempt to justify it by doing good work with the stolen money."

"One step at a time," Kevin said, and then added, "Thanks for being who you are. I really don't want to do anything that threatens you and me, because you are amazing and I love you like crazy."

She nodded and responded, "Yeah, I love you, too." She paused and looked at him with concern. After a time she said, "But it feels like I have lost you. And maybe you're not who I thought you were." She shook her head and said, "I'm not sure that we can be together, Kevin. We seem to have different ethical and moral standards."

Chapter Twenty-Nine

Twenty-Five Days After

Michael Sayer flew to Los Angeles for several meetings and to talk to a group of newly sworn agents. He was introduced and walked to the front of the large room to applause from the enthusiastic new team members. "Thank you, new team members and welcome to the Agency where we will demand a great deal of you, but give you a great deal in return. You will do important work for your country. You will protect our nation and its citizens from crime, and from those who would attack our citizens for their own religious or political purposes. You will be at the forefront of protecting this country." There was an eruption of applause. After a few moments, he continued, "We are purposeful in everything we do," he said to the attentive crowd of agents. "We do what others can't do and we stand behind one another. If a fellow agent needs a resource, we try to provide it. And that goes all the way to the top. We have a job to do and we are not political, no matter what politicians choose to say. Whether the government is run by Democrats or Republicans, we are the same. We hunt those who would harm our citizens and our allies and we stop them." He took a moment to look around the room and added, "You can be proud that you made this one of a kind team. You will have the opportunity to do good things for our citizens, to protect our country's values and to be a big part of the future of this Agency. Welcome to each of you. Please know that you can call on supervisors up the chain. Know that we will be there to help you. Thank you and welcome to your future. Your country is grateful to you."

As the room burst into applause, an assistant walked over to Sayer and whispered, "Mr. Tanner needs to speak with you. He says it's important."

"Thank you all," Sayer reiterated and walked from the room. From an adjacent office he called Tanner.

The phone rang once, and the response was immediate. "Michael, we have a problem," Tanner said.

"What are they up to?" Sayer asked, referring to Paul Mason and Brian Gallagher.

"It's not them," Tanner said. "Bob Danner of the New York Times just posted an article stating that they have multiple sources saying that the FBI is investigating itself for involvement in the California Bank robbery last month. The Washington Post just called for comment on a similar article that they plan to post."

"Holy shit," Sayer responded.

"Yeah," Tanner said, "we have a leak."

"Okay. Get with the communications director and fashion an appropriately strong denial." He paused for a moment and asked, "What about Mason and Gallagher? What have they been doing?"

"Nothing. Fucking with us a little. Gallagher took a three hour drive across Los Angeles as fast as he could through all the traffic he could find. Never stopped anywhere and never used his phone. Then he parked in his garage. It was just to tell the team that he knew they were following."

"Or maybe he was running a test to see if they could stay on him," Sayer said. "What about Mason?"

"He took a long drive to a restaurant, had lunch and drove home. Then he called the Agency and reported the license number of the car following him. He suggested that they should be a little more subtle."

"Jesus," Sayer said. "All right. Let's deal with the crisis at hand and we'll worry about these two clowns later. Find out who is leaking. Start with anyone with an ax to grind. Someone we let go recently, anyone likely. You know the drill."

"I'm on it," Tanner responded. "The reporters that received the leaks are in touch with the fraud unit frequently, so I'll get a good look at them, too. I'll let you know what I find."

Sayer was quiet and then said, "Mitch, this is critical. We have to find a way to make sure there is no more of this. You know what I mean, right?"

"I do."

There was a protracted silence, and then Sayer said, "My gut tells me that the leak is Mason or Gallagher."

"That's what I thought, too," Tanner said. "But I've had two agents on both of them around the clock. We're looking at every email, reviewing every phone call and watching every move. I have good teams on each of them and they have seen every move they have made."

"Mason and Gallagher know they're being followed, so they aren't going to overtly do what they don't want us to see."

"Sure. They know we're out there, probably spot our guys frequently, but we still see everything they do."

"What about burner phones in their own houses? Our guys wouldn't see that, right?" Sayer asked.

Another protracted silence. After a few moments, Tanner said, "We can hear everything that is said in their houses."

"Jesus, Mitch, we don't have the authority to wire our guys at home. If that gets out, we are in deep shit."

"I know. But I also know that they haven't had contact with the press from home."

"So who is it then?" Sayer asked.

Tanner replied, "I've been looking at everyone in the Agency and I have no clue where the leak is coming from."

"Keep on it, Mitch. We have to find this leak. Expand the team if that's what it takes and get back to me with some information soon."

"Yes, sir," Tanner said.

Sayer put down the phone thinking about the impact of these stories. The alt-right would have a field day firing up their deep state conspiracy theories with these leaks. He had no real choice. He would have to cut the trip short by a day. He would make an announcement to the Los Angeles group that there is a matter he has to address back in Washington and get on the plane before this hit the press or anything else beyond his control happened. He had to get this stopped before the Agency was under attack by the same politicians that praised the Agency's work on a regular basis.

* * *

At 2:20 p.m., Paul Mason went from the gym to his car. He observed a partially hidden unmarked car fifty yards away, with two men in the front seat, waiting to follow him. He threw his gym bag in the back seat and climbed into his gray Jeep Cherokee. He drove from the parking lot and watched in the rear-view mirror as the distant car followed. He grinned and drove directly to the plaza where Montel Dry Cleaning was located. He made a show of fishing two suits from the back seat and taking them into the cleaners.

"Hi, Dirk," he said to the thin man behind the counter.

"Good morning, sir. And how's your day?'

"Everything is as it should be," Paul said, smiling.

"How about Thursday for these suits?"

"Yep. That's perfect."

Paul took the ticket from Dirk. "Thanks," he said, and turned and walked from the store. As soon as he exited, Dirk reached into the left interior jacket pocket of the blue suit and pulled out a carefully encrypted page of notes. He put the notes directly into the nearby suit jacket pocket that he had at the ready. Don Evans would be in to pick up that suit in about an hour. Evans was Paul's college roommate and knew exactly what to do with the encrypted page. Evans had already set up a second delivery of information to Bob Danner of the New York Times.

As expected, one of the agents ran into the dry cleaner and spoke to Dirk. "Jack Stark, FBI," he said, showing his badge. "That guy who just came in, you know him?"

"Sure, he's a regular."

"What did he give you?"

Dirk shrugged. "Just a couple of suits."

"Let me see them."

"Sure," Dirk said, cooperatively, and handed Agent Stark the suits.

Stark quickly probed all pockets and then examined the suits for access to the lining. Apparently satisfied, he handed the suits back to Dirk. "Thanks," he said, and then added, "And don't tell him we were here."

"Okay, man. You got it," Dirk said affably. He smiled to himself as Stark walked from the store.

* * *

It was almost 9:00 p.m. when Michael Sayer's cell phone rang. He looked at the number and answered, "What have you got, Mitch? Something on Mason or Gallagher?"

"Negative. We have another headline about to be posted on the websites of the New York Times and the Washington Post."

"Shit. Saying what?"

"Saying that two sources reveal that the FBI suspects and is tailing its own agents in connection with the California Bank Robbery. They asked for a response."

"Did you respond?"

"I sent them to communications to get the standard denial, but this is getting more than a little uncomfortable." He paused and added. "I can't find the source of the leaks and we are looking hard."

"I know. I'm flying back to the office from Boston in the morning. Get Mason and Gallagher in the office at 5:00 tomorrow afternoon and let's chat with them a little further. Meet me in my office at 4:00, okay?"

"I'll be there," Tanner said. "I don't like this shit," he added. "It's like someone has turned our own tactics on us."

"It's very much like that," Sayer said. "And I don't know how they are doing it, but I think it's being engineered by Mason and Gallagher."

Part 8
Squeeze 'Em Till They Bleed

Chapter Thirty

Twenty-Six Days After

Kevin Roper was in one of a dozen chairs near the entrance to the Detective Division of the LAPD. He had been waiting twenty minutes so far and didn't know why he was there.

Uniformed and plain clothed officers strolled past him on their way to somewhere without ever noticing his presence. He could see about fifteen desks in an open workspace with glassed offices forming a "U" shape around them. Stacey Gray emerged from one of the offices and walked over to Kevin and extended a hand. "Sorry to keep you waiting, Mr. Roper. Please come with me." She turned and he followed her down a hall and into a conference room where Jeff Butler waited.

"Please, Mr. Roper, have a seat." She pointed to a chair.

"Why am I here, Detective?" he said, sounding annoyed. "Why was I asked to be here on a moment's notice by two uniformed officers at my door early in the morning?"

"Well, Mr. Roper, it's because we need to talk," Stacey said, calmly. She leaned back in her chair and eyed Roper carefully. She allowed the silence to fill the room and then said, "You have not been honest with us, Mr. Roper."

"Not again," he responded. "What now?"

"Do you know that it is a crime to lie to the FBI or the FBI task force, Mr. Roper?"

"No, but that reminds me. Wasn't this investigation put in the hands of the FBI? Why are you guys still questioning me or anyone?"

"Well, today we get to ask the questions and you get to answer them." She paused and then added, "Or you are free to leave and we can come for you with an arrest warrant."

"For what?" Kevin asked.

She looked him directly in the eyes and said, "You told me that you never saw Linda Caldwell at the Sheraton. You remember that?"

"Yes."

"You want to change your mind about that?"

"Why would I?"

"That was evasive, Mr. Roper. That was not an answer." Roper was quiet. "Were you at the Sheraton, Mr. Roper? Did you see Linda Caldwell there?"

"No."

"Well see, now we really have a problem."

"Why is that?"

She smiled. "We know that it happened. How about a direct quote: 'We just want you to forget you that you saw someone approaching us during the robbery. Be unsure. That's it.' "

He froze. He knew that she had seen the shock that was on his face before he could recover from his initial reaction. He could see the recognition that she had hit pay dirt on her face. "Where did you get that?" he asked.

"Got your attention now, right, Mr. Roper?" She paused a moment, and then she looked directly into his eyes and asked, "So, sir, would you like to confirm that were you there?"

"Do I need to have a lawyer here now?"

"I don't know, do you? Were you there?"

"Am I under arrest?"

"Nope. Were you there?" she persisted.

"What do you want?" he asked. "Why am I here?"

"I want you to know that I can establish what happened at the Sheraton. I know what was said and what happened there. It's all on tape." She paused and then added, "I want you to know that you can't use her testimony about what happened at the Sheraton to burn her as a witness. I want you to know that her testimony will be as strong as ever and the three of you will suffer because of what you tried to do to her. I believe that messing with a witness the way the three of you did constitutes obstruction of justice. One more pretty serious felony, you know?"

"I don't know anything about this," Kevin said, starting to recover.

"Right. Well, good thing you're not involved or you'd be aware that everyone involved has some real problems and it's just a matter of time until the arrests come, right?"

Kevin nodded, but said nothing, turning all this over in his mind and wondering if any of what they had would identify Mason and Gallagher.

"Anything you'd like to say at this point?"

They sat in silence for a while, and then Kevin replied, "Not that I can think of."

Stacey said, "You want to give it serious thought, Mr. Roper. You may think that we don't have Mr. Abbott and Mr. Costello yet, but you know that we have you. You can help yourself get significant time off your long sentence by identifying the others involved or you can go down the path of self-sacrifice which I am sure the others will appreciate. I fear that Ms. Parson will not want you to select that route however." She watched his eyes and added, "Think hard." She stood and said, "I think we are done for now, Mr. Roper, but I know we'll see each other soon."

* * *

Kevin drove to his neighborhood shopping center and walked among the crowds, wanting desperately to feel inconspicuous. He felt a rising panic that he had never known before. He could feel the blood pulsing through his veins. His heart raced and he felt compelled to look behind him frequently for Detective Gray and the FBI. They were on to him. He would go to jail. His career was over and worse, he would lose Kelly and the life they might make together to a twelve foot cell. He was trying hard to get enough oxygen as he walked into the mall, knowing there was only one thing left to do. He pulled the burner phone from his pocket and called the emergency number. He got a voice mail that said, "Not unless critical," and then there was a beep.

As he walked through the mall, Kevin spoke as softly as possible. "It's critical. They have me and I think they have you. I don't know what to do and we need to meet right away." He hung up and waited. If there was no call back within ten minutes, he was to destroy the phone and move to another designated location to receive a message. He walked into Starbucks and joined a line waiting to order, looking in all directions behind him but spotting no one. It wasn't reassuring because he wasn't trained for this. Mason and Gallagher would spot a good tail. Kevin had no clue what to look for and he felt like the walls were closing in on him. He made it to the front of the line and ordered a latte, then joined the crowd further down the bar watching the baristas and waiting for their drinks to appear.

As his name was called and his latte appeared at the end of the bar, the burner phone rang.

"Got the message," Gallagher said.

"We need to meet," Kevin said, speaking rapidly. "They have us on tape at the hotel. Where can I meet you?"

There was silence and then Gallagher said, "Go to the Mayflower Hotel in Pasadena at 8:00 tonight and ask for the green room. Take all precautions to assure you aren't followed. Got it?"

"Yes. I have it."

"Kill this phone," Gallagher said and then there was a click.

Kevin checked his watch. It was 4:30 p.m. He would leave for his meeting about 6:00 p.m., to assure that he could do everything he could think of to avoid a tail. He felt momentarily reassured. Then he looked up from his coffee and saw Detective Stacey Gray sitting on a bench in the mall about twenty feet away. She smiled when he looked in her direction, but she didn't move. He looked away quickly, but he knew she had seen the terrified look in his eyes before he did so. Kevin sipped his coffee and suppressed the urge to throw up. He told himself that if she was there to arrest him, she would have already. He looked at the phone she had probably seen him using and decided that he had to find a way to get rid of it before she took it from him. He left Starbucks and walked into the mall with coffee in hand and the phone in his pocket. He walked toward Macy's. He decided to walk into the store and then exit directly into the parking lot. He looked back and saw that Detective Gray was following him through the mall, and making no effort to avoid being seen. He walked faster, periodically glancing behind to confirm that she was still following. She was. He saw the restroom sign ahead and turned down the long, narrow corridor toward that men's room. He made it half way down the corridor when he saw Detective Jeff Butler standing outside the men's restroom door looking his way and smiling.

Kevin momentarily froze. He looked behind him to see Detective Gray waiting at the end of the corridor. Butler walked toward him and said, "Good day, Mr. Roper." Kevin said nothing. "I'll just take that phone."

Kevin attempted to regain his composure, forcing himself to speak calmly and evenly. "You have a warrant?"

Butler smiled. "Nope, but I could take you in and put you in a cell while I get one if that is your preference."

Kevin looked at Butler's unflinching expression. "What's the probable cause to support a warrant?"

"Well, let's see. You are a suspect in a bank robbery. You had a meeting with a witness for purposes of destroying her credibility in which a shooting was feigned for her benefit. And that was all so you could destroy the witness who saw you personally working with Mr. Abbott and Mr. Costello." He paused, and then added. "Oh, and the meeting at the Sheraton where the fake shooting took place—you know, the meeting you denied happened? We have that whole thing on tape. Sounds like more probable cause than we'll ever need to me. Of course, if you want to test it, that is perfectly okay with us."

The two men stood looking at each other in silence. After a short time, Kevin took the phone from his pocket and handed it to Butler.

Butler smiled. "Thanks so much for your cooperation, Mr. Roper. We'll get this analyzed and get it back to you as soon as possible. Unless of course it was just a burner that you were planning to get rid of anyway." Roper was silent. "Have a nice day, sir," Butler said. He walked back down the corridor to where his partner waited as Kevin stood frozen, assessing the significance of what had just happened. It wasn't good.

* * *

Linda was still shaking as Brad held her tightly. "What are we going to do?" she asked.

He was quiet a moment and then said, "I think maybe you have to disappear again."

"What?"

"These guys faked a killing in front of you just to undermine your testimony. They want to make sure that you don't testify against Kevin Roper or that if you do, that you won't be believed."

"Yeah, that's right," she replied with a questioning expression.

"It didn't work. So do they just give up?" He hesitated and then added, "Or do they come after you in some other way? I think that maybe you need to go away until we know that they aren't coming after you."

She was quiet for a few moments and then began nodding. "Okay, if you think so."

"What about the kids?"

"The kids and I will be okay. And you can come home as soon as we know it's safe."

They walked upstairs and she began packing a bag. She haphazardly threw in clothing for about a week, then she looked at him. "I'm so scared," she said. "How can this be happening?"

He held her close and said, "I love you so much. I just want to make sure that you are going to be okay. You can't stay with anyone you know. You can't be findable. Get a hotel room off the beaten path and stay put."

She nodded. "This is so awful, Brad. I just want my life back."

"I know," he said, softly.

She finished filling the suitcase and then looked around the room, as if taking in familiar surroundings for the last time. She turned to Brad and said, "I have to be available to testify when I'm needed. My plea deal is tied to that."

"I understand and we'll figure that out. We have to make sure you're safe before that happens," he said.

She stood and carried her suitcase to the bedroom door. When she looked back at him, they were both fighting tears. He walked over and kissed her tenderly. "I love you," he said. "Be safe for me."

Linda nodded and then made her way downstairs. She put her hand on the handle of the front door and then she froze. She put the suitcase down on the floor and turned to look at Brad, who eyed her with concern. Linda shook her head and looked at him. "I can't do it," she said. "I can't run again." Brad was quiet for a time and she added, "I have to see this out to the end. I've made mistakes before and I really need to do the right thing now. If they come after me in some other way, we will deal with that, too."

He nodded slowly, and then said, "Okay, I understand." He smiled and then added, "Come back upstairs and I'll help you unpack before the kids get home."

* * *

"The FBI may believe its own agents robbed California Bank," was the bold print headline posted on line by the New York Times. Tomorrow's newspaper headline today. It quoted two sources inside the FBI, talking on condition of anonymity, stating that the Bank of California was robbed by FBI agents to carry out Agency business. The article concluded, "We are attempting to learn precisely what business the FBI could have been trying to carry out by robbing a bank and taking hostages."

Right wing cable was all over it. Fox News hosts had talking points like, "This is the deep state abuse that we all fear and at some level, we all knew existed. Now we're learning that it's all true and even worse than we thought. We need to subpoena the reporters and make them talk or put them in jail."

Michael Sayer denied the allegations when asked for comment and then called Mitch Tanner. "What the fuck is this, Mitch? Who is talking?"

"We have checked everyone and have not identified any leakers."

"Well, what is your gut?"

Tanner was quiet a moment and then said, "My gut still tells me that these two sources are Mason and Gallagher, but we can't prove it. Shit, we're following them around the clock and monitoring all of their calls. We have no evidence that they have done anything, but I know it's them."

"So what the fuck do we do?"

"We could bring them back to work. We've given them a lot of free time to do whatever they're doing. At least we can watch them more closely if they are at their desks."

"Do it. Get them in at 7:00 a.m. and chain them to their fucking desks."

* * *

It was 7:25 p.m. and Kevin had been taking his circuitous route to the Mayflower Hotel for the past hour and a half. Two Ubers, one bus and one car ride later he was still seven miles from destination. He would make one last stop in a parking garage to trade the Honda he was driving for a Chevy Malibu, then he would park almost a mile from the hotel and walk the remainder of the journey. Kevin was constantly looking in the rear-view mirror. His blood pressure hadn't returned to normal since Butler had taken his phone. It felt like walls were closing in on him; on all three of them. They were going to be caught, there was no longer any doubt and what sounded like a great adventure at the outset now seemed like a horrible mistake. He was going to jail for a long time. And he was going to lose the woman of his dreams and there was nothing he could do about any of it.

When he arrived at the hotel, it was sixty-two degrees and a slight westerly wind was blowing. Under other circumstances it would have been a beautiful evening. He was trying not to be too obvious about looking all around for anyone following, but his composure had slipped in the wake of the previous screw ups. He was not a field agent and couldn't appear and disappear at will.

Kevin walked into the Mayflower Hotel and proceeded directly to the front desk, still scrutinizing the crowd around him to assure he wasn't followed and feeling much less confident that he was doing things right. Seeing nothing but the ordinary, he looked to the young woman with large breasts and purple hair behind the counter and said, "I need the green room, please."

The woman looked at a document and said, "That is room 1242, sir. Take the elevator bank down the hall to your right."

"Okay, thanks," Kevin said, looking around furtively as he made his way toward the elevator bank. Still nothing unusual to see. No one was following him. He climbed into the waiting elevator and pushed the button marked 12. The doors closed and the elevator rose rapidly.

When the elevator came to rest and the doors flew open, Kevin made his way down the hall that said rooms 1240 to 1265. He found room 1242 on his left and turned the handle. He walked in to find a small table and one chair. On the table was an audio speaker. The telephone rang and Kevin hit the answer button on the speaker. "Hello," he said.

"Good evening," Paul Mason said.

Brian Gallagher said, "I'm here, too."

"Why aren't you actually here?" Kevin asked. "This is an emergency meeting, remember?"

"We remember," Gallagher said, "but you haven't exactly been successful at avoiding attention, right? So we didn't think it was a good idea to all be physically in the same room."

There was a brief pause, and then Kevin said, "Are you guys hanging me out to dry?"

"What do you mean?" Mason asked.

"I mean, I'm the only one they can identify and you guys seem to be leaving me exposed all alone. Isn't that plain enough?"

"No, Kevin, we won't leave you out there alone. So update us."

"Linda Caldwell recorded our meeting at the Sheraton. She has it all on tape and took the tape to Detective Gray."

"Actually, they don't have jurisdiction anymore," Mason said. "The joint team she was part of was disbanded and this is strictly an FBI investigation now."

"Great, although no one seems to have told her that and I'm not sure how it helps."

"How do you know about the tape?"

"They brought me in and told me about it. They convinced me it was real by using quotes from the meeting. They had the words that you told me you were going to use with her. Then they told me that they know we did it to discredit a witness who can put me on the team with you guys."

"And what did you say?"

"I said nothing."

"Anything else we need to know?"

"Yeah, one more thing. After I called you earlier, I looked up and Gray was right there watching me. Then she and her partner followed me through the mall and took the burner phone before I could destroy it."

"For an operative who manages to go anywhere and get any information needed, you were pretty easy to take down today."

"I go behind curtains using a computer. I'm not a ghost like you people." He paused. "These guys are coming for me and I am not going to go to jail," he said excitedly. He drew a breath and then asked, "So what are we going to do?"

"We get it, Kevin, we really do. First, don't panic. They haven't arrested you because they don't have the evidence yet."

"Maybe, but I feel like it could be anytime now."

Mason said, "They are likely to pick you up to squeeze you. If they get you to identify us, then they have a case. If not, they are still stuck."

"So that's the only advice you have, don't identify you guys?"

Gallagher said, "That's the first step. If you identify us then all our leverage is gone. You understand? Kevin, we won't leave you out there alone. You've worked with us a long time. You know us pretty well, right?"

"Yeah, I do."

"All right. Give us two days. Lead your normal life because you're likely to be closely watched. If they pick you up, call the number. Otherwise, wait for us to get back to you."

There was silence for a moment, and then Kevin said, "Okay, but this is getting hard. I thought you said this investigation is solely FBI now."

"It is," Mason said.

"So why are LAPD detectives all over me?"

"Persistence. They're operating outside of their authority, but they think they've got something and they aren't letting go. Looks like they are also determined to protect Caldwell's credibility so that they can hang you out to dry and flip you to identify us." He paused and then added, "We hear that Gray is a smart cop, so be careful."

"Be careful?" Kevin said, incredulously. "You've got to be kidding."

"Forty-eight hours, Kevin. Hang in there," Mason said.

"Sure thing," Kevin replied, shaking his head.

When they hung up, Gallagher asked Mason, "What do you think?"

"He'll hang in there," Mason replied. "But we better have something worked out in the next forty-eight hours."

Gallagher was quiet a moment and then said, "They're bringing us back to work in the morning. I think that the latest New York Times piece will have a big impact. I still don't think that they can find enough evidence to get back to us, but if they find a way to connect the dots, the national articles will provide us with some leverage to negotiate. It's not good for the Agency to be looking at their own as perpetrators."

Mason nodded and then replied, "You and I both know that if they are going to connect the dots back to us, it is going to be through Kevin."

Gallagher nodded. "I think that detective knows it too."

* * *

Kevin took the elevator down to the lobby. As he walked toward the massive glass entry doors of the hotel, he saw Stacey Gray and Jeff Butler walking directly toward him. They approached and stopped, looking into his eyes. "Another hotel meeting that didn't really happen?" Gray asked.

"Why are you following me?" Kevin asked lamely.

They both stared at him through a prolonged and uncomfortable silence. He walked outside and toward his car, wondering how they had managed to follow him through two hours of circular travel. He looked behind him to see that they had disappeared into the hotel. Soon they would have an employee showing them the green room and tracing the call. It occurred to him that they were hoping he would not emerge alone, but would be accompanied by Mr. Abbott and Mr. Costello, so that they could be identified and apprehended. They left him quickly because they were thinking the others might still be inside. He knew he would be seeing them both again soon. He decided that there was no longer reason for him to go through the gymnastics of multiple vehicles to go home. After all, they had already found him. He got into the car and decided he had to see Kelly. Maybe he could convince her that he wasn't going to spend his life as a would-be Robin Hood and that she should keep him around. She was the best thing that had ever happened to him and he wouldn't lose her without a fight. He dialed her number and waited nervously as it began to ring.

* * *

Stacey Gray and Jeff Butler stared into the green room, seeing that there had been no meeting, simply an audio set up for a conference call. Those bastards knew better than to show up in person. They flashed their badges for the hotel manager and asked him to trace any outgoing calls from this room, but they were convinced there would be none. These guys thought about every move. Stacey considered that they seemed to know how to avoid leaving a trail, just like someone in law enforcement.

Maybe the New York Times was right and these two guys were FBI.

"How do we make him tell us who these two guys are?" Butler queried.

"We arrest Kelly Parson and keep her in jail until he talks. That would work. Or did you mean some action consistent with the Constitution?" She grinned.

"You're scaring me, Gray, and I'm finding you less amusing all the time."

"Relax, partner," she replied. After a moment, she added, "But I know that if we scare Roper enough, he'll talk. And Parson is his point of vulnerability." She paused and then said, "So let's go talk to her."

"Okay, but we need to tread carefully. I mean, we're trying to turn a non-suspect to get information she might have received from someone else in connection with an investigation that we have no authorized role in pursuing, right?"

"Sounds like a bad thing when you say it that way," Stacey said. "But yeah, that's right." She paused a few moments and then added, "If we get nothing, I want to take him in and roll him. He'll tell us who the other two are if he thinks he's facing charges alone."

"Are you kidding?" Butler asked. "We don't have enough to bust him and, like I just mentioned, this is not even our investigation and we have no authority to act. We're in this because you have a soft spot for Linda Caldwell, not because anyone in the food chain said we could be."

"I know we can't hold him, but maybe we can scare the shit out of him before we're forced to kick him loose."

"Shit, Gray, I don't know if you can scare the shit out of him, but you are scaring the shit out of me. Our asses are on the line here."

"Yeah, I know." She smiled. "I'll understand if you want to sit this one out, Jeff. I really will."

He shook his head. "Dammit, Gray. You already know I'm not going to do that."

"Yep," she said grinning. "I do know that." Her eyes grew wider as she finished speaking. "Thanks, partner."

"So how do we do this?" Butler asked.

"We move at him slowly. We let him get word to Mr. Abbott and Mr. Costello that we are coming for him. These are smart guys and once we have him in custody, they will have reason to be nervous that we might flip Roper to get to them."

"When you get us fired, Gray, I hope you have a back-up plan. I would like to go on eating."

* * *

Kevin stared in the rear-view mirror all the way home. He was about to cross the subtle line between scared shitless and completely paranoid. He was sweating and working hard to get enough oxygen. He wanted all of this over. He wanted to be with Kelly and he wanted peace of mind. No more Abbott and Costello, no more cops following him, and no more threats of a long prison term.

When he got home, Kevin ran into the house and threw his arms around Kelly. He held her tight and tried to slow his heart rate.

"What? What is it?" she asked.

He shook his head and said, "I love you and I don't want to risk us for anything." He held her tight and said, "I've been thinking about this a lot and I think you were right. The ends don't justify the means." He looked her in the eyes and said, "I'm sorry for all of this."

She nodded. "Do you mean it?" She looked into his eyes and said, "I really need to know that, Kevin. I love you, but I just don't think I could be with a man who thinks that robbery is okay if you donate the money."

"I mean it," he said, and then cautioned, "This may get worse. The detectives have been following me and I don't know what they are going to do next. I'm going to find a way to put an end to all this, but if they come and get me, I need you to make a call for me, okay?"

She nodded, fear filling those beautiful eyes. "Yes, okay."

Chapter Thirty-One

Twenty-Seven Days After

At 7:30 a.m., Detective Stacey Gray parked the unmarked car directly across the street from Kelly Parson's house. Attempting to be as obvious as possible, she and Butler took a couple of extra minutes before getting slowly out of the car. They moved casually towards the house, and past Kevin Roper's car parked in the driveway. It was an overcast morning, unusually cold, portending the delay of spring's arrival.

Stacey was contemplating just how far out on limb she and Butler were about to go. They didn't have the authority to visit witnesses' homes, attempt to flip a suspect, or even interview witnesses. The case was the exclusive province of the FBI and they were going rogue—or even further rogue than they had been so far. She knew that she should turn around now, but she wasn't going to do it. She wanted to protect Linda Caldwell's chances of living a decent life, but there was something else. Her gut told her that she could get Roper to identify Mr. Abbott and Mr. Costello and she wanted to stop these guys.

Butler looked over at her as they walked up the driveway. He gave her the wide eyes and the shake of the head that asked what the fuck she had gotten them into. She shrugged in return and zipped her jacket to fend off the cold morning air. As they walked toward the house, Stacey's phone rang.

"Detective Gray," she said.

"Hi, Stacey," Carlos Morton said.

"Hey, Carlos. What have you got for me?"

"Nothing helpful," he replied. "The phone you took from Roper was a burner used one time to call a message number. Messages were retrieved from that number by another burner phone and no track left." He paused and added. "So I have nothing because whoever is doing this knows exactly what they are doing."

"I figured as much," Stacey said. "That has been the story all the way through this investigation."

"What investigation?" Morton asked. "If you'll remember, we don't have this one anymore."

"I know," Stacey replied. "But thanks for trying."

"Anytime," Morton said. "But not anymore on this case because I don't want to get my ass kicked."

"Yep. I appreciate the favor." She reflected and added, "One more question.'

"Yeah?"

"How does a brilliant Latino lab rat get named Morton, anyhow?"

"Long story of family entanglements with gringos. I'll tell you about it sometime over a beer."

"I'm buying." Stacey said. "Bye, Carlos." She hung up as they approached the front door.

Stacey knocked on the door and Kelly Parson promptly opened it, but only wide enough to let them see a pretty face dominated by worried eyes. "Yes, officers, what do you need?"

"We just have a few more questions for you," Jeff Butler said.

Stacey asked, "Is Mr. Roper here? We need to speak with him as well."

"I think we've had enough," Kelly said. "We don't have more to say and you're going to need a warrant to come inside."

"Why the sudden concern about a few questions?" Butler asked.

"Like I said, we've had enough. We just want to be left alone."

Stacey nodded and said, "I'm going to need to hear that from Mr. Roper directly, you understand."

Kevin Roper appeared in the doorway behind her, opening the door just a little further so that he could be seen. "What Kelly says is right. We just want to be left alone."

"Not quite that simple, is it, Mr. Roper. I mean we're talking about a serious crime committed by you and members of the FBI," Stacey said, carefully watching his eyes.

"I'm sorry, Detective. No more questions."

"Okay," Stacey said. "Mr. Roper, please come with us."

"Where?"

"To the Detective Bureau where we can question you further." Everyone froze. "We can arrest you if we need to?"

"For what?"

"For lying to us, obstructing justice and attempting to intimidate a witness. That would be Ms. Caldwell."

"So what do you want?" Roper asked.

"We want to know the names of your two partners. You know, Mr. Abbott and Mr. Costello." She allowed this to sink in and then added, "And we're prepared to recommend leniency where you're concerned if you tell us."

"I don't know what you are talking about," Roper said after a moment of contemplation.

"Very well, Mr. Roper. You're under arrest. You have the right to remain silent. Anything that you say can and will be used against you in a court of law. You have the right to speak to an attorney and to have that attorney present during questioning. If you cannot afford an attorney, one will be provided for you at government expense. Do you understand these rights?"

"Yes," Roper said with wide, reluctant eyes.

Kelly Parson looked at Roper with fear in her expression. "Kevin," she said, "please." Roper just shook his head at her.

"Let's go," Butler said and they walked him towards the car leaving Kelly standing in the doorway, near panic. "I will get you a lawyer, right away," she yelled. "It will be okay." She watched them pull away and then raced through the house to find the burner phone and the number he had left for her. She had one emergency call to make before she called the lawyer.

Kelly felt a rising sense of panic as she dialed the number Kevin had given her and left the message that Kevin had been arrested by the LAPD.

Five minutes later, she got a return call. A voice said, "We got your message."

"And what?" she asked. "You have to get him out."

"We'll work on it," the voice said, and then hung up.

* * *

Kevin Roper was placed in a small conference room in the detective bureau. It was without the cameras and one way mirror of the interrogation rooms. Stacey sat across from Roper and smiled. She punched a button to start recording the conversation. "Mr. Roper, I am recording this conversation." He shrugged. "I need a verbal response."

"Not much I can do about it."

She nodded and looked him in the eyes. "You sure you know what you're doing here?"

"What do you mean," Roper asked.

"Ms. Parson is a great catch, don't you think?"

"Yes," he said, "I know."

She looked at him thoughtfully. "Aren't you risking a great deal, Mr. Roper? I mean, are you okay with losing her?" Roper was quiet, but considering, so she continued, "You go to jail for a long time and it's over. I hope that you're not telling yourself

264

that she can wait years for you. You know that's not realistic, right? I see that fantasy quite a bit. But the true love doesn't sit waiting for ten or fifteen years. The caring ones wait a while, but even they burn out. They realize that they are missing life because of what their partner has done." She shook her head and added, "I mean you can't blame them, you can't maintain a relationship with someone who's not there; someone who is locked away in an environment where they gradually become a different person." Stacey leaned back in her chair. "I understand that you are successful in business. This can't be how you want to spend the next fifteen years or so, Kevin."

"What if I did know something, and I'm not saying I do, but then what?"

"Then I'll get a DA recommendation for leniency and you'll be looking at a much shorter time."

"What about immunity?" Kevin asked.

Now Stacey knew that she was getting somewhere. "I don't know, but it can be explored. You want me to talk to the DA and the Feds about it?" He hesitated. She said, "You really want to leave your woman and your career behind to spend your time in a cell?"

"I don't want to talk anymore," Kevin said. "Let me know when my lawyer gets here." Stacey felt deflated. She shook her head and stood up. It was then that Kevin added, "But let me know about the immunity deal."

"I'll work on it right now," Stacey said. She turned off the recorder and moved quickly across the room. She stopped at the door and turned around. "Or, there is an alternative."

"Which is what?" Kevin asked.

Stacey walked back to the table and sat down. This time she never turned on the recorder. "You don't admit anything legally binding. You do nothing more than give me a little information that I need and I won't use it against you. If it works out, you walk away and there are no charges."

"I'm listening," Kevin said. "What do you need from me?"

* * *

Paul Mason and Brian Gallagher had been at their desks since 7:00 a.m. For almost an hour, they worked through files with no interaction from anyone. Then, shortly before 8:00 a.m., Paul retrieved a message from Kelly Parson and went out to his car to return the call on a burner phone. "What the fuck," he thought to himself. Kevin Roper had been arrested by that rogue LAPD detective, who wasn't even on the case anymore.

He called her and, without identifying himself, assured a panicking Kelly Parson that he would work on helping Kevin right away. She thanked him and he hung up. Then he put the burner phone under his back tire and backed up. His actions would be caught by the video cameras scattered throughout the facility, but he hoped it wouldn't matter. At 11:00 a.m., Mitch Tanner was expected in and they would request to see him. They had Roper in custody and it was time to end this before something went wrong. Today, it would all come to a head—one way or another. And they would be fine or they would go to jail, but this would play out today.

When he got back upstairs, his cell phone rang.

"Paul Mason," he said.

"Hi, Mr. Mason. This is Detective Stacey Gray."

There was an extended silence while Mason considered his response to this crazy person. She was off the fucking reservation. "How can I help you, Detective?" he asked as evenly as he could.

"You and Brian Gallagher can meet me in fifteen minutes."

"Why?"

"Because as I'm sure you know, I arrested Kevin Roper. He and I had a good talk and he told me some fascinating things about activities that he was engaged in with you and Mr. Gallagher."

She paused and added, "Right now you're wondering just how much I learned from Mr. Roper. The answer is a great deal."

"Why should I believe you?"

"You don't have to believe me," she said evenly. "You could elect to wait and see what happens."

"You don't have any authority over this case," Mason countered.

"Well, you can complain to my supervisors if you like. They won't much care by the time all of this comes out. It's going to be quite a story. Consider the possibilities. Some will think you're a hero and some will think you're guilty of treason. It should make greater dinner conversation all the way through the time of your trial."

"How do you even know who I am?"

"That's a good question to ask yourself until we get together," Stacey replied.

More silence, and then Mason asked, "Where do we meet you?"

"Starbucks on Kelman Drive. Fifteen minutes."

"Okay. We'll be there."

"I thought you might. It should be an enlightening visit," Stacey couldn't resist adding.

* * *

Mason and Gallagher walked into Starbucks and glanced around. Picking cops out of a crowd was seldom difficult. Cops not only looked like cops, they were looking at or through everything around them, eyes moving. They walked directly toward Detectives Gray and Butler, who sat facing the door at a tall table in a far corner that had two unoccupied stools.

Mason and Gallagher sat down and said nothing.

Stacey recognized Mason immediately as the witness to her promptly aborted coffee date. Stacey said, "Good to see you again, Mr. Mason. Hello, Mr. Gallagher. This is my partner, Detective Butler." They glanced at him, but neither spoke a word.

"So you guys think that you have the Bureau by the balls?" Stacey said.

Gallagher was turning an angry red. Mason furrowed his brow and said, "Last I heard, the LAPD was off the case and has absolutely no jurisdiction to do anything."

"Is that what you heard? Well, stick around and we'll show you what we can do."

"What do you want?" Gallagher asked.

"We want you to do the right thing."

"About what?" Mason asked.

"See, now you're fucking with us," Stacey replied, shaking her head. "Come on, Mason. You want to have a conversation or not?"

"Like Brian asked, what do you want?"

"First, I want you to know that we have it all." She was quiet and then repeated, "All of it."

"All of what?" Gallagher asked.

"Let's begin with the events that took place at the Sheraton for the purpose of destroying Ms. Caldwell's credibility. You remember, everything you denied. All recorded." There was silence and both Mason and Gallagher were expressionless, so Stacey asked, "You understand what I just said?"

"I understand."

"So, maybe you have some good reason for faking a homicide at a hotel after luring Ms. Caldwell there for a meeting. And maybe you have a good reason for denying that the whole thing happened. Maybe, but I doubt it. The tape Ms. Caldwell made is pretty compelling." The silence continued. Stacey let her statements settle in and then she smiled. "Of course," she said, "that's just the beginning."

Mason folded his arms and said, "That's all you have."

Stacey was smiling now. "You'd be in a lot less trouble if that were true. But we know everything. We know that Mr. Roper was the computer wizard who set up the electronic thefts. We know that he was the only hostage not there by coincidence. We know that he left the room in which he was supposed to be searching for marked bills and a GPS device to come and assist you both on the computers. Pretty slick the way you gave three people that same job so that you could free Roper to help you without raising suspicion of the other hostages. But you know, there's always something you don't expect. You just can't foresee everything. In this case, there was Ms. Caldwell, who opened her door to see Kevin Roper walking toward the two of you and then visiting like it was old home week." More silence. "You don't yet look convinced, gentlemen. How about if I tell you that you started discussing this plan back in March. You called Mr. Roper and told him that you had the best gig for him so far. No money in it, but he was going to do some great things for his country and for a number of really good causes. You told him that he was the only guy who could help you pull it off. He was hesitant, to say the least. You had your first meeting eight days later at Mr. Gallagher's house. You sat in his back yard and drank Coronas and ate chicken wings." Their faces had become serious and Stacey asked, "How am I doing so far, guys?"

"What do you want from us?" Mason said.

"Just a little cooperation."

"Meaning?"

"You are about to discuss a resolution of your legal problems. You are in the process of blackmailing the FBI into silence because if it doesn't go along, your conduct implicates the Agency. All the deep state conspiracy theorists, including our own administration who constantly doubts our security agencies, will be proven right and the FBI will have to charge its own agents. Won't look good at all, so the Director might deal with you to keep you guys under wraps. We know all of that," Stacey said.

"And?" Mason asked.

"And all we want is to be part of that deal."

"How?"

"First, the Director uses his pull to get Linda Caldwell a deal on her prior conviction as Angela Bremmer."

"And what else?"

"You two resign from the Bureau. I don't care why, make it up. To spend more time with your ailing mothers or the grandchildren you plan on having some day."

"Why would we do that?" Gallagher asked.

"Because it's part of the deal like I just said. And you have no choice. You guys think you have the FBI because they want to keep this out of the papers just like you do. I get that you are counting on that leverage because they have to care about the image of the Bureau. But I don't have those concerns and I will happily blow the whistle on all of this. So, taking this deal is what keeps the real story out of the paper and your asses out of federal prison."

Mason looked perplexed. "Why do you even want that? What we are being accused of was good for this country, and many good non-profits that found more funds than they ever had, to do what they needed to do to help people all over the world. Some of them might even have gone under without the help. Now they can expand and do great work worldwide."

Butler spoke for the first time, leaning forward and looking intently at Mason and then at Gallagher. "As well as being self-righteous assholes, you are the ultimate illustration of attempts to have 'the ends justify the means.' And they don't. You are law enforcement and you violated the law. There are no exceptions for those who thought they might accomplish something good by committing crimes." Butler shook his head and added, "You think by creating some kind of moral and legal quagmire you can skate personal responsibility. Well, no fucking chance, gentlemen."

There was quiet and then Stacey said, "What we are proposing is a compromise. You walk away from law enforcement rather than going to jail." She paused and then added, "This is not a close call. If you violate the law when it's expedient, then you don't get to be law enforcement. So, you will both walk away from your careers, resigning today as a part of the negotiated resolution, or we will blow the whistle on this whole fucking gambit and you can go to prison. I assume that you've heard how well cops do in prison."

"You don't know who you're fucking with here, lady," Gallagher said, glaring at Stacey.

"First of all, I'm not 'lady,' I am a cop. Secondly, I know exactly who I am fucking with here. You want to take me on, give it your best shot." Stacey let that settle on her angry audience and then said, "I get that you don't like the deal, I just don't care."

After a prolonged silence, Mason calmed the conversation by saying, "We'll think about it."

"Well, think fast," Stacey replied. "You are about to try and make your deal. If it doesn't include Linda Caldwell's protection and your resignation, read the headlines in the New York Times tomorrow and pack your toothbrushes."

Mason and Gallagher stood and walked out of the coffee shop without looking back. Jeff Butler looked at Stacey and said, "Jesus, you're trying to get us killed as well as fired."

Stacey started to laugh as Butler watched in shock for a moment and then got drawn in, beginning to chuckle himself. "I need a partner without a death wish," he said. Then he asked, "What do you think they'll do?"

"They'll either run us over outside our homes or they'll take the deal," Stacey answered.

"Or both?" Butler posed.

Stacey smiled. "Yeah, or both. Any way it goes, I think we got their attention."

"Do you think they have any idea that we already met with Director Sayer and laid out the deal?" Butler asked.

"I don't think so." Stacey replied, shaking her head. "I think these guys think they are about to cut their own deal."

"I was surprised how receptive Director Sayer was," Butler said. "I thought he would balk at this."

"Desperate measures for desperate times," Stacey replied. "He doesn't want to do this, he's just stuck. And really, a pretty safe deal for him. He lets these two guys resign and walk, he gives up any claims on Kevin Roper and he helps us with Linda Caldwell." She smiled. "Pretty low cost and it's much better than having his Agency under investigation for felonies and international crimes. And the FBI remain heroes for their role in recapturing the stolen money. This is a deal that would make J. Edgar Hoover jealous."

* * *

Mason had been back at his desk for about ten minutes when he was told his presence was needed in a meeting in conference room 'J.' When he arrived in the conference room, he found not only Assistant Director Mitch Tanner waiting for him, but the Director himself. Michael Sayer said, "Agent Mason, please have a seat" and directed him to a chair across the table. One minute later, Brian Gallagher walked into the room and received the same treatment from the Director. He extended a hand toward the desired chair so that both Brian and Paul were now facing the Director and the Deputy Director.

Sayer got right to it. "You know why you're here. You did it, now it's time to own it." Mason and Gallagher remained quiet. "Something you don't know is that I just got a call from detectives at LAPD. Turns out Kevin Roper is in custody presently and he is negotiating the terms for his roll over on you guys. Seems like a good time to have this conversation, don't you think?"

Mason looked over at Gallagher and then back at Sayer. He said, "You know what a fear of the deep state this administration has. The right wing will go crazy with something like this. And my guess is that both of you would be unceremoniously dumped as organizational leaders."

Sayer stared directly at him. In a soft, stern voice he said, "I don't get blackmailed Agent Mason."

"No, sir, certainly not by me. I just want to point out the obvious implications of all of this becoming public." Mason reached into his pocket and pulled out a one-page document.

Sayer looked at the list of five sets of names with multiple cities shown under each. He showed the list to Tanner and then asked, "What's this?"

Paul Mason leaned forward in his chair and said, "Five very carefully selected groups who have been recently apprehended, each of whom have done at least three robberies, each were active at the time of the California Bank robbery, and each used certain characteristics similar to those used at California Bank, including the involvement of hostages."

"You want to pin the California Bank robbery on one of these groups?"

"I would just say that they are likely suspects. The press might be made aware that the Bureau is looking at them as suspects, whether or not it ultimately results in an arrest."

"Or," Sayer said with wide eyes, "if Roper rolls over on you two, then I have more than a suspect, I have a ready-made case."

Gallagher said. "Setting aside the fact that we didn't do it, pinning it on us wouldn't be good for the Bureau. Whoever did this brought down some people who had it coming and supported some great causes while they were at it."

Sayer narrowed his eyes and stared at Gallagher. "You people are not fucking Robin Hoods and crime isn't justified either by nasty victims or philanthropic use of the proceeds. You guys parted company with what this Agency is all about." He shook his head.

The room got quiet for several minutes and then Mason said, "We have a proposal."

"Which is what?" Sayer asked.

"You cast suspicion on one of the other groups. You can charge them or not, but you don't charge us and no one looks at the Agency for any of this."

"Is that it? If so, the answer is no."

"And we agree to resign as of today for our own individual bullshit reasons," Mason added. Sayer was quiet, and Mason said, "And one more thing. You support a reduced sentence for Linda Caldwell."

"One of the hostages?" Sayer asked feigning ignorance. "Why the hell would a hostage need our help?" Then Sayer sat back and listened quietly to Mason relaying Detective Stacey Gray's request for help with Linda Caldwell's conviction as Angela Bremmer like he was hearing it for the first time. He never disclosed that he had already met with Gray and Butler and knew all about Linda Caldwell.

"What does this case have to do with her prior conviction?"

"Only that her fifteen minutes of fame as one of the hostages shed a light on her prior identity. It put the skids on her life as a fugitive."

"So how does any of that relate to this case? Why do I support her?"

"Just part of Detective Gray's deal," Mason said.

Sayer suppressed a smile. Mason was not going to tell him that Caldwell was a witness that they had attempted to intimidate, or about the tape recording she had made. "Mr. Gallagher, can you tell me anything about how Ms. Caldwell relates to this case?"

"No, sir."

The room was quiet for a few moments and then Sayer said, "I want an under oath statement from both of you."

"Saying what?" Gallagher asked.

"That all of the matters surrounding the robbery and its investigation are to stay confidential; that there will be no conversations with the press or anyone else about the robbery, the investigation or any reason for your departure other than what you are about to put in a resignation letter."

"Agreed, so long as we are never charged with anything," Mason said. "If we have to defend ourselves in court, then all bets are off." He paused and added, "And one more thing, the Bureau agrees not to say anything negative about either of us to anyone. We have to be able to make a living, so we can't have the FBI telling anyone we want to work with that we are less than good, loyal employees."

"I won't agree to characterize you two as good, loyal employees. That would be pure bullshit. But I will agree that the reason we will give out for your departure is the reason that you put into your resignation letters, with one exception. If you seek work with any law enforcement or intelligence agency, you will never get the first interview, understood?"

Mason looked at Gallagher, who gave a nod. "All right," Mason said. "It is agreed."

"And," Sayer said, "if either of you violate any part of the agreement, all bets are off and we come after you."

Mason looked at Gallagher and drew a nod. "Okay," Mason said. "Done."

The Director nodded slowly. "This all happens today," he said, and then he stood and walked from the room.

Tanner said, "Resignation letters delivered to my office in twenty minutes. Your statements under oath will be ready to sign when you get there." He then exited the room.

Gallagher looked at Mason with raised eyebrows. They left the room together and as they walked down the hall, Gallagher asked, "Is this a win?"

"I'm not sure. I mean we're not in jail and we did hack the friends of Putin."

Gallagher smiled. "I guess it is a win."

"Time to figure out what comes next. We're going to have to make a living," Mason said.

"We talked about the security and protection business. We can join one or start our own."

Mason nodded. "We have contacts with money to help us get started." He paused and added, "But stealing was also a lot of fun."

"Fuck that," Gallagher said. "I've come as close to prison as I ever want to get."

"You're right, of course," Mason responded. "But still, it is a thrilling experience…"

* * *

"Detective Gray," Stacey said into the phone.

"Detective, this is Michael Sayer."

"Good afternoon, Mr. Director. So how did it go?"

"The deal is made. Resignations in hand."

"Good news," she said.

Sayer added, "We are also in the process of assembling the supportive statements for Ms. Bremmer. I guess Mrs. Caldwell these days."

"Thanks, Mr. Director. She really put herself on the line."

"She did. She did it when she came forward about what she saw during the robbery and again when she recorded these guys at the hotel. Seems to me that she is one strong woman. She earned our support."

"Yeah, she did."

"And you were a big part of getting it done for her. She should know that, too."

"No need for that," she replied. "I'm just glad we got there."

He was quiet a moment and then said, "Detective, if you ever think about a career change, call me. I think you'd make a good agent."

"Thanks," she said, "but I like what I do."

"If you change your mind, call me directly and I'll make it happen."

Before she could speak again, he was gone. She sat back in her chair and considered. FBI agent might be a more glamorous position, but quickly dismissed the prospects. She was happy as a detective and she remembered the down home wisdom, "if it ain't broke, don't fix it."

* * *

When Butler knocked on the door, Kevin Roper opened it immediately. He looked at Gray and Butler expectantly.

"Can we come in?" Stacey asked.

He stepped aside and they walked into the living room, where Kelly Parson joined them. "Can I offer you anything?" she asked the detectives.

"I'm fine, thanks," Stacey replied.

"I'm okay, too. Thanks for asking," Jeff Butler added.

Kevin and Kelly looked at the officers expectantly, not knowing if Kevin was about to be arrested again and formally charged.

Stacey saw the torment and said, "We want you to know that Paul Mason and Brian Gallagher resigned from their positions with the FBI. They are done working with all law enforcement and intelligence agencies. You understand?"

"No charges?"

"Not so far," Stacy replied.

"What about me?" Kevin asked.

"It is in your best interest never to work with those two guys again. So if they call you, make sure you're too busy to visit. They will be under close scrutiny for quite a while and you are the subject of some interest yourself."

Kevin looked at Kelly briefly and then said, "I just want to live every day with this wonderful lady here."

Stacey nodded. "So, I guess you can return to your corporate clients." She smiled. "Like I told you before, we know that the computer the FBI picked up isn't what you used for business. I mean, unless you had clients paying you a great deal of money to play Solitaire or view Facebook posts." Kevin was quiet. Stacey smiled at him and said, "You may want to be careful just how far you go to please your clients unless you want to bring a world of shit down on them and you. I mean, people are watching you now."

Kevin nodded slowly. "I understand."

Stacey nodded at Butler and they both stood. "Good luck to you, Mr. Roper and Ms. Parson. Something to keep in mind as you go back to your previous business. I think that an average life struggling to pay bills and being with someone you love is better than making lots of money in questionable ways. That is especially true when one is being closely watched, such that every violation of securities and unfair competition laws might be noticed and prosecuted. Does that philosophy make sense to you, Mr. Roper?"

"It does," Kevin said, nodding.

"Consider it a heads up. We have some sophisticated technology these days and getting rid of the computer you're using when the police knock at the door won't protect you. Your business activities were not the case that Jeff and I were assigned to investigate and we don't need to go any further, but some of your actions could have been fertile ground for felony investigations." Stacey was quiet. She looked at Kelly and then back to

Kevin. After a time she said, "I hope you understand that there is only one friendly warning like this one."

"Yes, I get it," Kevin said.

"Good day, folks," Butler said, as the detectives made their way to the front door.

As they walked to the car, Butler said, "He may look behind a few curtains for corporate clients, but my guess is that he stays clean from now on."

Stacey smiled. "Yeah. Our good deed for the day."

Chapter Thirty-Two

Twenty-Eight Days After

Stacey walked into the Franklin County Court of Common Pleas in Columbus, Ohio, on a cold and overcast morning. She made her way through the metal detectors and then found her way to Department 17. She saw Brad Caldwell sitting on the other side of the room and gave him a wave. He smiled and waved in return.

Stacey sat in the back of the court and waited through a series of pleas and arraignments on six cases. Then the clerk called out "The People of The Commonwealth v. Angela Bremmer."

Linda Caldwell stood up at the defense counsel table, next to Thomas Gibbs, the Ohio attorney she had hired. The prosecutor also stood up at the adjacent table. "Good morning, Your Honor. Jackson Peterson for the People."

"Thomas Gibbs for Ms. Bremmer Caldwell, Your Honor."

"Be seated everyone," Judge Alicia Hill said. The judge checked the documents in front of her and said, "I understand that we have a plea deal with special circumstances." She paused a moment and then looked at Linda. "You were one of the hostages in the California Bank robbery we've all heard so much about."

"Yes, Your Honor," Linda replied.

"And it was at that point that you knew you would be recognized and you would be held accountable. In other words, you weren't motivated to come forward before it became evident that your conviction was going to be discovered."

"I think that demonstrates a lack of genuine contrition and remorse, Your Honor," Peterson said.

"May I speak, Your Honor?" Linda asked.

"Yes, you may," Judge Hill responded, focusing on Linda.

"I had not owned my mistake before becoming a hostage and I was wrong not to do so. I hated the secret and I needed to make it right. I really want to be entirely forthcoming, Your Honor, and I am very remorseful for what I did and for the secret I kept all these years."

Gibbs said, "If I may, Your Honor, we have an abundance of evidence substantiating Ms. Caldwell's rehabilitation and excellent character. She lived through a hostage ordeal and then worked with the authorities to help find a resolution of the case in which she was a hostage."

Judge Hill nodded slowly and said, "That is true. We have statements from two FBI agents and two LAPD detectives about your dedicated service to helping them solve a crime. They say that you were brave, forthright and incredibly helpful." She looked into the audience and said, "I understand that we also have one of the LAPD detectives here to speak on your behalf. Detective Gray, are you here?"

Stacey stood and approached the front of the courtroom. "Yes, Your Honor."

"What would you like to say, Detective Gray?"

"Thank you, Your Honor. I came out from Los Angeles because of the strength of character that Ms. Bremmer Caldwell has demonstrated in assisting us. She came forward with information we could have obtained in no other way. She was brave enough to attend a meeting and record it when there was a clear danger to her. She faced threats against her safety and stood her ground. Ms. Bremmer Caldwell has been honest in her dealing with us throughout and I would characterize her as an upstanding citizen. She has my respect and that of my partner, as well as the FBI agents that we worked with. If ever I have seen conduct that should mitigate a sentence, Your Honor, this is the case."

Judge Hill nodded. She looked at Linda and said, "It seems that you have law enforcement fans in the LAPD and the FBI that were prepared to go to some lengths to establish your rehabilitation. I am impressed and I am persuaded." She paused and then said, "Under the circumstances, you are ordered to serve a sentence of one year, with credit for the days since you surrendered yourself into custody. That leaves a balance of 354 days to serve, starting today, less time for other credits earned. You will be on probation for one year after your release."

Linda nodded and said, "I understand, Your Honor."

Judge Hill then said, "I understand that you are now a resident of California with a family there, so upon your release, probation may be overseen in California if you choose to return there. That is the disposition. Thank you all."

"Thank you, Your Honor," came from counsel at both tables.

"Can I say good-bye to my husband, Your Honor?"

"Yes. The Court is in recess for five minutes." Judge Hill stood and walked from the bench.

Brad walked to the counsel table and kissed Linda. They held each other tight for a few moments, while a compassionate bailiff waited without attempting to hurry them. They teared up as they said good-bye, and then Linda turned toward Stacey and blew a kiss. She mouthed a 'thank you,' as she was led from the courtroom.

Brad walked over to Stacey and said, "Thank you so much for coming all the way here to help Linda."

Stacey shrugged and then said, "Linda is courageous and deserves all the support she can get." She smiled at Brad and added, "Hang on tight to her, she's a good catch."

"I agree," he said. "The person you came to talk about is the person that I've known since the day we met."

Stacey shook his hand. "Good luck to you and Linda. I wish you both the best."

"Thank you, Detective. You have been good to us and we will never forget it."

Part 9
Stockholm Syndrome: The Reunion

Chapter Thirty-Three

July 14, 2018
Ninety-Four Days After

The open meadow in Las Virgenes Canyon was covered by an expanse of deep blue sky, punctuated by periodic, randomly hovering white, billowy clouds. The late afternoon was cool and the hills seemed forever away from the bustle of Los Angeles. Just as the ceremony was to begin, Stacey and Butler followed signs and balloons down a dirt pathway. Stacey Gray wore a navy blue suit and looked as natural and elegant as she did in jeans. Butler wore a blue pin-striped suit and a striped tie that he could hardly wait to take off.

"How come you didn't bring Liz? Didn't you hear that when you have a spouse, you're supposed to drag them to this kind of event?" Stacey asked.

"Yep, Lord knows she dragged me to enough of them," Butler replied with a sideways grin. "But this time, she's visiting her mother."

They walked along the uneven trail until the decorated meadow came into view. They took a seat in the back row. It was a surreal sight to see a meadow full of seats filled by women in suits or long dresses and men in dark suits. The formality of the attire was in striking contrast to the dirt and grass of the open meadow. The urban world making a desperate attempt to escape back to nature for a couple of hours. The gazebo in front of them had been decorated with white roses. The seating was fifteen seats across with a middle aisle filled by a white carpet. The rows of chairs on each side of the aisle were connected by turquoise silk and white roses.

As soon as they sat down, music began and the groom, Kevin Roper, approached the center aisle in a gray and black tux, followed by three identically dressed groomsman, each looking a little more nervous than the last. When they reached their pre-designated marks and stopped, the maid of honor and bridesmaids appeared at the entry to the carpeted walkway in lavender and white. Then came Dr. Kelly Parson with a handsome, white-haired man in his sixties that Stacey immediately knew was her father. His face was a thin veneer covering the gamut of emotions faced by fathers when their little girls marry; pride, joy, loss and fear, all in some mysterious, undefined proportion. Kelly wore a gorgeous white dress with a flowing train and a veil that seemed to frame and illuminate, rather than hide, her beauty. As they took their first steps down the aisle, Wagner's 'Bridal Chorus' began and everyone stood and turned to see clearly. When they reached the front of the gazebo, Kelly Parson gave her father a hug and a kiss. For a moment, Stacey was taken to an imagined world where she was the bride, about to marry the man she adored.

She was brought back from her daydream when the officiant, a tall woman with a wide grin, walked to the microphone and said, "Thank you all for coming to this wonderful celebration. I am Beth Richmond. Some of you know me as an architect, and who doesn't call on their architect to marry them?" After brief laughter she continued, "Today, I am also a licensed officiant with the honor of marrying my amazing sister, Dr. Kelly Parson, to Mr. Kevin Roper. All of you who know them as a couple know that they belong together, and today, we get to help them make memories." Beth drew a breath and then said, "We come together to show our love and support for Kelly and Kevin, to show them that we love them and that we will always be there to support them. Kelly and Kevin have written the vows that they wish to exchange today. Kevin, it's all yours."

Kevin took several breaths, made a false start while he pulled back tears and looked into Kelly's eyes with a wide grin. "Kelly, you are my dream. You are brilliant, compassionate and the most beautiful woman in the world. You light up every room you enter and you light up my entire world. You are my moral compass." Only Kelly, Kevin and the cops in the back row knew exactly what that one meant.

Kevin took a deep breath and continued, "I am mystified that you could have chosen me, but I sure don't want you to change your mind. From the fateful moment that I re-met you, all those years after high school, I have been enchanted. Kelly Parson, I love you to my soul and I will spend my whole life showing you how much. With this ring I commit myself and my love to you now and forever."

He slipped the ring onto her finger and there was applause and cheering from the audience. Once the audience quieted, Beth said, "Okay, Kelly, your turn."

Kelly cleared her throat and said, "Kevin, I am in love with you because of who you are. You are caring and considerate, smart and insightful. I am grateful that our paths crossed, even given the extraordinary way that happened."

She paused to laughter from the audience at the reference to meeting as hostages, and it was then that Stacey realized that there were a number of the hostages scattered throughout the audience and that they laughed the loudest. Stacey looked through the crowd to see Josie Everett sitting with her husband, Tom. Don Silver sat alone a few rows back and on the other side of the aisle. Chris Morgan and his wife Connie sat near the front, holding hands. Stacey had heard that Chris pleaded to a misdemeanor unlawful possession of a firearm in the wake of recommendations from her and Butler to keep felonies off his record. Seventy-eight year old Mrs. Pierce sat in the front row and was seemingly hypnotized by the ceremony. It was hostage old-home week.

Kelly continued, "Between us I think we have some pretty good genes and we will have awesome kids." She paused a moment and then added, "Remind me I said that when they are teenagers." More laughter and then she said, "I promise that I will love you today and forever, that I will share our great moments and our saddest of times and that all of them will be important to me. I promise you that I will value the man you are, dedicated, intelligent, compassionate and loving, and that I will do my best to be open and share all of life's moments with you." With that Stacey was pushing tears away. "Kevin, with this ring I promise you my love and caring, now and forever."

Beth Richmond looked at her sister's face and was working hard not to cry. She said, "It is the job of each of you to love and protect each other and to be there for each other in good times and bad. Kevin, do you take Kelly to be your lawfully wedded wife, to love her now and forever, to be beside her in sickness and in health and until death do you part?"

Kevin lifted her hands in his and said, "I do, I do, I do."

"Kelly, do you take Kevin to be your lawfully wedded husband, to love him now and forever, to be beside him in sickness and in health and until death do you part?"

"I do," she said, looking into Kevin's eyes.

"By the authority vested in me, I now pronounce you husband and wife. You may kiss the bride, Kevin."

Kevin lifted her veil and they kissed as the audience cheered.

Beth Richmond lifted her arms to the crowd and said, "I now present Kevin and Kelly Roper."

Cheers erupted. They turned and walked down the aisle to thunderous applause and blown kisses. The wedding party followed them down the aisle. As they walked past Stacey and Jeff, both looked at them and gave them a smile.

"Shall we stop at the reception?" Jeff asked.

Stacey hesitated a moment and then said, "Yeah, let's do."

They followed the crowd down the dirt path as the sun began to set and made their way to the reception several miles away.

* * *

The reception was held at the Sheraton Agoura Hills conference center with a small stage and a large bar, where many of the guests were now lined up. The massive room was populated by round tables with long, white tablecloths, each table surrounded by eight chairs. There were four serving areas where different buffet entrees would soon be available. Stacey ordered a glass of pinot noir and Butler a screwdriver. They sat down at one of the tables and began to count former hostages in the room. They looked around the room and picked out all of the hostage alumni. By the time they were done, they had concluded that all of the former hostages were present, with the singular exception of Linda Caldwell, who was counting down the days to freedom in Ohio.

Stacey and Butler finished their drinks as Kelly and Kevin walked into the room and were greeted with applause. The bride and groom began making their way around the room, receiving congratulations and good wishes and thanking people for coming to witness their ceremony.

Kevin was one table away from Stacey and Butler when he looked over and saw them. He smiled, thanked the couple he was speaking to and made his way over to the detectives. "So glad you came," Kevin said, shaking hands with each of them.

"Congratulations," Butler said. "You are a handsome couple."

"Beautiful wedding," Stacey added.

"I'm still shaking," Kevin said, laughing. "And I am so lucky."

Butler smiled and said, "You got yourself a wonderful lady."

Kevin nodded. "I did. Part of me still can't believe it."

Stacey said, "Pretty amazing that all of the hostages are here. I guess with the exception of the one who couldn't be here."

He nodded. "We are connected by that unforgettable experience and we've actually become quite close. We stay in touch by email and even plan to get together once in a while." Stacey shook her head, speechless. "We actually began referring to ourselves as the Stockholm survivors."

Stacey's eyes grew wide and she spoke softly, so as not to be overheard. "The rest of the group would probably have a mixed reaction to the irony of that if they knew your role, don't you think?"

Kevin shook his head. "We are all just the people who were at the wrong place at the wrong time."

Stacey looked at him thoughtfully and said, "I guess some fictions are worth maintaining. I'm glad that a couple of people aren't here. We know that you haven't been associating with them and that's what counts to us."

"You're right. I haven't and I won't."

"Just so you know, we are also told that you are staying away from exposure to the wrong influence in your business, too. So congratulations. Looks like your new life is good for a lot of reasons."

Roper said nothing. Kelly joined them at the table and they shook her hand and congratulated her. "You are a gorgeous bride," Butler said.

"Thank you. And thanks for coming Detectives." She looked at her husband and then back to Stacey and Butler. "We want you to know that we are both grateful to you. Things might have gone badly for us if it wasn't for you."

Stacey smiled and said, "This is a new beginning for both of you in many ways."

"It really is. It is the ultimate irony that a terrifying experience is also the source of our re-meeting and our finding happiness together. We do have a great 'what brought you together story' to share with other couples though," Kevin said.

"That is for sure. I think you'll win the most unusual meeting contest every time," Butler said.

Kelly and Kevin shook hands with Stacey and Butler one more time. Then they joined hands and moved on to visit other tables. As they moved away, Butler looked at Stacey and said, "What was that stuff about reports we're getting on things he's doing in business? Nobody's watching him as far as I know."

"Yeah, but it's not a bad thing if he thinks we are."

"You are too much, Gray."

"Shall we get out of here?" Butler asked.

"Yeah, let's do it."

They took a last sip of wine and then stood and put on their coats.

As they walked from the table, a man appeared at the door and quickly scanned the room to assure all was what it should be. His gaze fixed on Stacey as she moved toward the door. His eyes grew wide and a smile appeared on his face. She smiled back as Marc Foster moved a few steps into the room to meet her. "Hello, Detective," he said grinning. "You look really nice."

"Thanks," she replied.

He shook her hand and added, "It is good to see you again."

"Yes, likewise," Stacey said. "Marc Foster, this is my partner, Detective Butler."

Foster shook Butler's hand and said, "Good to meet you, Detective Butler."

Butler smiled and said, "Hi, Mr. Foster. Good to meet you."

"May I have a moment of your time alone," Foster said to Stacey.

"I'll wait over at the bar," Butler said, giving Stacey a sly grin.

"How can I help you, Mr. Foster," Stacey said, after Butler walked away.

"First, please call me Marc."

"Okay, Marc," she replied with a smile, "how can I help you?"

"You can help me immensely just by saying you will go out with me."

Stacey was quiet a moment while she assessed. Foster said, "This is clumsy. I should have asked you if you have a husband or a fiancé."

"No," Stacey said, "I don't have either."

"Do you?"

"No, I don't either," he said. Foster smiled and his blue eyes lit up. "That is so good. Will you go out to dinner with me?"

Stacey grinned and said, "I will."

"How about tomorrow night?"

"That will work," Stacey said. "Shall we meet somewhere?"

"How about Davenport's in Encino."

"I can do that," Stacey said.

"I'll make reservations for 7:00 p.m. Does that work?"

"I will see you there."

There was a moment of quiet and then Stacey said, "It took you a while to get around to asking."

He shook his head. "Way too long for me. I knew I wanted to ask you out from the first moment I saw you. It's just that last time we talked you were all business, so I got the feeling that maybe you weren't interested."

"I have to admit that I was attracted to you too, Marc."

He smiled widely and took her hand. "I look forward to tomorrow," he said.

Stacey said good-bye and walked over to Butler who was smirking like he had a secret that he could barely contain. Stacey turned back and saw Marc was still watching. He gave her a wave that she returned. Something was up here because she noticed her heart beating more rapidly than normal. She didn't want to be too optimistic too soon, but early reaction to Marc Foster was pretty positive.

"So, how's the social life?" Butler asked, with a large grin plastered on his face.

Stacey smiled back and said, "It might turn out to be pretty good. I'll let you know. In the meantime, stop smirking at me like that."

As they walked out to the car, Stacey couldn't help feeling like a school girl, caught up in the excitement of a new relationship. She found herself grinning like an idiot as Jeff Butler looked on, shaking his head.

At that moment, Stacey's phone rang. "Detective Gray," she said, thoughts only half in the call.

She looked over at Butler and her face grew serious and then concerned. "For what?" Butler stared at her in anticipation. Whatever this was, it didn't look good. "Holy shit," Stacey said, and then, "Yeah, Butler's with me. We'll be right in."

She hung up and gave him a shit just hit the fan look.

"Last time I checked, this was our day off. What is it already?" Butler asked.

"The FBI just picked up Paul Mason. They have him investing 3.8 million dollars through three shell corporations. They say Brian Gallagher is not involved as far as they can tell so far."

"What? Where the fuck did Mason get 3.8 million dollars?" Then he stopped and said, "Oh, no. Tell me it isn't."

She was quiet a moment and then said, "Apparently, Mason did it again, but this time through several different remote computers rather than bank computers. They are following the money to see the route it took to get to him, but it looks like they have him cold. A former FBI agent is going to get prosecuted for theft and the media is going to be all over it in short order."

Butler looked at her with concerned eyes. "So does this out the California Bank robbery? Does it get made public when they investigate this new fiasco?"

Stacey said, "I don't know. If it does, it's going to hit the newlyweds we just left pretty hard." Butler looked worried. Stacey added, "Maybe the past never comes up. When you think about it, there's no reason for Mason to bring it up, because it just adds fifteen or twenty years to his sentence. And the FBI still doesn't want it out there. They aren't going to tell the world about the deal they made to keep a couple of rogue agents quiet. So maybe the connection to the California Bank robbery never surfaces."

"So, where are we going?"

"We're going to FBI headquarters to confer with Lowell about what they've got."

"Are they bringing the task force back together again?" Butler asked.

"Maybe. I'm not sure yet, but they sure want us all on the same page," Stacey replied.

Butler considered a moment and then said, "It is also possible that Mason tries to blackmail the FBI with the former episode. You know, either get me out of this or the whole story hits the headlines and you can deal with the deep state conspiracies that come about when two FBI agents rob a bank."

"That's not out of the question," Stacey said thoughtfully. "He may try to play that card. I mean he's going to be pretty desperate because it looks like they have him this time."

"This could be a real clusterfuck," Butler said. He looked over at Stacey who wore a concerned expression and nodded agreement. "Gray, you have to promise not to drag me into a world of shit. I mean, if we get assigned to this team, let's avoid violating the Constitutional rights of everyone we come across. I really want to keep my job. You with me?"

She looked thoughtful and then said, "Maybe we can find his Achilles heel and use it to keep him quiet about the last go round. What do you know about his family?"

"Jesus Christ, Gray, that's exactly what I mean. I am not getting involved in scaring the shit out of his relatives."

"It's the kind of tactic that works," she offered.

"You are worrying me, Gray. I don't want to be brought up on charges, fired or shot by some deep state guy who plays without limits."

Stacey looked at him sternly. "We want to nail this guy. To catch the ones who are good at what they do, we have to find their soft spot and get leverage on them. It's all about vulnerability and doing whatever it takes."

"Vulnerability? Ours or theirs?" Jeff asked loudly.

She smiled and said, "Maybe both. It's the ultimate game of chicken."

"You are seriously over the top. Between Mason's new gambit and your extreme responses, I feel like my ass is going to be on the line again soon." She was quiet. Jeff said, "Gray, are you listening?"

As he looked over, Stacey furrowed her brow and wore a serious expression that told him she was plotting something he probably needed to avoid. There was soon going to be another plan that put them in the middle of a brand new shit storm. At that moment, Stacey's phone rang again. She hit a button and said, "Detective Gray."

"Stacey, this is Marc. Marc Foster."

"Hi, Marc."

"I know that I just talked to you ten minutes ago, but I just wanted to tell you that I'm thinking about you and looking forward to our date tomorrow."

"Yeah, me, too," Stacey said, softly.

Butler looked over to see her expression had changed to a wide smile. He shook his head. Maybe she was going to be crazy and in love, or maybe just crazy. Either way, they were about to walk into another clusterfuck. And either way, she was a partner he could depend on to be there for him right up until the day she got him fired or shot. What more could he ask?